What kind of man was Chase Riboud? And…how did she feel about him?

Having watched Chase help Rose master the age-old childhood trick of grass whistling, Fiona had seen in him a flicker of the father he might become—strong, kind, and patient. And, without reservation, her daughter had accepted him as a friend.

Conflicting feelings swirled within her, threatening sensory overload. At the root of her conflict lay the undeniable attraction she felt for Chase. Even as he unsettled her, she felt a strange ease with him. Like now. She could almost imagine the three of them, a family, heading home after a regular Saturday outing.

Already she'd seen his military strength of bearing, his ability to take charge, his professional competence, and then, briefly, a glimmer of his fatherly potential. But she suspected there was much more to Chase than first met the eye…

Dear Reader

Welcome to Silhouette Special Edition®, the most emotional, satisfying romances around.

We have three novels which feature children this month. There's our THAT'S MY BABY! title from Amy Frazier, *Celebrate the Child*, which is deeply moving and quite unusual. Then there's a mix-up at the sperm bank and two strangers want the same baby in Teresa Carpenter's *The Baby Due Date*. And in *Forever Mine* from the talented Jennifer Mikels, there's a secret child.

Tracy Sinclair imagined what it would be like to fall in love with a king—*The Bachelor King*—and Joan Elliott Pickart has finished her Bachelor Bet trilogy—*The Most Eligible MD*—while Gina Wilkins tells us a new one of her Family Found stories—*That First Special Kiss*.

Great books one and all, so have fun!

The Editors

Celebrate the Child

AMY FRAZIER

SILHOUETTE
SPECIAL EDITION®

First published in Great Britain 2000
Silhouette Books, Eton House, 18-24 Paradise Road,
Richmond, Surrey TW9 1SR

© Amy Lanz 1999

ISBN 0 373 24270 0

23-0008

Printed and bound in Spain
by Litografia Rosés S.A., Barcelona

To Chris Crosier,
who keeps the home fires of friendship and
encouragement burning in Point Narrows.

AMY FRAZIER

has loved to listen to, read and tell stories from the time she was a very young child. With the support of a loving family, she grew up believing she could accomplish anything she set her mind to. It was with this attitude that she tackled various careers as a teacher, librarian, freelance artist, professional storyteller, wife and mother. Above all else, the stories always beckoned. It is with a contented sigh that she settles into the romance field, where she can weave stories in which love conquers all.

Amy now lives with her husband, son and daughter in northwest Georgia, where the kudzu grows high as an elephant's eye. When not writing, she loves reading, music, painting, gardening, bird watching and the Atlanta Braves.

Dear Reader,

Each of us wants to be thought of as special. One dictionary defines special as 'distinguished by some unusual quality, unique, individual, peculiar.' So it's a fine line we walk between distinguished and downright odd. Although we wish to be seen as individuals , we don't care to be considered abnormal. Although differences define us, we don't wish to be so different that we're excluded. As humans, we need acceptance. The line between the usual and the unusual, between abled and disabled is one perception. I gave birth to two 'normal' children; I've taught children in 'special' educational classes. There were many times my own children behaved in such a bizarre manner even child-care experts offered no solace; and there were times when my special ed students demonstrated behaviour so wonderfully astounding that I couldn't help but ask myself if that wasn't what normal *should* be. We must not prejudge. We must celebrate that which is unique in all of us.

Some people might think that Rose is special because she's a Down's syndrome child. I believe her specialness arises out of her zest for life and her capacity for love, and because she is able to bring Chase and Fiona together.

With love,

Amy Frazier

Prologue

She'd given up their child for adoption, dammit.

Without his knowledge. Without his consent. And now retired Army Lieutenant Colonel Chase Riboud was determined to gain custody of the daughter he hadn't known he fathered.

He'd been cheated and he'd been betrayed, and he sure as hell wasn't going to stand for it.

Icy water sluiced over his naked body as he stood in the hotel shower, trying to cool down, trying to plot his next move over the anger, frustration and disgust that threatened to tear rational thought apart.

Just today, people and forces beyond his control had ambushed him, had destroyed his plans for the future. Rage rising like a poison within him, Chase smacked the shower tiles so hard with the flat of his hands the fixtures rattled. Retired or not, he was military through and through. He didn't accept that anything could remain beyond his control for long.

With a jerk, he cut off the flow of water. The shower having done nothing to cool him down, he stepped out of the stall only to see the sink vanity strewn with the contents of his pockets: appointment cards for further medical tests. The sight of them jolted the memory of the doctor's words this afternoon when Chase had shown up for the results of the routine job physical.

Some irregular results that need further exploration…more and more common with military personnel who've seen action…especially with these new chemical and nuclear agents…sometimes the effects don't show up until the next generation…some individuals choose not to have children….

He might never be able to father healthy children. The thought slammed into him like shrapnel.

It was a crap shoot, the blunt doctor had said, especially considering the lieutenant colonel's past special assignments. A risky business. At the very least, Chase and a future wife would need to go for genetic counseling.

Like a heat-seeking missile, the news sought to destroy the very foundation of his manhood.

Chase grabbed a towel and vigorously rubbed his chilled and reddened skin. An army veteran, he'd trained to anticipate the unexpected. But no amount of training could have prepared him for the possibility that at thirty-eight, ready to take his place in the civilian world, to find a good woman, settle down and raise a family, he would be told that he might never father a healthy child. And then, in a bizarre coincidental meeting, that he'd already fathered a daughter seven years ago, a little girl the mother had given up for adoption without his knowledge or consent.

How was that for a retirement package?

He reached for a piece of paper nearly lost amid the appointment cards cast upon the side of the sink. A torn corner of bar napkin with a scribbled name and partial address, it was at once an accusation, a weight and a challenge.

Pinching the insubstantial scrap between thumb and forefinger, he read, still disbelieving: "Dr. Fiona Applegate—Bertie's Hollow, NC."

Dr. Applegate had adopted his daughter.

She might be a fine woman, an adequate foster parent—he refused to accept the adoption—for his child, but blood should live with blood.

"I'm going to find her," he vowed aloud to cement his resolve. "No matter what I have to do, no matter how long it takes me, I'm going to gain custody of my daughter."

Somewhere out there Dr. Fiona Applegate had nurtured his child for six years. For that he would always be grateful. Now he needed to convince her that he would carry on in her stead. He had to. This little girl he'd never met was his own flesh and blood. His chance for a family. Perhaps his only chance.

Chapter One

Dr. Fiona Applegate sensed change—big change—in the air.

The imagined undercurrent arose not merely from the promise of a Blue Ridge Mountain spring, although plump buds everywhere strained to cast off winter's hold. No, spring always soothed Fiona's soul, whereas this sense of impending change had her fidgeting and restless, looking over her shoulder and pacing the corridor of her small Bertie's Hollow family practice clinic.

"Oh, for pity's sake, come on!" Sadie, her nurse, receptionist and only assistant, came up behind, startling her. "We can close for half an hour. There are no appointments until three and no walk-ins waiting." She pinched Fiona as if to rouse her. "Let's go meet him."

Him. Retired Lieutenant Colonel Chase Riboud.

Could the prospect of meeting this stranger be the source of her agitation?

Riboud was the new mercy flight helicopter pilot out of Asheville. Fiona had experience with the two paramedics who'd been assigned with him in the test program, so maybe the pilot—a man not from these parts—was the source of her unsettled state of mind. It wasn't often folks saw an unfamiliar face in this remote area of North Carolina, but when they did, they reacted with conjecture and an edgy caution.

"Hellooo?" Sadie waved a hand in front of Fiona's face.

"Okay. Let's go." She rubbed her arms as an unexpected chill sent goose bumps racing over her flesh. "We've certainly waited long enough for this day."

"And the fact it's come at last is due to your efforts and your efforts alone." Sadie was Fiona's chief and unabashed cheerleader. "This man needs to meet the woman responsible for his paycheck."

"I'm not responsible for his paycheck," Fiona replied quickly. "I just nagged the powers that be over at Asheville General until someone saw the need for an airborne ambulance to serve our isolated mountain population."

"Whatever." Grinning, Sadie tugged at Fiona's sleeve as if she, the grown nurse, were an impatient child and the doctor an unyielding parent. "Come on. I hear this Chase Riboud is too handsome for words."

"How professional!" Fiona rolled her eyes but smiled nonetheless. "Besides, he's retired from the army. How old must that make him?"

"Not too old, not too young. Thirty-eight. Just ripe."

"You're married, Sadie."

"You're not."

Fiona wasn't and she didn't intend to be. Her life, held in a delicate balance, was a rewarding challenge, unneedful of change. She had her daughter Rose. She had her practice. She had a hometown with the emphasis on *home*. Her life was settled, busy and fulfilled, lacking nothing. She didn't need a husband disrupting the equation.

Why then, if she was so satisfied, did she feel so on edge? Her well-known sensitivity was more curse than boon today.

"Sadie…?" Sadie, a good friend and co-worker, wouldn't think her crazy. "Do you feel a major change in the air? It fairly hums."

"Spring. Definitely spring." With Fiona in tow, her assistant pushed through the front doorway into the abundant mountain sunshine. A fresh and fragrant breeze wafted around them. "Ta-daa!"

"No." Fiona felt the vernal pull, yes, but it didn't tie her in knots. "Something bigger. An energy. A challenge. Oh…I don't know how to word it." And, quite frankly, not knowing what *it* was, she didn't know how to cope.

She should be used to these *feelings* by now. As a child, the old folks in town had called her a "special one." Her professors had called her intuitive. But it wasn't until she'd participated in an extrasensory perception workshop that someone had given her the label "empath." Whatever the term, Fiona was sensitive beyond the norm. Most often, as with her healing, the added insight proved a remarkably helpful gift. Sometimes, however, it could be an unsettling burden.

"Hmmm." From the small storefront clinic, Sadie bustled along the shoulder of the state two-lane that doubled as the Bertie's Hollow main street. "If you're talking about a challenge, I have a hair appointment after work. I've asked Jo Beth to do something different with this rat's nest. Now, that'll be a challenge. Or maybe," she added, kicking a large stone out of her way, "we should get our good-for-nothing town manager to put a sidewalk along this stretch of road."

"I'm serious, and I'm not talking about hairstyles or

sidewalks.'' Fiona stopped to pluck a long wand of winter-dried grass. ''I'm thirty-two, and I feel as unsettled as a teenage girl. There must be something in the air.''

''Something as old as the hills.'' Sadie laid a gentle hand on Fiona's shoulder, then winked. ''Mating fever,'' she whispered. ''Perhaps this handsome lieutenant colonel…''

''Sadie!'' Fiona exclaimed, warning her friend and co-worker with an exaggerated frown. ''Don't go there.''

Her nurse, happily married, thought astute matchmaking could cure most ills.

''Suit yourself…but…he's single!'' the pert assistant blurted, then quickly raised her hands in mock surrender.

Fiona might *feel* things, but Sadie collected fact and rumor as a static mop did dust.

Shrugging with an I-know-better-than-you-do grin, Sadie turned then cut through the convenience store parking lot to a well-worn path in the field out back, leaving Fiona in her provoking wake. Despite her retreat just now, Sadie wouldn't rest until she'd seen Fiona paired, courted and settled into married life. Of this Fiona was certain.

''Doc!'' The adolescence-cracked voice coming from behind could only belong to twelve-year-old Rush Harmon.

Sure enough, Fiona turned to spot the boy loping down the roadside, overalls flapping, a beagle clutched to his narrow chest.

''Doc, you got a minute?'' Rush's stick-straight blond hair jutted into his eyes with each bony-legged stride he took.

''Sure!'' Fiona always had a minute for any man, woman or child in Bertie's Hollow. This community, her birthplace, had literally put her through medical school. She owed them. Moreover, she loved each and every one of the residents with a devotion that surpassed indebtedness.

Bertie's Hollow had embraced her special condition and her special daughter.

She called to her nurse, "Sadie! Go on without me. I'll catch up."

Glancing at his watch, Chase punched in the familiar numbers on the hospital pay phone. Although it was time to fly to Bertie's Hollow—really only a couple minutes' hop over the ridge—for today's public demonstration, he needed to talk to someone who understood his gut-wrenching sense of anticipation.

While waiting for his father to pick up on the other end, Chase fingered a frayed photograph he'd taken from his jumpsuit pocket, a photograph of the Riboud clan. Two proud parents. Seven sons and daughters—Chase and his siblings. Fourteen grandkids. A great-grandbaby on the way at the time and very evident from the proud maman's stance. The picture, nicked and creased from travel and inhospitable bivouacs, had been Chase's talisman through many a dark and uncertain hour. Family was his anchor and his strength. He'd looked forward to the day when his future wife and children of their union would join the Ribouds and smile out from just such a photograph.

Fat chance now.

"Riboud here." The clipped voice, Cajun inflected, crackled through the line.

"*Papa.* It's Chase."

"Where the devil are you? Your *maman* wants to know when her now civilian son is bringing her new granddaughter for a home-cooked meal."

Chase shook his head. "I have to meet her first. Perhaps today."

"*Perhaps?*" The elder Riboud muttered a colorful expletive under his breath. "Your maman and I grow older by the minute. We can't wait to meet this little angel."

"Neither can I." Chase replaced the family photo in the pocket next to his heart. "The paramedics and I are giving a demonstration of the helicopter and the program today. My daughter's…temporary mother will be there along with the whole town. Maybe even the children." In a town the size of Bertie's Hollow, the darnedest events were treated as out-of-school holidays. He hoped this demonstration would prove such an occurrence.

"Maybe? Too slow," his father grumbled. "I don't know why you don't just call up General Switzmore, Senator Landry—"

"*Papa,* this isn't a military operation or a lobbying exercise." Although Chase, throughout his career, had attracted the attention and gained the admiration and support of people in high places, this challenge was his alone. "I have to be careful. I don't want to jeopardize my chances at custody. I don't want to frighten the child. She doesn't know me."

"How could *that woman* have done this to a child of her own flesh? To you, the father."

Chase felt a sharp sense of betrayal rise at the thought of the birth mother's treachery. Only coincidence had revealed her secret. He'd begun his civilian job search at the hospital near his last stateside base, where years ago he enjoyed a brief affair with a lab technician before shipping overseas. Marcia. Still on staff at the hospital, she'd seen his lab results, had heard the doctor's troubling diagnosis, and had sought him out with the truth at last.

Did a sense of guilt make her reveal that although he might never father a child in the future, he had in the past?

They hadn't loved each other, Marcia and he, had barely known each other, but they could have made it work. Against all odds, his mother and father had made it work.

The Riboud parents had built a relationship of love and respect, of joy and laughter from a marriage of convenience. Marcia and he could have made it work, too.

"You okay, son?" His father's voice roused him from his dark thoughts.

"What's done is done, *Papa.* History. Let's concentrate on the future. I'm going to get my daughter." Perhaps the only child he would ever have, he added in a bitter mental note.

"When you do, we will throw a party the likes of which Lou'siana's never seen. There won't be enough crawfish for the étouffée your *maman* will make."

Tammi, one of the paramedics on his mercy flight crew, patted him on the arm.

"Gotta go, *Papa.*" Chase felt determination settle deep into the marrow of his bones. "Wish me luck."

"Go with God."

For a brief, unsettling moment, Chase wondered how God would interpret this upcoming custody struggle.

Fiona heard the beat of a helicopter rotor in the distance. Standing on the shoulder of the road next to the convenience store, she felt chilled as she told the panting boy who'd come to a dust-raising halt beside her that his dog would indeed be fine. The little beagle's slight scratches from a fight would heal without her intervention.

"You take that dog home," she said, rising. "Give him plenty of water to drink. And while you watch him, recite your math tables and memorize this week's spelling list so you're prepared when you go back to school *tomorrow.*"

"Aw, Doc." Rush rolled his eyes. He might be adult proud, but he was still a boy. Scooping up the beagle, he escaped as quickly as he'd come, without promising to think a lick about school.

He'd take good care of his dog, Fiona knew, but she

had no illusions he would pay any attention to homework today. Having been assured his dog would recover, the youngster would revel in his own freedom. A kid out of school. There was no headier situation.

Feeling herself as antsy as any truant, Fiona empathized with the boy even though she hadn't a clue as to why she felt so wired. In fact, she still felt as if her life was about to take a dramatic turn. Obviously, the roadside examination of Rush's beagle hadn't precipitated the change in store. Odd. The strange anticipatory sensation had felt so *male.*

Perhaps she needed a break. Perhaps she should go with the compelling truant feeling and play hooky in earnest. Perhaps she should postpone meeting the area's new mercy flight pilot. Perhaps she should head home for an afternoon of fun with Rose.

Ah, Rosie and she could find endless frivolous ways to amuse themselves…but today Martha, Fiona's housekeeper and Rose's teacher-caregiver, had taken the six-year-old to the Jakes' farm to see the new lambs as part of a home-schooled science lesson, leaving Fiona alone in the convenience store parking lot with a restless sense of anticipation and no outlet.

With an uncharacteristic sigh, she headed toward the well-known path Sadie had taken. Fiona would stick to the familiar; that was good advice. She'd meet this new member of her medical support network, she'd complete her afternoon office hours, and then she'd head on home to her daughter who forever made life worth living and in whose presence the world blossomed.

Life was good. She had Rose.

Brightening as she always did at the thought of her daughter, Fiona did a little skip on the meadow path that led to the clearing all of Bertie's Hollow considered their park, their fairground, their ball field and their common.

In fact, it was an out-of-the-way, not-too-level acre of non-arable pasture donated to the town by Increase Murdock. The farmer had hoped to appear the homespun philanthropist and get a tax write-off at the same time. But the residents of Bertie's Hollow were too practical to get their collective nose out of joint over gift-giving motives. A gift was a gift and should be enjoyed and utilized. Murdock Field got used. A lot. And for countless reasons.

Today on that gift patch of land, retired Army Lieutenant Colonel Chase Riboud was to set down Asheville General's brand-new mercy flight helicopter so that folks here could take a firsthand look at the shiny technology, and listen to its pilot and paramedics explain the updated emergency service to the area's precarious peaks and inaccessible hollows.

The pilot had his work cut out for him, Fiona mused.

Her neighbors would attend today out of curiosity, but it would take a while before this Chase Riboud—this outsider on the team—gained their trust no matter how important his services.

When he'd called to set up a time and place for the demonstration, she'd been struck by the smart military authority in his voice. She hoped he wouldn't press that authority as he presented the mercy flight program. An independent lot, people around here took their sweet time when making up their minds about something new, no matter if that something was entirely for their own good. Hill folk didn't take to being pushed or manipulated.

Fiona hoped Chase Riboud was a patient man.

As she cleared a rise, she looked down upon Murdock Field and discovered to her dismay that she trailed almost every able-bodied Bertie's Hollow adult who had taken a little time midday to check out the stranger and his incredible machine. The town, minus its schoolchildren, milled about the blindingly bright red, white and black helicopter.

"Doc!" The small group sang out in chorus.

Fiona hurried to join them, then halted as a man unknown to her stepped away from the little crowd and faced her.

He wore a dark-blue, military-style jumpsuit that contrasted sharply with the white uniforms of the two paramedics behind him. He stood out from the others, his bearing erect, his build large and solid, his sharply chiseled features a mask to any inner thoughts or feelings. His closely cropped dark hair capped a no-nonsense demeanor. This man meant business.

She knew it was pure foolishness, but the intent way in which he stared at her, the ready posture of his body made her feel as if he'd been waiting for her. Specifically her.

How silly.

Of course he'd been waiting for her. She was his contact person in this area. Even though she told him that her appointment schedule might hold her up, she should have been the first one on Murdock Field. To welcome him. To introduce him to the people he—and she as part of the team—would serve, and to reassure her neighbors with her presence that this man was a potential lifesaver. But here she'd hung back like some cantankerous hill granny.

She blushed with chagrin even as she completed the distance between them, hand extended. "Lieutenant Colonel Riboud, I'm Dr. Applegate. I'm sorry I was held up…with a patient." The fact that the *patient* had four legs blanched the lie.

"Call me Chase." The directive held no invitation to friendship. With a regimental sternness he stepped forward to take her outstretched hand. "We might never get down to business if we have to run through titles every time we meet." Not even a hint of a smile touched the corners of his beautifully sculpted mouth or the depths of his inscrutably dark eyes as his hard right hand enveloped hers.

"Fiona, then." She suppressed an urge to add a *sir,* so powerful was his handshake, so intense his regard. The man had cool command down pat, and because he did, she felt the slightest bit off balance, found herself wondering what it would take to make him relax, to smile.

The townspeople watched the two of them with hushed interest. Trusting their doc implicitly, they would take their cue from her.

She tried to withdraw her hand, but he held it just a second longer than necessary. Staring with an unsettling calculation, he took her measure as she took his. A tiny chill ran down Fiona's back even as she reminded herself that the two of them would essentially work as a unit. She wasn't the only one in this situation who needed to assess the situation, to size up the other team members. From his standpoint he'd want a capable liaison, not some hick general practitioner. She tried to give him the benefit of the doubt while she attempted to appear professional and unruffled under his unwavering inspection.

Patience, Fiona, she mentally chided herself. *After all, you pushed for this much-needed program.*

"Reg and Tammi say they know you already." Turning to the two paramedics, Chase Riboud released her hand and broke the spell.

"Hey," Fiona offered in greeting. Glad for social amenities and Reg's and Tammi's familiar faces, she smiled a little too broadly and felt her cheek muscles strain.

"Have I missed much of the presentation?" She plunged on, determined to ignore her unaccustomed awkwardness.

"Nothing. We just touched down." In a move both authoritative and intimate, Chase Riboud took her elbow and guided her to the front of the group, right next to the massive helicopter.

It was strange how much warmer that hunk of metal seemed in contrast to the imposing ex-military man who commandeered her elbow. In Fiona's opinion, the man needed to loosen up. He needed a good laugh. Needed a carefree afternoon with a child such as Rose who laughed easily and loved picnic food, silly songs and all manner of creepy-crawly things. Fiona would dare Retired Lieutenant Colonel Chase Riboud not to smile after fifteen minutes with her irrepressible Rosie.

But he wasn't going to get that afternoon with her child. Aside from the contact Fiona and Riboud would have as members of the same medical support team, he was no concern of hers.

"I was about to explain," Riboud said, his words clipped, "how the four of us—" he included her with a nod and a quick, searing glance "—would be acting as a well-oiled unit."

He towered over her, his pressure on her elbow holding her unaccountably close by his side.

And close up, this man exuded an aura of indisputable quiet mastery from his broad, intelligent forehead to his unshakable, military stance. Ultimately self-possessed, he seemed accustomed to standing at the helm. Alone and in charge.

If he had simply been all macho posture, Fiona could have found it easy to dismiss him. She made the mistake, however, of looking into his eyes. Dark, almost black, his eyes close up showed flecks of umber. And an intense gaze that Fiona had automatically labeled as solitary and off-putting, upon closer inspection, seemed to flicker with a yearning to connect.

Compelled by she knew not what, Fiona experienced a distinct emotional pull toward this stranger. She suddenly felt too warm. As a hint of perspiration trickled between her breasts, she found herself short of breath.

What was wrong with her? She'd just met him.

A psychobabble article in one of the women's issues magazines, with which Sadie loved to stock the clinic waiting room, claimed that standing close—really close—to a man at first meeting could give a woman an instant reading on a future relationship.

If that was true—and Fiona sincerely hoped it wasn't—she could expect an association with Chase Riboud that unfolded like a mountain summer: hot, humid and unsettled.

Chase scanned the assembled citizens of Bertie's Hollow and tried to keep his thoughts on the business at hand.

As his mouth explained his part in the new mercy flight program, his brain tried to tell his fingers to release the elbow of one Dr. Fiona Applegate. A direct order they refused to obey. Now that he'd found the woman who had custody of his child, he couldn't seem to let her go.

He wanted to tell the paramedics to take over while he escorted Dr. Applegate beyond the small assembled group, then explain to her why her services as interim parent, although appreciated, were no longer needed. Why he must now take custody of his daughter.

It wasn't easy. In fact, military search-and-rescue missions had been easier.

"Lieutenant Colonel!" This crowd seemed loath to extend him a first-name-basis familiarity. "What made you choose work in this neck of the woods?" The speaker was an older woman with a gimlet gaze.

"I needed a job. You needed a pilot." *I needed to find my daughter.* He felt a twinge of conscience at what he left unsaid.

"You plannin' on settin' down roots, or you just passin'

through on your way to a better opportunity?'' The question from a stocky man in overalls held a jaded note of accusation.

"I'll give the job my all.'' Chase bristled with professional pride. He'd never given any task less than his all. "As for roots…I've taken a house here in Bertie's Hollow. I'm here to stay, to make this program work.''

That was the truth. The fact that the program would provide him the means to reunite with his child did not diminish his allegiance to duty. Perhaps, he would eventually settle for good in this town. He'd considered such a permanent move to ease the disruption his daughter might feel upon coming to live with her unexpected father.

"Will you have family joinin' you?'' The question hit too close to home.

"I'm not married, if that's what you're asking.''

Dr. Fiona Applegate glanced between his and the audience's intent faces. "We're not being rude,'' she offered. "We're so isolated that we always want to know if our children can expect new playmates.'' She seemed to be sending a message to those assembled that their questions had indeed bordered on rude. Moreover, she seemed to be sending him a message that he could count her on his side.

She didn't have a clue yet as to how many sides there actually were—professional and personal. And in that respect he didn't warrant her trust, he thought with discomfort.

Realizing suddenly that he still had a hold on her elbow, he snapped his fingers wide apart, releasing her, and tried to regain a mental equilibrium.

"Speaking of children,'' he replied with a motive, "we'll need to have the children see us and the chopper so they won't be frightened should they ever need our services.''

He needed to have his daughter see him and see him in a favorable light.

"Yes, well..." the good doctor demurred. "Perhaps we can set something up with the school."

He wanted to say, *We could have set it up for today.* He could have met his child today. But Tammi and Reg had warned him that the residents of Bertie's Hollow were a wary lot, that by setting up this adults-only meeting with him—a stranger—they'd withheld and thus, in their eyes, protected the most vulnerable among them: their children.

Having shown off the chopper and explained some of the challenges of an airborne ambulance service in this area, he let the doctor and the two paramedics explain the medical aspects of the program, all the while, watching the doctor.

She was obviously a woman who commanded the respect of the Bertie's Hollow citizens. Too, she seemed to know her stuff and had the ability to put medical concepts in layman's terms without condescension. Neither fact surprised him. The staff at Asheville General had sung her professional praises—her skill and her devotion to her patients—at the same time they made a point to mention the extreme privacy of her personal, single-parent life. One doctor had jokingly called her Saint Fiona.

He fought the urge to find traces of his daughter in her face. She was not, in fact, the biological mother. But she'd cared for his little girl these past six years. Standing next to Fiona Applegate, he was only once removed from his child, and he hungered for some clue as to his daughter's looks, personality, likes and dislikes.

What had she inherited from him, her father? Did she love baseball? Spicy food? Foot-tapping music? A good story?

"Do you have anything to add, Lieu...Chase?" The

doctor's hazel eyes focused upon him, catching him off guard.

"Negative." He frowned. "I think we've gone over the basics."

"Well, you won't see me up in that thing," someone in the crowd muttered. "I'll take my chances waitin' for the ambulance on four wheels."

"I hate to hear you say that, Silas," Fiona replied instantly. "The difficulty has been that there were times— because of mud slides or washed-out bridges or ice, to name a few problems—when the ambulance drivers couldn't get through. Period. Making a bad situation worse. The helicopter can reach places the ambulance can't. Hopefully, now, emergency situations won't escalate out of control."

"I was here when that contraption landed," another voice called out. "It's noisy enough to stop my hens from layin'. If you were pickin' me up for a broken leg, I'd have a heart attack from the noise alone before I reached the hospital. That's what I call a situation escalatin' out of control."

"The noise is actually greater when you're outside the chopper." Chase, sensing that mistrust had quickly replaced curiosity in this demonstration, joined Fiona in reassuring the group.

"And I suppose you're going to tell me the ride is as smooth as my Uncle Billy's sedan on the interstate."

"In fact it is," Chase replied with pride in his piloting skills. "I'd be happy to take anyone up. Right now."

"I've flown with Chase for a week now, and he's the best," Tammi piped up. "I trust him. So should you."

"She's right," Reg added with a grin. "If I were you, I'd take Chase here up on his offer of a free demo ride. It's better than the Ferris wheel at the state fair."

Now, that was not the diplomatic thing to say. Distrust was etched on the crowd's faces.

"Believe me," Chase insisted, "my chopper is better manned, better maintained—safer, in fact—than any carnival ride. It's not an amusement. It's a lifesaver."

"Doc?" With that single query, a portly woman returned her neighbors' attention to Fiona for reassurance. "You been up?"

"No." The doctor suddenly seemed to go green about the eyes. "But I will—right now—if makes you accept this program."

People began to talk amongst themselves.

"I will," Fiona repeated with great deliberation, turning to Chase, Reg and Tammi. "If you do it now before I change my mind," she added in a whisper.

"Have you ever flown before?" Chase asked, taken aback by the raw exposure apparent in her words.

"Once," she replied softly. "It inspired a deep-seated fear of flying. But if it will get the program off to a positive start…" Her voice trailed off on the mountain breeze.

At that moment, with her admission, a change came over Chase.

As the woman before him looked up with a clarity of gaze and a sharp sense of purpose tinged with vulnerability, he saw not a doctor, not a necessary member of his team, not even an obstacle in a custody mission he pursued with military single-mindedness. He saw a person. An individual with goals and personal preferences, strengths and weaknesses. A human being with real feelings.

This humanization of his child's adoptive mother made his mission all the more difficult.

He considered himself a fair man. A decent man. Ruthless when dealing with obstacles, but not with people. Until this moment, he'd thought of his daughter's mother as an obstacle, not a person. He'd had to, to make himself take the steps that led him here. Now, however...

"Are you sure about going up?" he asked, trying desperately to regain professional focus.

"I'm sure," she replied and held his gaze. "This program is bigger than my personal phobia."

He had to admire her strength of purpose.

"Shall we run through a complete routine?" he asked Reg and Tammi. "Stretcher and all?"

"You bet." The paramedics sprang to action.

By instinct Chase snapped an order for the Bertie's Hollow residents to stand clear of the chopper, then climbed into the cockpit and took the controls as Reg and Tammi retrieved the stretcher. Positioning his headset and checking to see that the area was indeed safely clear, he waited for his paramedics to give him the all-clear signal to take off, watching as they expertly positioned their "patient." Dr. Fiona Applegate.

Until only a few seconds ago Chase had seen her as some objectified symbol, holding the fate of his future in her hands. Having seen a glimpse of her as an individual, he realized that it was he who held an awesome power over her future.

This new turn of events—this new perception—created a setback to his mission, required him to rethink his plans.

He still wanted custody of his daughter, oh, yes. But a deep-rooted code of ethics wouldn't allow him to ambush this unaware woman—this *human being*—with the forthright hazel gaze. It might help his cause if she first came to see him as an individual as he now saw her, then came to understand the injustice that had been done to him. He counted on the fact that she appeared a fair and caring person.

With characteristic self-assurance, Chase altered his plans. He would wait, not long, but a decent interval, until he and Fiona better knew each other—until at least he was able to meet his daughter—before he presented his case.

Chapter Two

Gracious sakes alive! An entire morning of restlessness had led up to this unexpected and unwelcome helicopter ride. Fiona glanced with nervous anticipation at the monster machine. Talk about a dramatic turn in her life!

For the sake of her watching neighbors and patients, she tried to be a good volunteer, tried to relax and cooperate fully as Reg and Tammi strapped her onto a stretcher. But then a horrifying thought struck her.

"You're not going to swing me from a basket outside the helicopter, are you?" she squeaked.

"Don't worry, Doc." Laying a reassuring hand on Fiona's shoulder, Tammi smiled gently. "You'll be traveling first class. Inside."

"I'm sorry. I'm not at my best," Fiona offered, glad, for some reason, that she couldn't make eye contact with pilot Chase Riboud. She bet he had no silly weaknesses. Obviously not a fear of flying.

"This is good practice for us." Reg gave Tammi the sign to lift Fiona, now on the stretcher, into the helicopter. "Our patients won't be at their best, either."

"For many a different reason," Fiona murmured, mortified by her phobia as the copter's dim interior swallowed her whole.

"Put on your best brave smile and wave to your practice out there before we close the door for take-off," Tammi said with grin. "Remember, right now you're our program's chief goodwill ambassador."

With great determination, Fiona stared out into the bright beyond where the residents of Bertie's Hollow followed her every movement from a safe distance. Putting on her game face, she waved energetically and viewed a hesitant group response before Reg slammed the helicopter door shut with excruciating finality.

"Now can I close my eyes, grit my teeth and say a silent prayer till this ride's over?" she asked as Tammi gave an all-clear signal to Chase at the controls.

Rotors roared to life overhead.

"Actually," Reg suggested, "tension gives you a more gut-wrenching ride. Remember how on the Ferris wheel the butterflies go away when you unclench your muscles? Relax, Doc. Let go."

"I'll try," she muttered, feeling the liftoff and the subsequent somersault in her stomach. At least the rear section of the helicopter didn't have windows. She didn't want to watch her world falling away.

"Pretend you're on a highrise elevator, climbing to the top floor," Tammi offered. "And at the top is something or someone you've been looking forward to for a long, long time."

Fiona could do this. She visualized Rose's hand in hers. They were shooting upward to a penthouse suite outfitted like her daughter's favorite burgerland playground. They'd have the equipment all to themselves. She could even hear Rosie's squeals of delight as the child scrambled through the tunnels while she, Fiona, sank slowly into the ball pit, a cool and plastic secret adult pleasure.

She giggled at the image.

"That's the ticket," Tammi said and jolted Fiona out of her fantasy.

Instead of primary playground colors, she stared at the sterile gleam of medical equipment. "I'd rather be in burgerland," she muttered.

"How are you doing back there?" The deep voice from the cockpit sent a shiver down Fiona's spine.

"Just fine!" she chirped. She wasn't about to let Mr. Firm-as-a-Rock think she was anything but copacetic.

In fact, the time to stop coddling her weakness had come. If she could pretend serenity, she could be serene. She had ridden attendance—professional and cool-headed—in ambulances before, in real emergencies. Heck, this was just a demonstration.

She could do this. "May I sit up?" she asked.

"Sure." Tammi loosened the stretcher's security straps. "In fact it would be a good idea if the folks on the ground saw you return upright and under your own power. Cured, so to speak." She winked.

Fiona doubted anything could cure her fear of flying. But in this enclosed rear section of the helicopter, surrounded by machinery she understood and two people who seemed genuinely calm, she could cope.

"Come forward." Chase Riboud's voice was more command than offer, ruining Fiona's plan to stay put until they touched down, pulling her out of her tenuous comfort zone. "I'll give you a bird's-eye view of Bertie's Hollow."

Her stomach lurched. "Thank you, but I'd just as soon remain in the area of my expertise." She wasn't about to go forward, not with that terrifying view, not with that disconcerting man.

"Go on," Reg urged. "Chase is the best. It would do a lot for the program if we landed with you riding shotgun. Would go a long ways in reassuring folks."

He was right, of course. This demonstration was about getting the residents of Bertie's Hollow to accept a life-saving program. In all good conscience she couldn't let her own qualms stand in the way.

"Okay." She put her feet on the floor. It seemed substantial enough.

Placing one hand on Reg's shoulder and one on Tammi's, Fiona stood and discovered she could keep her balance. Riboud seemed to be doing his job. No dips, no pitches, no barrel rolls. Taking a cautious step toward the small opening between the rear ambulance section and the cockpit, she transferred one hand from Tammi's shoulder to the entryway's framework. She released Reg, took one more step, then ducked into the cockpit. The wraparound windshield made the world freefall away, made her knees go weak and her senses reel. In an effort to avert her eyes from the awful void between her and the ground below, she caught sight of the small jump seats on either side of the craft just behind the pilot. In misery, she flopped into the seat diagonally behind Chase, reached automatically for the safety belt, took an enormous gulp of air, snapped herself securely to the helicopter's framework, then squeezed her eyes shut tight.

"You won't see much that way." Did his voice hold just a hint of amusement? Damn him if it did.

"Shut up and talk to me." Normally a rational woman, she didn't care now if he thought her completely, rudely bonkers. Blood roaring in her ears, she couldn't waste effort on being either polite or lucid.

Chase glanced behind him at Fiona's ashen face, contorted with an effort to keep her eyes closed. It had obviously taken courage for her to come forward. He admired courage in any form and refused to feed her suffering by insisting that she relax and enjoy the view. He wouldn't patronize her even though she'd told him to shut up. That was anxiety talking. He suspected that Dr. Applegate, securely on the ground, would never have allowed herself such an unprofessional outburst.

Unaccountably, at the same time she told him to talk to her, and he seized that opportunity. "I'll need help getting used to this area, getting to know individual families."

"We'll all pitch in," she responded, her words taut, her eyes still closed. "Tammi and Reg are first-rate. They'll be wonderful, well-informed partners."

"They have been already." Which led him into the perfect segue. "They've each promised to introduce me to the families in a specific area along with any special considerations of terrain and weather patterns. Reg knows the area surrounding Deer Run especially well. Tammi, Frenchman's Peak. They suggested I get you to help me with Bertie's Hollow."

Fiona seemed to balk at this idea. "The area I know so well from the ground I wouldn't recognize from the air."

"You sure won't if you don't open your eyes." He glanced over his shoulder.

She opened one eye. He had a gut instinct that this woman never shrank from a challenge.

"We could make rounds at ground level. You needn't go aloft again," he said quickly in an effort to reassure her. He didn't want to lose communication. "I'm used to forming a mental ground-to-air transition, and I am getting to know the area bit by bit. I've flown over it for the past week. But there's a difference between flying and flying with intent."

When he cut her another glance, he saw that she'd opened both eyes.

"This whole mercy flight purpose is people," he persisted, trying to hold her attention, to involve her professionalism. "You'd be an invaluable help if you'd take me to your neighbors' homes. Help them further understand the service and become comfortable with me as a member of the team. That's what will make my job more efficient and save lives in the long run. I need to be seen around town with someone people trust. I need to be seen as an insider, not an outsider."

Averse to speech making but knowing he played on her love of her patients, as well as her professional sense of duty, he pressed on. "Perhaps we could meet for coffee and..."

"No!" Her refusal was sharp. "I'd be more than happy to talk if you make an appointment through my office. If you need more, perhaps Sadie could take you with her when she makes her regular visiting nurse rounds on Tuesday and Thursday mornings. I'm sorry, but I'm the only doctor for miles and there are just so many hours in my day."

He knew right then that, for whatever reasons, she'd seen him as overstepping an invisible boundary line. The tightness in her words said that she would not be pushed. Nor persuaded. Not today.

"Of course." He tried to inject a human note so that he didn't lose her completely. "You must have a life, too. Family responsibilities."

"Yes," she agreed but didn't elaborate.

"I guess I'm not quite used to civilian life." He attempted a smile in her direction. "The military never lets you think of time as your own. You tend to view all twenty-four hours as part of the same job."

She seemed to respond to this more personal approach. He could sense her leaning toward him from the jump seat.

"This program is extremely important to the people in these mountains," she said in a quiet, forthright manner. "I've waited for the day when we could finally implement it. I don't want to appear contrary. Despite what you might think, I do want to be a team player." She paused. "Perhaps mountain living has made me too solitary for my patients' good."

He noted she didn't say *for her own good*.

The staff at Asheville General had emphasized that she kept her private life just that—private.

So she was a solitary individual, as he was. He tried to push the thought to the back of his mind. He didn't want to identify with her. He wanted eventually to be completely honest with Fiona Applegate, but he couldn't afford to form too close an identification that might leave him or his mission vulnerable.

"This is solitary country," he said, attempting to get the conversation back to the need for her to help him meet the area's residents. In order to get to know his daughter, he needed her adoptive mother to get to know him as an individual. They couldn't become better acquainted unless they spent considerable time together. Work provided a good excuse. Besides, he really could use her help in familiarizing himself with this tricky area and its wary residents.

He wanted to do an excellent job. He wanted to prove himself worthy of his daughter.

"I can better serve this program," he suggested, "if I know the people and the terrain inside and out. For example…"

He pointed to his right below. "Now that house near the meadow would be easy to get to in an emergency. Plenty of clear space for safe landing." He then pointed off to his left. "But that cabin—the one with the red roof almost hidden in the trees farther down the mountain— that location presents a real access problem. I'd like to scope out that property from the ground."

Fiona leaned practically over his shoulder. "Why that's my house! On Smoke Mountain. I'm the only one around with a red roof."

She lived alone with his daughter on a remote tract of inaccessible land? How safe could that be? Concern for the welfare of his child jumped to the forefront of his thoughts.

"How far are you from the center of town?" he asked testily.

"Ten miles." She seemed to have lost her flight anxiety as she stared below at her home. "It only seems farther because the last seven are dirt road winding up the mountain."

"You said you had a family. How in blazes do your children get to school?" He didn't know if she had other children, but, coming himself from a huge clan, he couldn't envision otherwise.

"It's just seven miles of the dirt road. It's not the Oregon Trail."

"But do your children have to walk it to a school bus stop?"

"Child." She sat back, a wariness creeping into her voice. "And she's home schooled."

What kind of parent would isolate a child so? Chase could barely conceive of an only-child situation, let alone a self-imposed exile halfway up a mountain. And home schooling…did his daughter receive a quality education? Was she happy?

"She doesn't get lonely?" That was the least confrontational question springing to his lips.

"I don't leave her alone, Lieutenant Colonel!" Fiona

snapped. She didn't like this turn in the conversation, this skid into interrogation, this hint of accusation.

From the moment Rose had been born, Fiona had safeguarded her with a fierceness normally reserved for a biological mother. She'd created a loving environment, as secure and natural as she could find, and then had let people into that world only after careful forethought. Through this cautious process the residents of Bertie's Hollow had become an extended family for her daughter and herself. Loving, supportive, protective Bertie's Hollow. Fiona's communal benefactor and cheering squad. Home.

She didn't like a stranger thinking she neglected her daughter in any way. Lonely, indeed.

"I didn't mean to pry." Chase seemed to hold something back in tight check. "It's just that the more I see of this remote area the more I realize each airlift situation will be unique. I'm trying to understand and anticipate."

"Yes, of course," Fiona agreed absently as she watched the red roof of her beloved cabin fade into the distance.

Chase Riboud, an outsider, didn't yet understand the joys and challenges of living in this isolated region. As a newcomer, he couldn't possibly anticipate just how unique every individual was on every peak and in every hollow. Countless family stories—each one rich, convoluted and different—unwound with those long dirt roads snaking through these mountains, and she and Rose made up only one tale.

Theirs was a story with a happy ending, and Fiona intended to keep it that way by closely guarding their privacy. So she wouldn't tell Chase that the seven-mile hike to their cabin wasn't a barrier to civilization so much as a buffer zone between the sometime hectic outside world and a serene and loving retreat.

She couldn't be certain that now, in his present professional mode of problems and solutions, pilot Riboud would understand so esoteric a goal as preserving emotional balance and peace of mind. She suspected he still saw not the people but the job primarily, and that in black and white.

The airborne view began to make her dizzy again. Closing her eyes, she leaned her head against the inside wall of the helicopter and, to center herself, thought of Rose. She remembered the first time she'd held her daughter in her arms, just seconds after the baby had been born. The tiny girl hadn't been her daughter then. She'd been Marcia's.

How distant the relationship with Marcia seemed now.

Fiona had been finishing up her residency. Marcia had been a lab technician in the same hospital. It had been coincidence that their paths had crossed in the cafeteria that day. Marcia had spilled tapioca pudding on Fiona, and Fiona noticed the desperation in Marcia's eyes. To apologize, the technician had bought the resident a cup of coffee. They shared a table, and Marcia shared her dilemma, a dilemma Fiona had sensed even before the other woman had put it in words.

Marcia was single and pregnant, the result of a one-night stand. The man was no longer in town. No longer in the picture. She contemplated an abortion.

As a physician, Fiona made certain Marcia knew all her options and all the consequences. As a woman, she wanted her new friend to know that she had choices.

That first cup of coffee turned into many as the two women met often to discuss the situation. After several weeks Marcia decided to carry the baby to term. After the birth she would reassess the situation, would consider adoption. She asked Fiona if she would be the birthing partner, not as a doctor but as a friend. Fiona felt honored.

"There's the field." Chase Riboud's voice cut into her thoughts. "I think we've had you up long enough."

"Amen to that," Fiona breathed, squinching her eyes even more tightly closed as she felt her stomach flip-flop with the descent.

"I know this wasn't easy for you, but I appreciate the show of support."

"I want this program to work." She felt a gentle thump as the helicopter touched down.

"So do I." Chase Riboud sounded as if he meant it. Sounded, too, as if he were turned in his seat and looking straight at her.

She opened her eyes only to find herself lost in his dark gaze.

There was that compelling depth of focus she'd sensed in him right from the beginning, right from the moment she'd cleared the ridge and seen him apparently waiting for her in Murdock Field. Waiting with intent. And an unsettling intensity.

"I understand that you're busy," he said, "but I'd be glad for any input you can give me. Any information. Any access into everyday life in Bertie's Hollow...."

"I'll be certain to speak positively of your piloting skills." She knew he wanted more. Knew he wanted her—as the respected local physician—to introduce him round. To smooth the way for his challenging job. It was only logical. It could only benefit the program.

So why did she find herself resisting?

There was *something* about the man.

It might have to do with the vitality of his regard. His unwavering stare harbored a disconcerting hunger. What fueled it? Personality? Professional drive? Some inner need?

She didn't want to think of retired Lieutenant Colonel Chase Riboud's inner needs. He disturbed her in a profound and emotional way. She must remember to interact with him in a purely businesslike manner, must avoid any personal connection. A tiny well-controlled part of her feared that in acknowledging his inner needs, she might just unearth some of her own.

"Reg and Tammi and Sadie will spread the good word, too," she offered, suppressing her anxiety. "You have to understand, however, that progress comes slowly to these parts. You have to have patience and faith that things will work out."

"Oh, I have faith things will work out," he replied, marked self-assurance underscoring his words as he slipped out of the copter with a strong masculine grace. "It's patience I've always had trouble with." He cast her a pointed glance. "Here. Let me help you down. There's not much room to maneuver."

She resisted his outstretched hand, but he was right. With so little room to move in the cockpit, she felt off balance after her less than relaxing flight. As much as she hated to admit it, she could use a little assistance until her feet were firmly planted on Blue Ridge soil once again.

She slid her hand into his and instantly regretted it.

Before Fiona could react, he put his other hand on her waist. He removed the first hand from her grasp and put that on the opposite side of her waist, his wide reach of fingers nearly spanning her middle. Then he lifted her from the helicopter to the ground so that she stood before him. Close. Too close for comfort.

With a quickening in her pulse, she flattened her hands against his chest and pushed away.

Still, he didn't release her. "I want you to remember that we're on the same team." His gaze bored down upon her as if he were trying to convey more than just those simple words, was trying to impart some deeper meaning.

"Of course we're on the same team." Unable to bear the intensity of his regard any longer, Fiona looked away, looked toward the Bertie's Hollow residents who had stayed to see if she in fact would survive her flight.

When he finally released her, she felt as if she could breathe again.

Yes, she survived the flight, but her life wouldn't quite be the same hereafter. That change she'd sensed in the air earlier had blown through her day like a persistent wind. She was now part of a team—a very important team for her cherished patients—that included a man who rocked her well-maintained emotional balance.

At the same time she wished she could shirk her responsibilities and never see Chase Riboud again, she anticipated their next meeting with a subversive little thrill.

Sitting in the clinic waiting room, Chase tried not to rub his itchy, watering eyes. A sneeze caught him unaware and triggered a new round of irritation. This was not how he'd planned his next meeting with Fiona.

"Doc will see you now." Sadie motioned for him to follow her.

He rose, although he didn't want to see the doctor now, not when he felt this miserable. He hated feeling out of control. Of his body. Of circumstances. And here he was reduced to sniffles.

He knew what was wrong—allergies—but he didn't know how to cope with them without strong medication that would impair his piloting skills. He was on call, however, and had to remain alert. He might not want to see Fiona, but he needed to.

Perhaps she had some nondrowsy herbal cure. In the past few days folks he met had sung her praises as a doctor, as a vet and as an herbalist. They'd told him nothing, however, about her personal life.

"Sit right up there," Sadie commanded, indicating an examining table, "and I'll check your blood pressure."

Chase held out his arm, annoyance dogging him.

The goals he set himself this week had seemed simple: meet his daughter and find the appropriate opening to tell Fiona who he was. But at each turn he'd been thwarted. Although he'd used his spare time to hang out locally, he hadn't caught a glimpse of the good doctor. She'd been lost in her work. And without her he had no chance of meeting his daughter who remained out of sight, alone on her mountaintop like some enchanted princess.

"My, but you're a healthy specimen," Sadie said, finishing up the blood pressure reading. "You have a girlfriend?"

Chase nearly choked on the nurse's blunt question.

"Let's not grill the man and scare him off." Fiona stood in the door, an unreadable expression on her face. "This area needs his skills."

Sadie didn't seem in the least bit cowed as, with a Cheshire cat grin, she exited the small room.

Fiona left the door open. "What brings you in today?" she asked, her manner professional.

"Allergies, I think." He reached into his pocket to retrieve a handkerchief.

"The pollen has been frightful this spring." With practiced movements Fiona stepped before him and shone a light into his eyes, his nostrils, his mouth, his ears. "Are you bothered every year?"

"Never before."

"Where have you been stationed then?"

"In the arctic briefly. In the desert mostly."

"Well, no wonder. A North Carolina pollen season would come as a jolt to your system." Her gaze sympathetic, she picked up the end of her stethoscope, warming it between her two hands. "Untuck your shirt, please."

Following instructions, he wasn't prepared for her touch on his bare skin. Her fingertips were warm and smooth and sent a shiver of pleasure down his chest despite the fact that she was a doctor and he was, at present, a patient with a very runny nose.

"Breathe deeply."

He consciously tried to slow his breathing and felt strangely vulnerable as the stethoscope slid over his skin.

"Again." Moving the instrument to his back, she leaned so close he could smell the clean, fresh scent of shampoo from her hair.

He found it difficult to breathe at all. Ridiculous. His immune system must have wreaked havoc on the good sense he'd been born with.

"Your lungs are clear." She took a step back and looked directly at him. He was taken by the clear woodland green of her regard. "But you have a rip-roaring allergic reaction settling in your eyes, nose and throat. Do you have trouble with any medications that you know of?" She took a prescription pad from her lab coat pocket.

"I don't want any medication—"

"Now isn't the time to be macho."

He bristled. "I'm not." What did she think of him anyway? "I'm on call. I certainly can't take anything that forbids me to operate heavy machinery."

"This stuff is approved by the FAA for pilots." She scribbled on her prescription pad. "Don't worry." She cocked her head and looked up at him with a half grin. "I may be a rural doctor, but I keep current with my meds."

"I never questioned your expertise." He questioned her soft touch and her wildflower fresh scent and the physical response she'd elicited in him, but he never questioned her professional expertise.

She handed him the prescription. "If you're going to settle in the area, you might want to consider allergy testing and injections."

Injections. He couldn't say he was partial to anything that involved needles. "What about herbal treatments?"

Her look turned to one of surprise.

"What? I don't strike you as an herbal kind of guy?"

She smiled. An unexpected high-wattage smile that cast a glow into the deepest shadows of his heart. "No," she admitted, her eyes sparkling with what almost seemed like mischief. "I never—"

He sneezed hard, cutting off whatever personal acknowledgement she was about to make. When he opened his eyes, he found a tissue box thrust under his nose. With a frown he accepted a tissue, all the while hating that he might appear weak in any way before her.

"Saline nose drops can help," she offered, becoming strictly professional once more. "Drink plenty of clear fluids and an occasional tomato juice with lots of Tabasco sauce. Keep your sleeping area free of dust. Never go to bed without taking a good long shower." She glanced at him, her eyes clear and forthright. "Wear a sterile mask when you're outside. These are ordinary nonmedication measures you can take once we get you stabilized."

She turned to the sink, then ran a paper cup full of water. Opening the cabinet below, she pulled out a handful of individual sample meds and cracked the hard plastic wrapper on one.

"But we do need to stabilize you by turning off this allergic reaction right now." She held out the cup of water and a large tablet with a look that said she understood and empathized with his misery. "Take this. I promise it won't in any way impair you." Funny, but she seemed to understand, too, how important it was for him *not* to feel incapacitated in any way.

"Trust me," she said, extending the medication closer toward him.

Trust. A two-edged sword.

Although he would rather not have needed them, he accepted the water and downed the tablet with a quick swallow. He felt too awful not to. She'd given her word that this medication wouldn't make him feel worse, and—strangely—he trusted her. At a gut level.

He frowned, reluctant to rely on a tablet for good health and not wanting to trust the woman he'd formerly considered an adversary.

She stared at him in a curious manner, and he quickly said, "Sorry, but I don't like feeling under the weather," to cover his true feelings.

"No one does." Her smile was gentle. Disarming. "It just makes you human." She said this last as if his show of humanity came as a surprise to her. As if it actually pleased her. "You know…" She hesitated. "If you're really interested in natural treatments, I could introduce you to Alva Biggs. She keeps bees and claims that eating honey every day made from local pollens builds a natural immunity. Perhaps the two of you could talk."

"When?" He didn't know if he wanted to experiment with doses of honey, but he did know he needed to spend more time with Fiona Applegate.

"I'm going to make a house call now." Fiona flushed slightly as if she now thought better of her offer. "Alva's eighty and cut herself in a nasty fall. I need to remove some stitches, but she finds it next to impossible to make the trip to the clinic. You could…ride with me."

"Now?"

She took a deep breath. "Right now."

He couldn't believe his luck. Days of trying to get close to Fiona Applegate had produced no results. But a runny nose, and what he considered an irritating display of human frailty, had won him precious time by her side. It was odd how his life twisted and turned unexpectedly in this new civilian world.

Chapter Three

"Hellooo!" Announcing herself, Fiona pushed open Alva Biggs's unlocked front door as Chase stood right behind her on the small front porch.

Bringing him along had been a bad idea. Once his allergy symptoms had subsided, he'd lost the grumpiness, had, in fact, become an attentive and observant companion, wanting to know everything about the terrain, the weather, and the families in the areas they'd passed in their ascent up Smoke Mountain. She knew now that his questions came from a deep professionalism, but she'd still withdrawn when they'd driven by the mailbox with Applegate stenciled upon it—the box was her own; Alva lived several miles higher up the mountain on the same dirt road—and he'd begun asking questions about Fiona's family. She told herself he was simply making plans in case he ever—God forbid—had to airlift anyone from her property.

Although she had no reason to mistrust Chase, she still

didn't want to talk with him about her cherished mountain retreat, Martha her indispensable right hand, her own state of single motherhood, or her precious daughter Rose. To do so would seem, somehow, to leave them all vulnerable.

"Fiona, honey, is that you?" Alva's froggy voice came from the kitchen in the back of the house. "I'm making biscuits and greens for lunch. Come pull up a chair."

"I brought someone I'd like you to meet."

"Any friend of yours, dear girl, is a friend of mine, but you have to come to me. I have my hands plumb full."

Chase reached to hold the door open and, in doing so, grazed Fiona's shoulder with his hand. His touch made her jump.

"Smells good," he said, his voice a low, sensuous rumble close behind her. "Is eating part of a normal house call?"

"Too often," she replied, trying to keep her words light. "It's a wonder I'm not the size of a Sumo wrestler."

To get away from his disconcerting self, she marched through the little house to the kitchen in the back where the aroma of biscuits fresh out of the oven assailed her.

"Auntie Alva, are you sure you're not doing too much?" Thinking of the elderly woman's fall and subsequent stitches, Fiona's gaze automatically went to the bandage around Alva Biggs's calf.

"Not as long as I move at the pace my body dictates. You can check me out after we've put away these vittles." The woman whom everyone in town called Auntie, out of respect, turned from the stove. Her weathered, apple doll face broke into a grin. "Now come give an old lady some sugah."

With a swell of affection, Fiona stepped to Alva's side and felt herself enveloped in a soft, warm embrace that sent up a puff of flour between the two.

With a low whistle, Alva pulled back. "My, my," she

murmured as her gaze riveted on the kitchen doorway. She'd spotted Chase.

"Miss Alva Biggs, I'd like you to meet retired Lieutenant Colonel Chase Riboud. He'll be the mercy flight pilot out of Asheville General. His services will augment the ambulance services we now have."

"My pleasure, ma'am." Chase stood erect and smart, his dark eyes focused on Alva, awaiting her move.

Oh, but he was handsome. Moreover, Fiona sensed an energy underlying that still, straight stance, an energy that moved the man beyond handsome to compelling.

Alva extended her hand. "You wouldn't be one of the highland Ribouds, now, would you?" she asked, suspicion clouding her features.

Chase accepted her hand with a curt military inclination of his body. "Negative, ma'am."

One might describe him in many ways, but neither affected nor flowery would be among the descriptions. The strong, silent type, he might yet win over folks with his no-nonsense courtesy.

"Good," Alva snapped. "Those highland Ribouds always were no 'count."

"It's almost impossible to be of no account in the army." A pride laced his words.

To Fiona's amazement, the eighty-year-old blushed as she self-consciously withdrew her hand and patted the flour-spotted apron pinned to her dress. "My great-granddaddy was a colonel in the army," she said picking up two bowls of greens and bringing them to the table. "The Confederate army, of course," she added with what Fiona could have sworn was a coquettish flutter of eyelashes. "You sit next to me, suh; and I'll attempt to overcome my regional allegiances."

The old girl was flirting!

Suppressing a grin, Fiona retrieved the third bowl of

greens and the covered platter of biscuits kept warm on the back of the stove, turning just as Chase pulled a chair back for Alva to be seated. His small act of gallantry touched Fiona.

"Will you do the honors of pouring the lemonade?" Rubbing her wrist, Alva never took her eyes off Chase. "My rheumatism acts up now and again." Only seconds before she'd been hefting pots and pans and crockery as if she were chief cook on a tramp steamer. "And you seem like a mighty robust young man. Married?"

"No, ma'am." The corner of Chase's mouth twitched as he glanced at Fiona. "But I think a bachelor can handle the lemonade pitcher."

There was genuine warmth in the depths of his dark eyes, with a flicker of amusement. Who would have guessed that the spit-and-polish pilot would actually enjoy the attention of a flirtatious and prying hill granny? But he seemed ultimately at ease in this country kitchen.

"Sample some of the famous Biggs honey on your biscuits," Alva insisted. "Of course, our Fiona here doesn't need any. She's sweet enough all by herself. She's single, too, you know."

Sensing a round of matchmaking efforts on the horizon, Fiona moved to head them off. "Chase would like to talk to you about your theory of honey's natural antiallergenic properties."

"It's not a theory." Alva harrumphed. "It's a fact. I've had honey in one form or another every day of my life, and you don't find me sneezing and wheezing come spring."

"Well, it certainly can't hurt." Fiona poured the rich amber sweet onto her biscuit and took a bite.

"I was organic before it was fashionable," Alva sniffed with no small degree of pride. "Take these dandelion greens. I pick a mess every year before they blossom.

Cooked, they're a spring tonic my granny swore by.'' She winked broadly at Fiona. ''Makes the blood run hot and swift in your veins.''

''They *are* rich in iron.'' Fiona ignored the woman's nonmedicinal intimations.

''However you want to put it,'' Chase interjected, ''this is delicious.'' Taking a bite of biscuit and honey, he fairly beamed at Alva. ''Ma'am, I thank you. I've eaten enough army food and lately enough fast food to appreciate a home-cooked meal.''

''My pleasure.'' Alva actually reached over and patted Chase's hand before turning to Fiona. ''You can bring your friend to visit any time, sweetie.''

Nearly choking on a mouthful of greens, Fiona felt color rise to her cheeks. ''Chase and I are co-workers.''

''As part of the same team, Fiona's offered to introduce me to residents in these hills.'' Bless his heart, Chase backed up her assertion. ''She's taking me on the back roads to scout out locations where I could safely land the mercy flight helicopter.''

''Lordy!'' Alva exclaimed, throwing her hands to her chest. ''I sincerely hope I never have to be hauled out of my home in a helicopter.''

''Nor do I.'' Fiona reached out to the elderly woman. ''But as you always tell me, forewarned is forearmed. We're checking out landing sites that would benefit not only you but your neighbors. And that includes me.''

''And dear little Rosie,'' Alva added, affection clear in her faded blue eyes. ''You know, she and Martha were here just before you arrived. Brought me some fresh eggs. I used 'em in the biscuits.''

Fiona may have imagined it, but it seemed as if Alva's mention of Rose's visit sparked Chase's attention. Professional curiosity? A more personal interest in Fiona perhaps? Or was he simply settling into Bertie's Hollow, absorbing all he could about its residents, young and old?

Her own and her daughter's privacy always a priority, Fiona changed the subject. "I wonder if that clearing where you had the blighted apple trees removed wouldn't be a perfect place to land the helicopter."

"Oh, that's no airstrip."

"I don't require an airstrip," Chase said, wiping his hands on his napkin. "Just a clearing."

"Why don't you take him outside for a look-see, Fiona honey." Alva rose from the table. "I'll just do up these dishes."

"First I'll attend to your stitches." Fiona issued her most professional stare. "That is, after all, the real reason for this visit."

"Party poop," Alva muttered. But she sat down.

"I could check out the spot," Chase offered. "If you give me directions."

"Oh, it's easy enough. Out the back door." Alva waved her hand. "Through the peach trees. Past the beehives. And you're there. Then come back and I'll tell you tales about our fair doctor growing up."

Fiona cut Chase a quick glance. "I'll meet you outside as soon as I'm done here. We need to get back. I have a full schedule at the office this afternoon."

"You won't leave without taking some of my honey, will you?" Alva flashed a winsome, southern belle smile at Chase.

"No, ma'am." He returned her smile with a white-toothed grin that would have put poor ole Rhett to shame.

"The man doesn't say much." Cackling softly, the old woman turned to Fiona as if Chase were no longer in the room. "But what he *does* sure sets a body humming."

"Your stitches, Auntie…" Reaching for her medical kit, Fiona began the work at hand, at the same time she struggled within to build up an emotional immunity to the new, warmer, more charming Chase Riboud.

Chase tried to keep his thoughts on business as he surveyed the clearing on Alva Biggs's back property. From this spot on Smoke Mountain, he felt like king of the universe. Below him treetops in new leaf sloped to the valley floor where streaks of white and pink mixed with the yellow-green. In the far distance, other mountains faded to purple and then to mist. Under the expansive Blue Ridge sun, the cosmopolitan world seemed far, far away. Even farther seemed the areas of strife that had been his assignment on too many occasions.

"Will it do?" Fiona's voice from behind made him start.

How long had he been standing alone, daydreaming? For him, a most uncharacteristic occupation.

Would it do? A hard lump grew in his throat. This land would do for paradise.

"How long have you lived here?" he asked without turning to face her as a rush of pure mountain freedom swept mercy flight business and even his personal search-and-rescue mission from his thoughts.

Fiona stepped to his side. "I've lived here all my life, except for the years I spent in college and med school." Her voice was as clear and fresh as the breeze. And somehow spellbinding.

He turned to look at her. "You are one lucky woman."

"I remind myself of that daily."

Her lichen-green gaze was forthright, her complexion smooth and creamy, with pale freckles sprinkled liberally across her nose. Her long, honey-colored hair rebelled against the single braid with which she'd tried to capture it. The sun shone through errant single strands and wisps to form a golden corona around her head.

Not thinking, Chase reached out to brush one such wisp behind her ear. "This week I heard someone refer to you as Saint Fiona." He resisted the urge to touch her cheek. "But I hadn't seen the halo until now."

She rolled her eyes. "That had to come from Max Edelmann, Asheville General." She was right. "He thinks anyone who won't date him must be frigid. A real saint. Untouchable." She held his gaze, smiling with amusement, not irony, and appeared very touchable.

Why hadn't she withdrawn at his personal remark as she had on so many occasions before? The meadow must be enchanted, he decided.

"How about you?" she asked. "Where do you come from if you're not one of the no'count highland Ribouds?"

"From the bayous of Louisiana." He felt a sudden regret. "But I've had little time in the past twenty years to go back."

"Do you still have family there?"

"Do I." He whistled long and low as he ran his fingers through his hair. "I swear Ribouds have overrun the state. A family get-together isn't a party, it's a convention. We're a force to be reckoned with, that's for sure. Hardworking. Hard playing. Good-natured till you cross us." He ran on, unable to stop the flow of words. "I keep in touch by phone, but somehow that's not the same as a raucous Riboud *fais-do-do*. Fiddle music. Dancing. Crawfish étouffée…"

"Why didn't you go back when you retired from the army?" Her question brought him up short.

"The job that fit my skills was here."

"Lucky for us." Her words held a sincerity that snagged his conscience.

"Is Alva Biggs a relation of yours?" he asked, trying to deflect the attention from himself. "You seem so comfortable together. You called her *auntie*."

"No blood relation. *Auntie's* just a hill country form of respect." Fiona's expression became soft. Vulnerable. "But I love her as if she were kin. She's been a wonderful neighbor. And she was the one who headed up the drive to pay for my medical schooling."

"I don't understand."

"My father died when I was young. My mother during my senior year in high school." Fiona looked down at her hands for a moment before holding her chin high and resuming. "I earned a full scholarship to undergraduate school in Chapel Hill. But nothing beyond that. Auntie Alva knew of my dream to become a doctor, however. She stumped the entire area to raise pledges for a scholarship. The stipulation was that I return to practice in Bertie's Hollow. I lost one family and found another right here in this very town."

The depth of determination and commitment on the part of Bertie's Hollow residents and on the part of the woman standing before him moved Chase beyond words. Fiona had been alone in the world, but a town had knit themselves around her in support. Her hazel eyes showed a peaceful satisfaction, a sense of real belonging.

He came from a big, loving, biological family ready to welcome him back into the fold at a moment's notice. Why then did he feel so restless, so displaced and so lonely?

"We...I came back after my residency," Fiona said, "and have been here ever since. I've never regretted a moment of it."

"That's quite a story." Chase found it difficult to speak even those few words.

"You know," she said, touching his arm briefly, "I thought it might be difficult—your fitting into Bertie's Hollow. Even though the program is absolutely necessary, you're...well...an outsider."

"Alva Biggs didn't seem to have any reservations when

I came calling as an acquaintance of yours." He couldn't allow her to forget that she hadn't wanted to introduce him around. "It seems it's all in who you know. You're my key to community acceptance."

"I realize that." She lowered her gaze. "I'm trying to admit that you were right, and I was, at best, a heel dragger. I've been accepted—unconditionally—for so long, I'd forgotten what it's like to be on the outside."

"I don't want to be on the outside." As though compelled, Chase reached out and slid his fingers under her chin until she looked at him once again. "I want to fit into Bertie's Hollow. I want to be an asset. Eventually, I want what you have. A sense of belonging."

His heart fairly ached with a hunger to belong. For his own branch on the family tree. But, in a bizarre turn of events, he no longer saw Fiona as an obstacle to that dream.

But what then was she?

Right now she was a beautiful woman standing beside him in a sweet-smelling meadow, her beauty blooming deep from within as well as from without. She had listened with genuine interest while he opened up to her, and then she responded by sharing a little bit of herself. She had touched him, however briefly, both physically and emotionally.

She now looked deep into his eyes. "It's important you follow your dream. To my way of thinking, we love or we perish."

No one had ever put it to him that way before.

When she reached up and brushed her fingertips along his cheek, saying, "I wish you Godspeed in your quest, Chase Riboud," he felt a well-guarded, sharply honed severity loosen within him.

He didn't want to end up a severe old man. Alone.

Because she was light and hope and intuitive kindness,

and she was so very, very beautiful, he sensed that in holding her, he might hold the promise of a rainbow; might touch the dreams of the future, might bring his wandering soul a degree of peace. At that moment he wanted to hold her with a want that would not be stilled.

Without considering the consequences, he drew her into his arms and lowered his mouth to hers.

Fiona could never say that she hadn't seen the kiss coming or that she'd searched for a way to prevent it.

From the moment she had joined Chase in the meadow, she sensed matters were different between them. She had seen that unexplained hunger return to his eyes—a need to connect—and it had struck a responding chord deep within her. For all her satisfaction with her life, she was hungry, too.

And so, against all common sense, she met his kiss, and kissing Chase rattled her world into tomorrow.

Whatever else was starched and military about the man, his kiss was not. It was hot and demanding and made her forget where they were, who they were. It was pure pleasure and startling in its intoxication. It made Fiona realize what a sober person she had been up to this moment.

Perhaps what had been missing from her life was not any certain individual but a certain wildness. She had been so careful. So responsible. So very bland.

She didn't feel bland now as she touched the fingers of both her hands to his face to make certain he was real. His hard and sharply defined cheek and jaw bones under skin tanned and tough were real indeed. Running her fingers into his hair, she felt surprise that it wasn't spiny in its shortness, but soft as the bristles on a baby's brush. She slid her hands down the back of his neck corded with firm muscles that joined broad shoulders. As his lips claimed her, as his tongue explored hers, as her breathing became

more rapid, her last thought that made any sense was that
here was a man of substance and passion.

Here was a man who could turn her existence upside
down.

He wrapped his strong arms around her, pulling her
tight…and then he released her with a suddenness that
took her breath away.

"I'm sorry." He held her at arm's length, a dazed expression in his eyes. "I thought kissing you would help
me get my head on straight."

"And did it?" She touched her fingertips to her swollen
lips.

He almost smiled. "I'd have to say it screwed it on in
a whole different direction." Noticing his hands on her
shoulders, he released her.

"It was a crazy moment." She took a deep breath.
"Call it spring fever. You don't need to apologize."

"What then?"

"Nothing. We're both adults."

They might not need to do anything about the kiss, but
the kiss itself, the moment, was far from nothingness. It
had awakened Fiona. For years she had cared for others,
advised them, encouraged them to indulge themselves a
little. When was the last time she'd truly indulged herself?

"I'm not saying I didn't enjoy it. I did." He rubbed his
jaw and looked at her in a way that hid more of his feelings
than it revealed. "It's just that normally I'm a rational
man."

"Have you never done anything on the spur of the moment?"

"Rarely."

How interesting and how sad. For Fiona, one incredibly
impetuous moment had brought her Rose. And happiness
beyond measure.

"Why not?"

"I like to know I can control a situation before I get into it." His gaze grew dark and distant.

She tried to lighten the situation. "Then you wouldn't have danced the polka with my Uncle Pete."

"Beg your pardon?"

"At a wedding a long time ago. Girls were dancing with their dads. Standing on the tops of their fathers' shoes so that they wouldn't miss a step in those country waltzes. I wasn't dancing because I didn't have a dad. Then the band starts up this really wild polka. Nobody could dance it except my Uncle Pete who'd moved to Pittsburgh and married a Polish woman. He asked me to dance, but I told him I didn't think I knew the steps. He told me not to think. Not to look at my feet. To jump into the music instead. I did. Just because I didn't want to be left behind. I've never danced again the way I danced that polka." She smiled. "I think he carried me most of the way, but that isn't the point. The point is the joy I felt in seizing the moment. An innocent moment."

Now why had she just told him that story? She'd never shared her feelings about it with anyone.

Perhaps she wanted to let him know that, as with the polka years before, she didn't regret seizing an ultimately innocent opportunity with a kiss minutes ago.

A kiss was, after all, just a kiss.

Chase's thoughts danced in turmoil. He'd just held in his arms the woman from whose arms he planned to wrest his daughter. He couldn't think of a more compromising situation.

What had gotten into him?

For a fleeting instant he'd forgotten that they were professional teammates, possibly personal adversaries. For a brief time they were just a man and a woman on a mountain in air so fresh it made his head spin. And he had wanted desperately to kiss her.

He wanted to kiss her again, which was the very worst thing he could do to either of them.

She was a most remarkable woman. A most desirable woman. And he needed to keep his desires under control.

"You said you had appointments this afternoon at the clinic." That was all he could think of to say.

"Yes." Was she relieved or disappointed in this return to the mundane?

Whatever she felt deep inside, she hid as she made her way through the meadow, back through the peach orchard and up to the back steps of Alva Biggs's small house.

"We'll be going now, Auntie Alva," Fiona called through the screened door.

"Take those jars of honey I left on the stoop." The voice drifted down from an upstairs window. "For that handsome lieutenant colonel."

Chase picked up the cardboard box containing the honey jars and felt a twinge of conscience. Alva Biggs had welcomed him into her house because she trusted Fiona, and Fiona trusted him.

He needed to clear the air. Right away.

Fiona had already made her way around the house to her truck. As he slid the box onto the seat between them, she smiled. "Ready?"

Climbing into the truck, then closing the door behind him, he said, "I think we need to talk."

"Not now." She looked directly at him, no upset in her eyes, no accusation, just resolve. "I'm operating on sensory overload."

"Not so much about the kiss," he began, "but about—"

"Please." She raised her hand to silence him. "Let's just concentrate on our professional relationship."

He backed off. There would be time aplenty. "When's your last appointment today?"

"Four-thirty."

"I'll pick you up at five-thirty for a cup of coffee."

"I need to get home to my daughter."

"I won't keep you long. But we need to talk."

Frowning, she put the truck in gear. "All right."

They drove down the dirt road in silence, until Chase spotted a woman and a child picking wildflowers on the shoulder a good twenty yards ahead. "Be careful," he warned, pointing.

"I see them." Joy bubbled up through Fiona's words. "It's Martha and my daughter Rose."

Rose. His daughter.

Rolling down the window, Fiona slowed the truck. She was going to stop. He was going to meet his daughter.

Chase thought his heart might hammer through his rib cage.

He was going to meet his daughter.

A beatific smile on her face, Fiona tapped the horn gently, then pulled the truck to a stop on the side of the road.

The woman, Martha, turned to look before the child did. The little girl, her hair dark as Chase's, continued picking wildflowers with a jubilant intensity.

Martha bent and spoke in Rose's ear. It was then the girl—his daughter—turned and, seeing Fiona, threw her arms wide.

Chase stopped breathing.

"Mama!" Rose's delight rang across the mountainside as she ran to meet her mother.

Fiona stepped out of the truck.

Hungry to take in every feature of his child, Chase watched, rapt. It took only seconds to absorb the round moon face, the gently sloping eyes, the happy-face grin, the slightly awkward movements and the spiky hair of his obviously mentally disabled daughter.

Chapter Four

Chase's thoughts tumbled in wild, sharp jabs of shock and confusion.

Was *his* daughter retarded?

Like any expectant father, he had projected a perfect child. Especially since she might be his only child.

He had never questioned his ability to be a good parent, but could he handle the challenge of parenting a child with a disability?

"Mama!" Six-year-old Rose wriggled with unabashed glee in Fiona's arms. "Look!" Drawing back, she thrust a fistful of wildflowers under Fiona's nose. "For you!" Then, with a total lack of inhibition, she began to thread the flower stems through Fiona's hair and down the open V of her shirt.

The little girl's smile was so wide that her apple-red cheeks pressed her eyes into twinkling, inverted crescents.

Fiona's reciprocal smile radiated with an obvious maternal love, the sight of which rendered Chase immobile and mesmerized.

"Open!" Rose ordered Fiona, holding a flower before Fiona's mouth.

Fiona cocked her head. "Please."

"Please." Rose uttered the word imperiously.

Fiona opened her mouth.

Ever so gently, Rose placed the stem of the blue, bell-like flower lengthwise between Fiona's teeth.

With a waggle of her slender eyebrows, Fiona straightened, placed one hand on her hip, the other behind her neck, tapped her heels in the roadside dust, then spun in three sharp circles, looking for all the world like a wild and free, flower-bedecked, honey-blonde gypsy.

Rose dropped her remaining bouquet and, without ceremony, sat where she had stood, amid the scattered wildflower blossoms, giggles engulfing her.

It seemed that Fiona and Rose were caught up in a world of their own, filled with love and joy and sheer silly fun. And Chase could but stare in rapt attention. An outsider.

With a laugh, Fiona stopped abruptly. "Where are my manners?" Her skin flushed, her eyes bright, she tucked the blue flower behind her ear. "Chase Riboud, may I present my daughter, Rose Applegate, and our friend and staunch right hand, Martha Ricker. Martha lives with us and takes care of Rose while I work."

Martha eyed him with an open skepticism while Rose, in a series of awkward movements, stood, then approached him, her limbs akimbo, her curiosity guileless.

"Chase is the new mercy flight pilot," Fiona continued. "Rose, you may call him Mr. Chase."

"Hello." Her *l*'s slightly rounded, Rose spoke the simple greeting as she stared intently at his face.

Chase couldn't help but notice that her eyes as well as her hair were as dark as his. "Pleased to meet you

Rose...Martha.'' It took an enormous effort to make his voice function, an even greater effort to tear his eyes away from his daughter to greet the older woman watching his every move with a wariness that unnerved him.

"Are you home for lunch?" Martha asked Fiona without taking her gaze from Chase.

"No. We ate at Alva's." Fiona ruffled Rose's short, dark hair, raising it in spikes that made the child resemble a startled cherub. "I hear you two took Auntie some of our eggs."

Her expression suddenly drooping, Rose looked over her shoulder at Martha. "I broke one."

"Rose didn't want to share my egg basket. She held on to her egg too tight," Martha said, her no-nonsense expression softening as she looked at the girl. "But I told her I'd make her a basket of her very own. From kudzu vines. She can even help me weave it."

"Do it now!" Rose crowed. "All of us!"

Without warning, stubby little fingers grasped Chase's thumb as the child pulled him with remarkable strength first toward Fiona, whose hand she next captured, then toward Martha. The little girl's touch sent a jolt of awareness through him.

This was his daughter.

And this reunion was not what he'd expected.

"Whoa, Rosie!" Fiona exclaimed with a broad grin and a wistful look in her hazel eyes. "Much as I'd like to join you, I have to work this afternoon." She scooped the child up in her arms. "You gather the vines with Martha, and I'll help you make the basket after supper."

"You, too." Rose shook Chase's thumb, which she hadn't relinquished even as Fiona gathered the girl to her. The child's grasp united the three in a symbolic manner only Chase fully comprehended. "Help make my basket."

"Mr. Chase has work to do, sweetie." Fiona extricated

Chase's thumb from his daughter's grip. With the motion, she seemed deliberately to distance herself and the child from him. "He has a very important job. Flying a very big helicopter."

"Let me see." Rose turned to him as if he could produce the machine. Despite a soft, slurred quality to her speech, she managed to make her meaning perfectly clear.

"I'm sorry." Chase shook his head. "My helicopter's in town. I rode with…your mother." The last two words stuck in his throat, the result of a dramatic realization.

From what he had seen in the past few minutes, Fiona and Rose had truly bonded as mother and daughter. Why hadn't he expected as much? How could he have deliberately set out to wrench a child from the arms of her mother? Having witnessed their loving closeness, could he now disrupt it? Could he cope as well as Fiona with the challenge of raising a child with special needs?

Sole custody of his daughter suddenly became a daunting task.

"Show me hel'copter." Rose slipped from her mother's arms, then tugged on his pant leg. Obviously, his explanation of the machine's absence hadn't satisfied her. "Show me."

"My helicopter looks like this." Chase knelt by the roadside and quickly sketched in the dust with his index finger a simplified version of the mercy flight chopper. "Maybe your mom will bring you into town some day to see it."

"Yes!" Rose's face lit up with expectation as she pumped the air with one fist.

"Perhaps," Fiona cautioned.

"No perhaps, Mama. Yes." Rose bent over from the waist to examine the dust sketch. "Draw Rosie," she ordered Chase, pointing to a spot next to the helicopter. "Here."

With a nagging sensation in the pit of her stomach, Fiona watched the taciturn pilot and his interaction with her daughter. Her sensitivity always kicked into overdrive when anyone new met Rose. Her Rosie was love. And sunshine. And laughter. And she happened to be a Down's syndrome child. Strangers, more often than not, saw only the latter upon meeting her.

What did Chase see when he looked at Rose? Did he see the loving little girl, or did he see a difference?

She watched him silently draw a stick-figure child next to the cartoonlike helicopter.

Fiona had almost forgotten how judgmental the outside world could be. When she had returned to her hometown a single parent, she had raised eyebrows initially. But the independence of the hill folk in this region had worked to her benefit. A private lot, they didn't pry. As long as Fiona served them well as their doctor, they wouldn't question her personal circumstances.

Now this stranger, this Chase Riboud, aroused Fiona's maternal preservation instincts like the hackles on a junkyard dog.

"We'd better get back to the clinic," she said to Chase, her tone more short than she intended.

"Yes." He scowled as he rose from his roadside easel, touching the pager clipped to his belt. "I'm on call. I need to stay close to home and the copter."

Fiona hugged Rose. "I'll see you, my darling, later."

"Now," Rose said, with a stubborn glint in her eye that Fiona knew all too well. *Now* was one of her daughter's favorite words.

"Rose." Martha, bless her heart, extended her hand for the save. "Remember the pie on the windowsill? It should be cool enough to eat. With ice cream."

Rose's face crinkled with delight as she ran her tongue

over her lips. She patted Fiona. "I'll save you some, Mama."

"You do that, love."

Unexpectedly, her daughter turned to Chase. "You, too."

"Thank you," he said, his deep voice cracking, his dark eyes revealing considerable emotion.

Fiona wondered at the emotion she witnessed in Chase. Did he have experience with Down's syndrome? With a relative perhaps? Or did he pity Rose? Fiona tolerated pity even less than she tolerated ostracism.

"Bye-bye!" Waving with both hands, her beloved child executed a rolling skip to Martha.

Chase raised his hand in a brusque, silent farewell.

Watching Rose and Martha walk hand in hand up the road, Fiona felt her heart go with them. Soon, but not soon enough, she would return to the snug cabin she shared with them. She couldn't wait.

"She's a trusting child." Chase's words broke into her thoughts.

"Yes. I'm lucky to have found Martha. She treats Rose as if she were her own grandchild."

"How did you *find* Martha?"

Perhaps his question was simply innocent conversation. But a swift, chill sensation swept her body, leaving her leery of confidences.

"It was just an expression," she replied infusing her words with nonchalance. "Martha's an old family friend."

His body language said he'd backed off this line of questioning. The look in his eye told her he might delay his probe, but probe he would—later.

"Thank you for bringing me up here today," he said, his tone even, his words turning the conversation matter-of-fact. "We accomplished several things that should help with the execution of the mercy flight program."

"How so?"

"Alva, Martha and Rose met me. A good first step. Familiarity's important." A clouded expression crossed his handsome features for a brief moment, then disappeared as quickly as it had appeared. "And I know that, should your household ever require a medical evacuation, the closest landing site would be the meadow behind Alva's house."

Mention of the meadow brought a sudden, hot reminder of his kiss. Fiona felt her cheeks flame.

Chase had been attracted to her for whatever reason. Would that attraction hold now that he had met her daughter? More to the point, why did she care one way or another?

"Let's hope we never need your skills," she replied. "Rose and Martha and I are as healthy as mountain mules." She grinned. "And Rose is sometimes as stubborn."

"Where's her father?" His unexpected question knocked the wind out of her.

"Let's just say he's no longer in the picture." Breathing in sharp, short spurts, she made her way to the pickup truck. She turned at the driver's-side door to level a cool, warning glance at Chase. "And let me add that such a direct question could get you in trouble in these hills."

Without apology, he walked to the passenger's side. Looking at her with a dark steady gaze through the open-windowed cab of the truck, he said, "I won't know if I don't ask."

"Why would you be interested?" Her heart beat a ragged tattoo in her chest.

"I'm interested in everyone who lives in these hills. It's all part of who I am and what I have to accomplish in this area."

Fiona shivered. He was an airborne ambulance pilot, not a social worker. He was her co-worker, not her confidant.

One stolen kiss did not entitle him to the story of her life. If anything, the kiss compromised their professional relationship. He needed to understand that.

The truck between them, she said, "If we're to be good teammates, I think we need to separate our work lives and our personal lives."

He cocked one eyebrow. "On the contrary. I think we need to get to know each other, to respect and understand each other in order to work well together. We need to talk—"

"Talk will keep my patients waiting, I'm afraid." For a fleeting moment, she didn't trust Chase Riboud. She'd seen in his eyes a power to disrupt her life. Maybe she didn't trust herself.

"Let's get back to the clinic, then." His words were even, but she sensed a weight behind them that pressed for future discussions.

Back in his rented cottage, Chase held the phone to his ear and waited for his father's response. The silence on the line did not bode well.

"You say you met your daughter and she is retarded?" The elder Riboud spoke low, his words held in check. "This cannot be."

"It is. I got the name, the town from the birth mother herself."

"That is not what I mean. The child cannot be yours. There must be some mistake."

"Meaning?"

His father hesitated. "There is no retardation in the Riboud family, son."

"This *is* Marcia's child. She showed me the legal work."

"Marcia's child, yes…another man's perhaps."

"*Papa,* what are you saying?" Chase had expected

shock from his family. He had not expected this searing negativity.

"Before you proceed any further," his mother broke in on the extension, "you must insist on tests. To prove paternity."

He had just undergone tests with disastrous results—results the nature of which he hadn't discussed with anyone, not even his parents. It wasn't easy sharing one's inadequacies. He didn't relish additional lab work, additional scrutiny.

More repugnant, however, was the thought of subjecting Rose to medical meddling. She was the innocent in this tangled set of circumstances.

And now his parents were suggesting DNA testing because they couldn't accept the fact that their grandchild had a disability. He'd counted on their support and counsel, not their denial.

"I don't think there's any call for genetic testing," Chase said, trying to keep his temper down, his voice even. "I believed Marcia when she swore the child could only be mine. And I've seen the child. Rose." His breath caught at the thought of the trusting little girl. "Her hair, her eyes are like mine. She has a Riboud stubborn streak, too."

"Chase," his mother implored, "don't rush into things—"

"You were both right behind me when I told you of my plans to gain custody."

"That was before—"

"Before what?"

"This is not a normal child. There will be difficulties—"

"Not *normal?*" Chase couldn't contain his anger. "You make her sound like some freak. Rose is a slow learner. I believe the clinical term for it is Down's syndrome. But she loves hugs and flowers and pie with ice cream. That doesn't sound too far from normal to me.''

"But what is Down's syndrome, exactly?'' his father asked. ''What are the challenges for both parent and child? What is the prognosis for the quality of her life? What are her educational needs? Her medical needs?''

''I don't know.'' And his ignorance drove him crazy.

"How would she fit into our family?'' his mother asked softly.

Chase gritted his teeth before saying, ''The same way any of the grandchildren have, *Maman.*''

''*Cher,* it would be so difficult. The other grandbabies are so quick—''

''You're seeing the disability, not the child.'' He caught himself. Wasn't that exactly what he had done? But only for an instant. In the seconds after meeting Rose, the love and sheer joy shared by adoptive mother and child seized and held him rapt. ''If only you could see her—''

''You should leave well enough alone, son.'' His father's voice was gruff and filled with disappointment. ''You will have other children.''

No, he would not have other children. The risk was too great.

Yet he couldn't bring himself to confide in his parents on that score. If they couldn't understand and accept Down's syndrome in a little girl they'd never met, how could he expect them to understand a skewed infertility in a robust Cajun man? A military officer. Their son.

He kept silent.

''Will you keep your job now?'' his mother asked.

''Yes.''

''Why?''

''It's a good job.'' Besides, he had some decisions to make—without the support or counsel of his family.

''Keep in touch,'' his father said, his voice softening.

"I will. Godspeed." Slowly, Chase hung up the receiver and felt as disconnected as the call.

A bitter sense that he was, at this moment, truly alone in the world washed over him. At this difficult juncture in his mission, he'd counted on his parents' encouragement, sanction he hadn't received.

Perhaps he should pack his bags and call it all a done deal.

But two images kept him from doing just that. The first was the memory of Fiona in his arms on top of Smoke Mountain. She had felt good in his embrace as no other woman had. Second came the vision of devotion and happiness Rose shared with her adoptive mother. A deep-down part of him craved that kind of unreserved attachment. Wasn't that why he'd set out on this journey in the first place?

The twists and turns and complications had made this journey almost unrecognizable from the black-and-white plan he'd devised in the beginning. Circumstances were far more delicate and convoluted than he anticipated, circumstances that required a reformatted plan. And before he could construct a plan, he must answer some vital questions.

First and foremost, could he handle fatherhood when his daughter had special needs?

To answer this question, he had to dispel his ignorance concerning Down's syndrome. He determined to use the resources of Asheville General.

A week later, Fiona stood by the water cooler at the back of her clinic, a cup of unsipped water in her hand.

"Raise a cup to closing time," Sadie chirped as she bustled by. "It hasn't come a moment too soon. I have a warm man and a cold beer at home, and my dogs are barking something fierce."

"It turned out to be a busy week," Fiona admitted.

"No emergencies, though. We should count our blessings."

"Mmm." No emergencies meant no appearance by the mercy flight team. No Chase. For seven whole days. Not even a casual encounter. Fiona thought that odd, especially since he'd declared they needed to talk.

"Of course," Sadie continued, her look a little bit of matchmaking provocation, "it would have been nice to rest weary eyes on that handsome pilot. You seen him around—off-duty—since you took him to see Alva Biggs?"

"No. Not since then." Despite her best intentions, Fiona blushed.

Sadie straightened. "Is there something you didn't tell ole Sadie about *then?*"

"I think maybe Chase Riboud might be deliberately avoiding me during his free time."

"What?" Sadie, reaching out, laid her hand on Fiona's arm. Concern emanated from the nurse's touch. "What could have happened between you two?"

"For one thing, he kissed me." There. She'd said it. Holding it in all week had just about given her a migraine.

"Where?"

Fiona pulled a moue. "On the lips, Sadie."

"Stop kidding around!" Sadie whacked her gently on the upper arm. "Where in town? When did he find the opportunity?"

"In the meadow behind Alva's house. The day I took him to meet Auntie."

Sadie whistled long and low. "The man works fast."

"It wasn't like that." She tried to explain. "I didn't get the feeling he was hitting on me so much as I sensed…a great yearning in him."

"Well, he has been locked away in the military."

"The military's not prison."

Sadie plopped her hands on her hips. "You're intent on not being serious, aren't you?"

"I'm just trying not to make too much of it."

"The man's attracted to you."

"I thought so too…until…"

"Until what?"

"Until we ran into Rose and Martha on the way down the mountain."

"And? He knew you were a single mom."

Bless Sadie. Like most of the residents of Bertie's Hollow, she'd all but forgotten Rose's differences.

"It takes a good man to date a single mother," Fiona began, her heart aching at the truth. "It takes an exceptional man to begin a relationship with a woman with a special child."

"Did he show signs of backing away?" Sadie's face flushed with indignation.

"Nooo…." Fiona tried to remember exactly his reaction. "He seemed shocked at first. But that military control of his soon reestablished itself. He was polite. And cool."

"How did Rose react to him?"

"As usual. She was ready to bring him home to eat pie with ice cream and make kudzu baskets."

Grinning, Sadie shook her head. "That Rosie. Such an accepting little one."

"That's precisely why I can't afford to let a man into my life who is capable of less than unconditional love for my child. Chase's absence tells me he's not willing to travel that road."

"Slow down!" Sadie held up her hands. "He didn't ask you to marry him. He just kissed you. He's attracted to you. You might enjoy each other's company. Might go out occasionally. Have some adult fun." She squinted at Fiona. "You do remember what adult fun is, don't you?"

"I don't know." Fiona ignored Sadie's lighthearted teasing. "I sense that this particular man wants more from me than I can give."

"Did he say anything to lead you to believe that?"

"No." Fiona rubbed the chill from her arms. "It was just a feeling that came over me."

"You and your feelings!" Sadie threw her hands in the air. "For every time they help you with a patient, they restrict your personal life. They make a harsh jailer holding you behind emotional bars."

Fiona hated to admit the grain of truth in her friend's words. In her practice, her empathetic skills liberated her, raised her to a new level of healing capabilities. But in her personal life—not with Rose, but with her own, private, hidden wants and needs—her supersensitivity made her cautious to the extreme.

When Chase had kissed her on Smoke Mountain, and when she kissed him back, she'd cast caution to the winds. And that momentary boldness had felt wonderful.

"Take a chance," Sadie persisted. "For a woman who took some daring steps in her life—becoming a doctor and adopting Rose to name but two—you sure are chicken when it comes to affairs of the heart."

Fiona stared at her assistant in surprise. "Neither becoming a doctor nor adopting Rose were daring acts. They were simply part of who I am."

"Then why don't you open up to the possibility of some kind of more-than-just-professional relationship with Chase Riboud? He might prove to be part of who you are."

The thought had occurred to Fiona. The issue, however, seemed moot. Chase hadn't attempted any contact professional or otherwise since he'd met her daughter.

She would put thoughts of his kiss and his dark eyes

full of longing and her one rash flight into personal freedom out of her mind.

Chase had made great strides in dispelling his ignorance
in the past week. He also made a couple of important personal decisions. The accomplishment called for some controlled R and R, R and R that would begin to bring his
decisions to life.

Hoping that the ticket window would be open for ad-
vanced sales, he pulled his newly purchased pickup truck
into the parking lot of the Asheville cinema.

His parents' denial and withdrawal of support on top of
his own shock at discovering Rose's Down's syndrome
had thrown his plans into a cocked hat. But once he realized he could make no new plans until he educated himself concerning Down's children, he galvanized his energy
to that end.

For seven days he'd used every minute of his spare time,
checking reference sources in the public library, scouring
the Internet, and talking with hospital personnel. The facts
about the condition were fairly clear-cut. He could absorb
facts without becoming emotionally involved. The thing
that had opened his mind, however, had been a declaration
on a kid-generated website. Across a rainbow background
a banner proclaimed, ''My problem isn't how I look. It's
how you see me.''

He'd repeated it to a social services worker at the hospital and she'd told him that retardation was a disability
to the extent family members viewed it as one.

Fiona hadn't seemed to view it as one at all.

Now Chase needed to spend less time with background
research and more time getting to know his daughter.

He got out of the truck and walked to the cinema ticket
window where a teenage girl sat, looking bored.

''I'd like three tickets to the one o'clock showing of *The*

Wish Machine,'' he said, anticipation rising at the thought of taking Rose and Fiona to this G-rated feature-length animation. When was the last time he'd seen a movie that didn't involve military hardware and a plot to save the world from assorted terrorists?

"That'll be twelve dollars," the teenager managed to reply between several loud pops of her gum.

"And do you have any of those posters left?" The marquee had proclaimed one poster free to a family while supplies lasted. Trying to redefine family, he felt himself eligible.

"Yeah." The girl slid the tickets, his change and a rolled-up poster through the arch in the window. "Enjoy the movie."

He planned to.

Slipping the tickets into his breast pocket and the poster under his arm, he jingled his change all the way to his new truck. He was about to begin the process of including his daughter in his life. After a week of research and hard introspection, he believed himself capable of living up to Rose's needs.

Although he hadn't been able to shake the feeling of Fiona in his arms, of her kiss, so warm and so receptive, he had to admit that if he pursued a romantic relationship with the adoptive mother of his child before she knew the truth, the results could be disastrous.

But he couldn't tell Fiona the truth yet.

To his own way of thinking, his reasoning made sense. Rose was his priority. His one real chance for a child of his own. He'd originally planned to find her, to reveal himself, to gain sole custody and to take her home to Louisiana. To the Riboud clan.

Now, circumstances had changed. His mother and father had all but pulled in the welcome mat. Of greater weight than that turn of events was the discovery that Rose and

Fiona had formed a tremendous bond. How could he remove his daughter from the only home she'd ever known without causing her incredible pain? Needing to offer her something more than she currently experienced, he had even gone so far in his replanning as to consider joint custody.

Before he could consider joint custody, however, he had to form a bond with his daughter without disrupting her sense of security. To do so, he needed Fiona's friendship, friendship unencumbered or fogged by hormones run amok. He needed the mother, this remarkable woman, to get to know him in a platonic way, to respect him, both personally and professionally; so that in the end, his dilemma would be clear to her and she would understand why he had to come to Bertie's Hollow.

But remaining just friends with Fiona Applegate might be the most difficult challenge he'd ever set himself.

Chapter Five

Fiona opened her cabin's screen door to find Chase standing on her front porch, holding a rolled-up sheet of paper, an almost bashful grin transforming his handsome features. She didn't quite know what surprised her more—his appearance after a weeklong absence or that grin. Until now, the stern pilot had not shown himself the grinning type. And this grin spoke of a vulnerability she would never have associated with Chase Riboud.

She prepared to put her professional-relationship-only vow to work.

"Am I needed at the clinic?" She closed the clinic, officially, on Saturday afternoons, but she always responded when called.

"No." He pulled three tickets from his shirt pocket. "I'd like you and Rose to go to the movies with me. One o'clock in Asheville. I know you're off this afternoon. The ground ambulance crew is covering for me."

"Oh, dear." Fiona's heart did a little flip, torn between want and reason. "I'm sorry you've already bought the tickets because we couldn't possibly go." Seeing a movie in Asheville with Chase Riboud didn't register on her list of professional activities.

"Why not?" Unfazed, he unrolled the sheet of paper in his hands to expose a poster for *The Wish Machine*. "Have you already seen it?"

Fiona groaned as she recognized the movie Rose had begged and begged to see. Unfortunately, her clinic schedule and her round of house calls had pushed the unseen movie further and further into the background. She'd hoped for a swift release to videotape. And now this man—the very same man she'd vowed to avoid on a personal basis—stood on her doorstep with three tickets, an invitation and the knowledge that her afternoon was free.

"I'll even spring for ice-cream sundaes afterward."

"Mama, who's here?" Rose's voice behind her startled Fiona out of a soda fountain reverie.

"You remember Mr. Chase? He just stopped by to say hello." Maybe Chase would take the hint and leave.

Too late.

"*Wish Machine!*" Rose had spotted the unrolled poster in Chase's hands. She rushed past Fiona, thrusting open the screen door, to stand before Chase, her nose almost pressed to the poster of the longed-for movie.

"I brought this for you." Chase handed the poster to Rose.

"Thank you," Fiona prompted.

"Thank you!" Unadulterated happiness lit her daughter's round face. "I want to see this movie!"

Chase said not a word as he looked over Rose's head directly at Fiona. His intense gaze said simply, *Please.*

In her mind Fiona ticked off all the reasons she should say no. She had just met this man. But her heart said, *He is already something to you.* She needed to protect Rose. But her instinct said, *Rose has already accepted him.* More than any other reason, she was hurt that, after one glorious kiss in the meadow, he could stay absent and silent for a whole week. But her head said, *Get over it, Fiona. You're not a teenager.*

Resolving to behave as an adult, she straightened her shoulders.

Knowing that her daughter would purely delight in a movie and ice-cream sundae outing, Fiona swallowed hard and nodded her head in assent.

Chase knelt before Rose as if, all along, he'd expected Fiona to say yes. "How would you like to see the movie now?"

"Yes!" Rosie planted a loud kiss on the poster, then started down the porch steps.

"Young lady," Fiona said, smiling in spite of herself. "First you have to turn off your computer and tell Martha where we're going."

Pausing on the bottom step, Rose shrugged, her almost perpetual smile energizing the area around her. "Oh, right." She trudged back up the steps. "Don't move," she cautioned Chase before disappearing within the cabin, dragging the poster behind her.

Not finished with suspicion, Fiona stepped onto the porch. "Why are you doing this?"

"I want to stay on your good side."

What an odd answer. "Why?"

His gaze, dark and sensuous, swept over her. "Because you're the key to the success of this mercy flight program." His cool, rational words didn't match his hot regard. "When you introduce me to the residents of Bertie's Hollow, you make my job of fitting in twice as easy. I need your professional sanction."

His hooded look said he needed more.

"I already agreed to introduce you round. I don't need a…what would you call it?…a kickback in the form of an afternoon at the movies."

He chuckled, a deep, throaty sound that sent shivers down Fiona's spine. "This is not a bribe," he said, his strong white teeth flashing. "But if you don't accept the you-scratch-my-back-I'll-scratch-yours idea, let's just say I'm new in town and I miss taking the Riboud grandchildren to the matinee."

"Let's go!" Rose burst from the house, slamming the screen door in her exuberant wake. She still clutched the movie poster under her arm.

Because of Rose, Fiona couldn't resist this field trip. "Don't you want to leave your poster in your room?"

"Nope."

Chase smiled. "I like a woman who needs no time to make up her mind."

Fiona slipped her arm around her daughter's shoulder. "Oh, this young lady can make up her mind, all right. Her's and everyone else's around her."

Tugging on her mother's shirt, Rose spoke very slowly, enunciating each word. "I would like to see the movie, *please*." She ended the request with a rather fierce show of teeth. Fiona recognized the exaggerated politeness as a mask for her daughter's eagerness. They'd been working on patience and good manners.

"Me, too." Chase's glance at Fiona held just a hint of triumph. "Let's take my truck. It's new and I want to break it in."

As Chase followed Rose down the front steps, Fiona took a gander at the new vehicle. It was big. The biggest model made by that particular company. And red. With an extended cab, four doors, and a back seat. Quite a truck for a single individual without even the requisite hill dog.

Now, who all was this bachelor planning to carry around in his shiny new purchase?

Chase opened both passenger side doors. "Where would you like to sit?" he asked Rose.

"Up front. I can do it myself," Rose declared as Chase attempted to help her climb the running board.

Over her daughter's head, he caught Fiona's gaze. "Independent too."

She laughed. "You don't know the half of it."

"You coming, Mama?" With a satisfied air, Rose buckled her seat belt.

"Yeah, Mama." Chase cocked one eyebrow. "You coming?"

Oh, my. If she hadn't already forged a resolute picture in her mind of Chase as a spit-and-polish, task-oriented, rational man, she might think he was flirting with her.

"After I get my purse."

Chase shook his head. "Treat's on me."

"I feel uncomfortable with that."

"I owe you for the diagnosis and sinus tablets the other day. I can finally breathe."

"Your insurance covered those, and you know it."

Rose threw up her hands. "Mama, are we going to miss the movie?"

"No." Surrendering her stubbornness to Rose if not quite to Chase, Fiona grabbed her purse and lightly skipped down the porch steps and across the front yard. "I'm coming."

It was just that, having taken care of herself and her loved ones with an ardent independence all these years, it was difficult for her to let others do for her.

Having closed Rose's door, Chase stood next to the rear passenger door as if he were about to help Fiona into the cab.

She smiled sweetly up at him, trying to suppress the

feeling that, in accepting this invitation to a movie and ice cream, she had made herself far too vulnerable. "I *also* can do it myself."

"Ah, yes, the self-sufficient Applegate women." Admiration echoed in his words as his regard assessed her with an intensity that made moisture form at her hairline.

She mounted the running board, careful not to brush against him, then slid along the narrow back seat.

"Comfortable?" he asked before closing the door.

No, she was not in any way, shape or manner *comfortable.*

Patting the fender as he circled the truck, he moved with the predatory grace of a wildcat. There were still wildcats in these mountains. North American panthers of terrifying beauty. She had, on rare occasions, seen them. Chase simultaneously unsettled and fascinated her in the same way those nondomesticated creatures of the forest did.

He slid behind the wheel and engaged the ignition.

"What's this?" Rose had discovered several CDs on the console. She opened one.

"Cajun fiddle music. Want to hear it?"

"Yes." Rose reached toward the player.

"You might want to let me do that although I haven't figured out all the bells and whistles yet."

"I can do it." Rose hugged the disc to her chest. "I have one of these."

Chase glanced in the rearview mirror, question in his eyes.

"She does." Fiona smiled, thinking he was about to learn an interesting aspect of some Down's syndrome individuals. Many, Rose among them, were uncannily fearless in the face of technology.

As Chase turned the truck around and headed down the lane, Rose slipped the CD into its player, then adjusted the tuning and the volume. When the strains of lively fiddle music filled the cab, she sat back in her seat with a loud sigh, her hands and feet moving to the music.

Chase looked at his daughter, a surprised but pleased expression on his face. "You like this?"

"Yes!" Rose bounced happily on her seat.

"How about you, Fiona?" Chase's reflection in the rearview mirror and her name on his lips gave her goose bumps.

"I like it fine. It sounds like party music."

"It is. Riboud party music." He glanced at her in the rearview mirror again, his quick gaze dark and probing. "Do you dance?"

"Mama and I dance," Rose declared.

Chase grinned. "I'll keep that in mind."

He'd better keep in mind that one normally—and safely—drove with eyes on the road, not on the back seat. Too, she wanted to remind him that their relationship was strictly professional. No parties. No dancing. She'd made a promise to herself and fully intended to keep it.

Just as soon as this afternoon of movie and ice cream ended.

Sitting outside the ice-cream parlor with Fiona at a picnic table under the budding trees, Chase pushed aside his empty ice-cream sundae container and watched Rose lying on the grass, inspecting the journey of a caterpillar. Oblivious to the world around her, the little girl softly hummed in a singsong rhythm as she stretched out on her stomach, her chin propped on her hands, observing but not touching the undulating green insect. She'd lain thus for ten minutes now.

The afternoon, for Chase as well, had been full of observations.

He'd noted that Rose's enjoyment—of the fiddle music in the truck, of the movie, of the ice cream, and now of the caterpillar—had been marked by an unfettered gusto. She didn't prioritize her pleasure. One entertainment was as agreeable as the next, and each received her undivided attention.

He glanced across the picnic table at Fiona. Sitting in dappled sunshine, she seemed to belong to the outdoors, seemed at peace, content to let the breeze caress her while she cast a loving and protective gaze over Rose.

In his plan to gain custody of his daughter, he hadn't expected her adoptive mother to be anything like Fiona. His goal would be so much easier to attain if Fiona were less Chase's ideal of motherhood. If she were stricter, more permissive, more self-absorbed, more domineering, less intuitive—to any degree—he could have said without a doubt, with biology on his side, *This child absolutely belongs with me. Her father.*

But Fiona had turned out to be…Fiona. Throwing absolutes out the window, making his tightrope-act mission all that much more difficult.

"Tell me," he said in an attempt to engage Fiona in conversation, "about Rose's home schooling."

She turned to him, leveling a gaze as cool and green as a mountain stream and making him feel a need to explain his interest.

"Just curious," he said. "Among my brothers and sisters, the choice seems to be between public and parochial school. We don't have any home schoolers in the family, so I'm not familiar with the concept."

"Home schooling is a wonderful way to individualize Rose's education." Her answer seemed guarded.

"Who teaches? You? Martha?" With all his Down's syndrome research in Asheville, he hadn't been able to run a background check on Martha. He still intended to.

"We both teach." Fiona almost visibly weighed the decision to tell him more. "And we share subjects with Martha's daughter, who home schools, also. Her family lives below us on Smoke Mountain. On occasion, we've even hooked up through computer with the regional elementary school for certain courses or special projects.''

Chase glanced at Rose, who had rolled over onto her back and was now staring with a beatific smile up into the branches of the trees. "Don't you worry about her social development?''

Fiona stiffened. "I don't think you need hordes of people to develop socially.''

"I'm sorry. I didn't mean to imply you weren't doing your job as a parent.'' Chase regretted his frank off-putting question. "Let me try to dig myself out of this hole. Rose seems so open, so curious, so sociable. I wondered if maybe she wouldn't love the activity of a regular school.''

"She might...'' Fiona gazed at Rose, then turned her attention to Chase. "But the bigger world can hurt as well as enlighten. She still needs me to act as a filter.'' She smiled. "In case you haven't noticed, my Rosie is pure unlayered emotion.''

Oh, he'd noticed. In fact, he'd even been a little envious. He was emotionally layered to the extreme. In his past line of work *covert* equaled *safe,* in more ways than one.

"It's a daunting task, raising a child,'' he said, shaking his head. "My brothers and sisters say the most challenging aspect is to raise independent individuals.''

"Even independence must be tailored to the individual.''

"How independent will Rose become?''

Fiona toyed with the spoon in her empty sundae container before she turned her clear gaze to Chase. "I've never made a casual acquaintance who asked such probing questions about my daughter.''

"We're not casual acquaintances.''

A deep blush swept Fiona's pretty features.

"Are you planning to have a family?" Gathering her composure, she turned the tide of questioning against him. "Is that why you're so interested in the details of child rearing?"

He felt the pang of her probing deep inside. He'd always wanted to belong to a family of his own, with a woman as warm and beautiful as Fiona and a child as unconditionally loving as Rose. But now...

"Howdy, folks!" A booming voice cut into his thoughts, saving him from a painful answer or an equally painful evasion.

Farmer Increase Murdock and his wife, Inez, approached them. Increase's hearty handshake and Inez's open smile surprised Chase, for the couple had been cool to him when he'd seen them on occasion in Bertie's Hollow. Now, however, they seemed most agreeable, accepting even.

"What've you folks been doing?" Inez asked.

Rose, having risen from her grassy bed, ran to the picnic table where she grasped the now very wrinkled poster of *The Wish Machine*. "We saw this movie!"

"Did you like it?" Increase bent to chuck Rose under the chin.

"Yes! Mama and Mr. Chase, too."

Inez eyed Chase. "If you like family entertainment, Mr. Riboud, you must bring Fiona and Rose to our community center's Friday night specials. Sometimes we show a movie, sometimes we play games, sometimes we dance. Square dancing. Clogging. Old-timey stuff."

Grinning, Rose poked Chase in the thigh. "Bring your fiddle music."

"Do you play, Mr. Riboud?" Inez's acceptance had not thawed to a first-name basis.

"Please, call me Chase."

Inez glanced at Fiona as if seeking assurance. "Chase, then. Do you fiddle?"

"I used to." He'd almost forgotten that long-ago pleasure. "But Rose was referring to my collection of CDs."

"Pity. A holler can never claim too many fiddlers." Increase's expression softened as he reached out to ruffle Rose's hair. "Have your mama bring you by to see the new chicks." He pumped Chase's hand again. "Don't be a stranger."

Well, if that didn't beat all. Stunned, Chase watched the Murdocks depart.

In Fiona's company, he'd become a member of Bertie's Hollow. The respect she generated in the community and her association with him made him downright respectable. Her quiet influence made her a force to be reckoned with…if he still considered her an adversary. He didn't. He admired her in much the same way her neighbors did, at the same time she fascinated him in a very personal way. That dual admiration and fascination complicated a goal he once thought simple.

"Come see my ca'pillar." Rose tugged on his sleeve.

"Okay." To diminish the mother's power over him, he concentrated on the child. "Show me."

"Oh, no!" Rose wailed, returning to her observation nest. "She's gone!" A look of utter desolation crossed the child's face. "Where? Where? Where?" she keened as she hunted frantically in the grass.

Chase felt his daughter's disappointment at the same time he felt powerless to assuage it.

Fiona stepped to Rose's side. "Rose, listen to me." With great calm she cupped the girl's chin in her hand, made eye contact. "Caterpillars, like you, need to eat and to rest. They also need to hide from birds who might eat them."

"She's hiding from birds, not Rose?" Rose didn't appear entirely satisfied with this possibility.

"Perhaps."

"Or resting?"

"Maybe building a cocoon in which to sleep and become a beautiful butterfly. Do you remember the caterpillar that turned into a butterfly in your terrarium?"

"I want to see her sleeping. Now." Determination etched on her face, the child pulled away from Fiona and began to search the grass again.

Chase thought of a diversion. "I can teach you how to play a lullaby for your caterpillar."

Rose's head snapped up. "Show me."

"Yes, do." Crossing her arms over her chest, Fiona cocked her head in amused interest.

"First I have to find the perfect instrument." Kneeling next to Rose, he plucked a broad blade of grass.

She watched him with an eager intensity.

Tightly stretching the grass between his thumbs, he raised the simple reed "pipe" to his lips.

"Dear Lord, you're not going to teach her that!" Fiona exclaimed, laughing. "I won't have a moment's peace."

Squinting, Rosie leaned so close to Chase he could feel her warm fudge-scented breath on his face. "Teach me."

With a wink at Fiona, he blew on the narrow space between the taut blade and his thumbs, creating an ear-splitting whistle.

At first he thought he'd frightened Rose, so wide did her eyes become. And then her face split into a wonderful impish grin as she danced around him.

"Teach me! Teach me!" she pleaded, the caterpillar forgotten in this new joy.

A simple happiness pooled in Chase's heart. His daughter wanted something of him. It was only a grass whistle, but it was a start.

* * *

Fiona leaned her head against the cool truck window and gazed out at the familiar passing scenery as Rose dozed in the front seat and Chase drove them home from a surprising afternoon.

Having watched Chase help Rose master the age-old childhood trick of grass whistling, Fiona had seen in him a flicker of the father he might become—strong, kind and patient. And, without reservation, her daughter had accepted him as a friend. Because of Rosie's unconditional acceptance, Fiona needed to ask herself two very important questions.

What kind of a man was Chase Riboud? And…how did she feel about him?

She could take his measure only through careful observation. Already she'd seen his military strength of bearing, his ability to take charge, his professional competence, and then, briefly, a glimmer of his fatherly potential. But she suspected there was much more to him than first met the eye.

As to the more personal question, conflicting feelings swirled within her, threatening sensory overload. At the root of her conflict lay the undeniable attraction she felt for him. Even as he unsettled her, she felt a strange ease with him. Like now. She could almost imagine the three of them, a family, heading home after a regular Saturday outing.

"Is this nap Rose's taking going to create a problem for you at bedtime?" His voice, rough and low, roused her.

She looked up to find his gaze in the rearview mirror upon her.

"Perhaps," she replied. "But Martha and I have learned to deal with situations as they arise."

"Have you thought of marrying? Giving Rose a father?"

Fiona nearly choked on his direct question. "You're not one for small talk, are you?"

"Negative." He shook his head. "I spent twenty years getting to the point."

"Well…" Fiona's fingers fluttered to her heart as she sought to lighten the conversation. They had fifteen minutes yet before they reached her cabin. She didn't want to cause a confrontation—although perhaps Chase's boldness deserved it. But not with her daughter sleeping in the front seat. "Maybe it's the storyteller in us, but here in Bertie's Hollow we get to know a person through a little more indirect route."

"Such as?"

"You might ask what my interests are. Do I hunt? Do I fish? Those are suitable questions for this area."

He actually grinned. "Even taking an indirect route, Fiona, those are not questions I'd ask you."

"Then let me ask you a few." Anything to turn the spotlight from her. "What are your interests besides Cajun fiddle music?"

He paused. "Baseball. Spicy food. And a good yarn told by someone who grew up without television."

"The yarns you can find aplenty in these parts, but I'm afraid you'll have to import your spicy food from Louisiana."

"My sister's already sent me a case of Tabasco sauce."

"Use it in private." Fiona smiled. "The cooks around here would take umbrage otherwise."

"I'll keep that in mind." He glanced over his shoulder. "Any other suggestions for fitting in?"

"Yes." She leaned forward in her seat, suddenly aware of a way he could begin to know the area and its people without following her around, driving her senses to distraction. "Shared history is important to the people of these hills. You'd do yourself a big favor by boning up on local events.''

''How do I do that when folks won't open up to me unless you're around?''

''Back issues of newspapers. Tobias Jones puts out a small weekly right here in Bertie's Hollow. It's mostly upbeat announcements and ads. But the Asheville public library would have more newsworthy regional newspapers on microfilm.''

''And you think this would be helpful?''

''Yes, I do.'' In her intensity, she leaned so far forward in her seat that she noticed several scars running along Chase's forearm.

Although she had a large *sense* of him, up until now she'd tried to avoid acknowledging him physically. His physical presence unnerved her. But now, as a doctor, she couldn't help but notice these curious scars, for they'd healed in a manner that suggested they hadn't been treated properly.

Without thinking, she reached out and touched his forearm with her fingertips. ''How did you receive these?''

He stiffened. ''So much for the indirect method of getting to know a man.''

''I'm asking as a doctor.'' She withdrew her hand from his arm. ''The scars suggest the wounds were treated inexpertly.''

''You do the best you can in the field.'' His answer was curt, unfeeling.

''I just assumed that in a peacetime military, you'd have immediate care.''

''Peace is a matter of perspective. Stateside, we're at peace.'' The muscles along his jaw rippled with an obvious tension. ''But there are many parts of the world in conflict. Parts that require a U.S. presence.''

''Was that the kind of duty you pulled?''

"Mostly."

She felt a darkness emanate from him. Was it a result of what he'd experienced or of what he'd become? In either case, this was not the man who'd taught her daughter to whistle on a blade of grass.

With a sharp intake of breath, Fiona sat back in her seat. "I'm sorry."

"You have no need to be sorry. I did my job." He hesitated. "But your ability to feel others' pain probably makes you a damn good doctor."

He seemed to offer an olive branch of sorts, and she accepted it. "Thank you."

Pulling his truck into the Bertie's Hollow convenience store parking lot and coming to a stop alongside the gas pumps, he said, "Do you mind if I top off my tank? It'll save me time later." He seemed a stranger, polite and distant.

"Go ahead. I need to get bread and milk anyway." She tapped Rose on the shoulder. "Sweetheart, come with Mama."

Rose rubbed her eyes. "Are we home?"

"Almost." Fiona opened her door, glad for the rush of fresh air into the too close cab.

As Chase turned his attention to pumping gas, Fiona took her daughter's hand and led her into the store.

"Hey, Jodi." Fiona greeted the cashier who leaned against the counter. Jodi was nineteen, nine months pregnant and obviously weary. "How are you feeling?"

"Big, Doc. Big." The young woman rubbed her extended belly protectively.

"You have my number. You feel the slightest twinge, you call me. Day or night. Otherwise I'll see you for your regular checkup next Wednesday."

"Okay." The mother-to-be offered a wan smile.

On her way to the refrigerated section, Fiona cast a

glance at the two booths near the plate glass window. Raymond Hickock, Jodi's out-of-work husband, sat in one, a can of beer in front of him. This was one family situation Fiona intended to monitor closely.

"Can we get cookies?" Rose had come fully awake.

"We have cookies at home, love. Help me carry the milk, please."

She heard the jangle of a bell, signaling the opening of the front door.

"Hi. Ten bucks. Pump number four." Chase's voice came to her from the front of the store. "I'm Chase Riboud. We haven't met."

"Jodi Hickock."

"When are you due?"

Oh, dear. Although she knew Chase asked these kinds of questions so that he could anticipate medical situations, his direct address would sooner or later land him in trouble.

Before Fiona could make it to the counter, she heard a clatter as if someone had pushed over a display stack.

"Who the hell are you to make time with my wife?" Raymond Hickock's drunken voice threatened the afternoon peace.

Trouble had found Chase sooner rather than later.

Chapter Six

"I asked you a question," Raymond Hickock snarled. "Who the hell are you, and why do you think you can make time with my wife?"

Fiona started toward the front of the store to intervene, but Rose whimpered and wrapped her arms around her mother's leg, stopping her.

"It's all right, baby," Fiona assured her daughter in a low voice. "Raymond's hurting, but we're going to make it all better."

Before she could make her way to Chase's side, however, she heard his steady voice. "I'm Chase Riboud, the new mercy flight pilot."

"And I'm Dale Earnhard." Sarcasm and rage dripped in equal measure.

Chase ignored the taunt. "I asked your wife when she was due in case she needed the airborne services."

"We don't want or need your services. The baby—*my*

baby's gonna be delivered at home." The soon-to-be father had a bad case of possessiveness mixed with one too many beers. "I'll teach you to mess where you're not wanted." Raymond lunged toward Chase.

Chase sidestepped, and Raymond slammed into the cashier's counter.

"Ray, honey," Jodi pleaded, "go home."

"And leave you with this lying dirtbag?" Chase's easy sidestepping maneuver had infuriated Raymond. He glared at the pilot with murder in his eyes. "Can you fight like a man, pretty boy?"

"Sweet Jesus!" Jodi wailed. "Take it outside! I'll lose my job, Raymond!"

Fiona's heart pounded in her chest. She didn't want to frighten Rose. She didn't want Jodi, nine month's pregnant, getting unduly agitated. And she didn't want a drunk Raymond taking on Chase. Chase could snap Raymond in two like a twig. And would he? The memory of the darkness she'd sensed earlier in the ex-military man haunted her.

"Raymond!" she called out in her most authoritative voice.

Three faces turned in her direction. Rose hugged her leg even more tightly.

"Doc, this ain't no fight of yours." Raymond slurred his words.

"There's no fight in the first place," Fiona declared, taking a step forward, drawing Rose with her. "This man is Chase Riboud, our mercy flight pilot. Just as he says. He's been making rounds with me, meeting folks, explaining the program. He's part of my team, and, as part of my team, he has Jodi's best interests—*health* interests—at heart."

Before Fiona, Raymond hung his head.

"What in tarnation happened here?" The front door

opened and Bert Ackworth, the manager of the convenience store, entered. "Hickock, you making trouble again?" He spied the two-liter bottles of soft drinks from the floor display tumbled across the checkered linoleum. "How in hell did you cause this mess?"

"We were just discussing who could give Raymond a ride home," Fiona declared, her words even, her emotions controlled. "Would you, please, do it, Bert?" She didn't think it wise to put Raymond—even a deflated Raymond—in the same truck with Chase.

"Not until he cleans up this floor display." Bert set his chin.

"I did that." Chase turned to the manager. "Sorry, I wasn't watching where I was going. I'll set it right."

Fiona quickly hid her surprise. "Would you drive Raymond home then, Bert?"

"I suppose," the manager grumbled, casting a pitying glance at Jodi. "C'mon, Ray. Let's get you home to sleep it off."

His eyes half-closed, Raymond paused before the cash register. He seemed unable to look Jodi full in the face. "I'm sorry, darlin'," he said.

Merely nodding, Jodi made a shooing motion. Without looking at Chase, Raymond followed Bert out the door.

"Oh, Doc, what am I going to do?" The young woman turned big, moist eyes on Fiona. "He's a good man, really he is, but being out of work has just about killed him."

"I know. And I think I can help."

"You do?"

"I have to discuss my plan with my partner, here." Smiling, she nodded at Chase who met her look with one of incredulity. Well, calling him *partner* so naturally had surprised her, too. "Then I'll explain it to you and Raymond."

The mother-to-be waddled to the front of the counter

where she threw her arms around her doc. "Fiona, you are sent from heaven!"

"Fiddlesticks!" Fiona blushed. "Now, let's restack these bottles."

Driving the last of the dirt road to the Applegate cabin, Chase turned to Fiona. "Are you going to share your plan for Jodi and Raymond with me, *partner?*" He still couldn't believe the little bombshell description she'd bestowed upon him.

"If you'll take a minute to have a glass of lemonade on the porch."

"Wild horses couldn't keep me away."

Rose patted Chase's arm. "Don't be scared. We have no wild horses."

He chuckled. It would be so much simpler to live in Rose's literal world.

As soon as he'd pulled up before the cabin and shut off the motor, Rose unsnapped her seat belt and bolted from the truck, dragging the now tattered movie poster behind. "Let's tell Martha about today!" she shouted gleefully.

"You tell her," Fiona called after her. "Mr. Chase and I have some things to discuss." Stepping out of the truck, she turned to him. "Just let me put away the bread and milk, and I'll be back. Make yourself comfortable on the porch."

It was too easy to make himself comfortable in Fiona's surroundings.

He liked this mountain retreat. He liked a place you needed a four-by-four pickup to get to. He liked the quiet. And he liked rockers on front porches, he thought as he lowered himself into one.

In a matter of minutes, Fiona returned, two icy glasses of lemonade in hand. "Martha's best," she said, offering him one.

She stood a distance away from him, straight and aloof, despite the casual nature of the porch. She may have called him *partner,* but she apparently wasn't about to consider anything but a professional partnership.

"Jodi was right," she said. "Raymond is a good guy. You saw the alcohol talking today."

"What's he doing, letting his pregnant wife stand on her feet all day?"

"He lost his job in a layoff."

"Because of his drinking?"

"No. He started drinking after he lost his job."

"There are other jobs. Why isn't he standing in line at the employment agency in Asheville?"

"His driver's license has been suspended."

"Don't tell me. DUI."

"Yes."

"Of all the immature—"

"Mountain pride's a double-edged sword," Fiona cautioned.

Chase rubbed the back of his neck. "Sounds to me as if Jodi's better off without Raymond. In a few days or weeks she'll have not one but two babies on her hands."

"Don't be too hard on Raymond. I believe he'd get sober if he got a job. And he'd keep the job he got because he loves Jodi to distraction."

"I noticed the distraction part."

Fiona ignored the comment. "He needs a purpose."

"You can't *give* a man purpose, Fiona."

She smiled at him, a lovely open smile that led him to believe he'd been the one spending the last twenty years cloistered in the mountains while she'd been the worldly wise traveler. "You can nudge him in the right direction, though."

"What do you have in mind?"

"I think Jodi and Raymond should take the series of

parenting classes Asheville General offers. Afterward, Raymond could check on prospective jobs at the employment agency.''

''Asheville's a twenty-minute drive, and he doesn't have a driver's license.''

''But you fly back and forth to Asheville at least once a day.''

Chase took a deep breath. ''I'm not a taxi service.''

''But you're not overworked as an ambulance service.'' Fiona crossed the porch, then knelt by his chair. An eager sparkle filled her eyes. Her complexion glowed. Her body tensed with a can-do energy.

All those qualities threatened to distract him from their conversation.

''This is an experimental program, Chase. We can mold it to the area's needs, emergency and otherwise.''

''Why would you be willing to bend the rules for these two?''

''Because they're a family, and families deserve to stay together.''

Stunned by how that sentiment hit home, Chase sought for words.

Fiona's expression became serious. ''Right now Jodi and Raymond's new family is in trouble. False pride and alcohol threaten its very foundation. I can't stand by and watch it fall apart. Watch Raymond desert his wife, his child.'' She laid a hand over his. ''Jodi's unborn child deserves to know its father.''

The child deserved to know its father. This was the crux of Chase's mission. Hearing it voiced by the very woman whose family he had the power to disrupt threw him into a tailspin. ''There must be social workers—''

''Jodi and Raymond trust *me*.''

Trust. Now there was a double-edged sword.

''You might see me as a simple country doctor,'' she

continued, "but I wear many hats in Bertie's Hollow. Family counseling is one of them. One of the most important."

"And you're dedicated to keeping families together."

"To my dying breath." She spoke those four words with such conviction that Chase felt his blood run cold.

Here lay a conundrum worthy of Solomon. Chase had found a woman who could comprehend his need to regain custody of his daughter, yet she was the same woman who would fight to her dying breath to keep that child from him.

Perhaps in helping to work out Jodi and Raymond's problems, he'd get a better handle on his own. "Where do I fit in?" he asked.

Breathing a deep sigh, Fiona smiled, then stood. "You, sir, have just acquired your second Bertie's Hollow hat." She gestured with her hands as if she were crowning him. "I hereby dub you Shuttle Director."

He returned her smile but couldn't feel it deep inside. Too much conflict lay heavy on his heart. He needed to retreat from Fiona's compelling presence. He needed to reassess—once again—how to achieve his goal of reuniting with his daughter without destroying this caring woman.

"I'll talk with the powers-that-be at Asheville General." He rose. "I'd better shove off."

"Come quick!" Rose burst onto the porch. "Henny Penny is sitting on eggs! We will have chicks! Martha says so!"

"Go ahead." Chase looked at Fiona. "I'll see you later."

"No, no!" Rose grasped Chase's hand as well as Fiona's. "You come, too!"

He hadn't meant to stay, but Rose's enthusiasm proved contagious. His daughter had quickly seized the power to move him.

He squeezed Rose's hand. "Lead on."

A quick glance told Chase that Fiona didn't share either the little girl's gleeful invitation or her total acceptance.

Fiona wished Chase had politely declined Rose's call to see the setting hen. She knew her daughter. The tour wouldn't stop with hens and prospective chicks. Having captured an audience, Rosie would happily conduct the grand tour of her domain.

Yet Fiona felt far too vulnerable exposing her home, her private and personal space, to Chase Riboud.

"Henny Penny, Henny Penny, Henny Penny," Rose chanted as she pulled the two adults down the porch steps and around the side of the cabin toward the chicken coop and wired pen.

Her daughter skipped and swung between Fiona and Chase with an emotional ease that suggested she'd been raised by them. Fiona wondered how Chase was reacting inside to this childish familiarity.

On the outside he seemed remarkably interested. In Rose and in their surroundings. Of course, he'd shown an interest in every Bertie's Hollow resident. Fiona reminded herself not to read too much into Chase's attentions.

Stopping outside the chicken coop, Rose raised a finger to her lips. "Shhh!"

"We'd better not go in if Henny Penny's broody," Fiona warned. "She might abandon her eggs. Let's look through the window in the door."

"Lift me up." Rose turned to Chase. *"Please."* She grinned at her mother for having remembered the magic word.

"Up you go." Like a natural father, Chase swung Rose onto his shoulders. Her daughter now sat so high she could see over the little coop's roof.

"No, no! Too high!" Rose crowed with glee, loving every minute of her giant status.

"Lower?" Chase asked, grinning.

"Lower!"

"Here goes." With an ease that came of untold strength, he lifted Rose off his shoulders, then swung her into his arms, bent at the waist and rocked her like an infant, at the height of his knees. "Low enough?"

Rose chortled so hard she hiccuped. "Too low!"

The man obviously had experience with children.

"Too high, too low." Chase rolled his eyes dramatically. "What could this girl possibly want?" He lifted her to the height of his chest and the little screened window on the coop door. "This?"

Rose turned to smile beatifically up at Chase. "This is just right," she said before turning to peer through the window at Henny Penny on her nest.

"I suppose you know," Fiona murmured dryly, "that with all your ruckus, we may now have scrambled eggs."

"I've had experience with chickens. Grandmère Riboud raised free-range fowl." Chase flashed a boyish grin that sent her heart into overtime.

Fiona wished she felt unflappable in his presence. She didn't.

"Look, Mama," Rose whispered, pointing through the window.

Obliging her daughter, Fiona leaned closer to the small opening, assuming Chase would step out of the way. He didn't. Instead he continued to hold Rose so that she could peek into the henhouse, at the same time he stood his ground.

To see the hen, Fiona had to brush against the man.

The memory of the shared mountaintop kiss of a week ago lay unspoken between them, at once a temptation and a caution. His muscle-corded arm holding her daughter while touching Fiona's back filled her with the sensation that this newcomer to Bertie's Hollow, this powerful male was in some way destined to connect with her, Fiona Applegate, and no other. Usually cautious, she should have raised an internal alarm. Rather, she leaned into an incredible yearning. And found herself leaning against Chase's very real, very hard, very warm body.

"Do you see, Mama?" Rose whispered.

"Yes," Fiona murmured, pulling away. She saw all too well.

She saw herself as a woman who'd rejected a social life to the extent she now gravitated recklessly toward the first available single man.

How foolish. And to end that foolishness, she made herself look Chase full in the face to determine his indifference, to quell her schoolgirl ache. No comforting detachment lay in his eyes, however. Instead his dark gaze burned with a fervor that rattled her emotional equilibrium. As though scorched, she winced, then quickly glanced away.

"Come see my swimming hole!" Wriggling from Chase's grasp, Rose extended an invitation to remain that Fiona sought to rescind.

"Mr. Chase has work to do, hon," she cautioned.

"It can wait." A chill late-afternoon breeze accompanied his words as he bent, hands on knees, to look her daughter in the eye. "How far is this swimming hole?"

A sly expression crept over Rose's features. "Not far if you carry me."

"Carry you?"

"On your shoulders!"

Before Fiona could protest, Chase swung her precious little girl high in the air for a shoulder ride.

Fiona didn't know whether the pain she felt around her heart was for the attraction she experienced toward this complex man, or for the resistance she manufactured in the light of Rose's unabashed acceptance of people, old friends and new alike. Or was there more? If Fiona was honest with herself, she might admit that seeing Chase horsing around with Rose brought home the poignant fact that her child had missed such simple fatherly pursuits as shoulder rides.

"Which way?" Chase asked.

"This way!" Rose sang out, pointing up the forest path that led to their secluded stream-fed swimming hole.

Chase set out in the direction Rose pointed, making his way even deeper into Fiona's territory. "Are you coming, Fiona?" he called out.

"Yes." She would follow if only to protect what was hers.

Trudging behind, she couldn't help but notice the economical sway of Chase's lean hips, the breadth of his shoulders and the easy strength of his arms as he held her daughter's legs securely around his neck. From her perch, Rose stretched her hands for leaves that had been, scant moments before, beyond her reach. Chase had changed not only Fiona's perspective but her child's as well.

A sudden rustling in the underbrush refocused her thoughts. A large shaggy creature broke from cover, raced across the path not six feet ahead of them, then disappeared again behind a thicket of rhododendrons.

"Oh, Mama, look!" Rose cried out. "It's Dustmop!"

"What was that?" Chase turned to Fiona, concern evident in his eyes. "Shall we turn back?"

"No, no!" Rose urged. "It was Dustmop!"

"And Dustmop is…?" Chase looked at Fiona for clarification.

"A harmless, half-wild dog we've tried to gentle," Fiona replied. "Rose nicknamed him Dustmop because of his unkempt coat. Everyone in town leaves food out for the creature, but he trusts no one. I'm afraid his wariness is counterproductive to his well-being."

"You could say the same for some people," Chase suggested, his eyes hooded and unreadable.

Uncomfortable under his regard, Fiona raised her hands to Rose. "Come down, Miss Fidget. You'll give Mr. Chase a brush burn with all your bouncing."

Rose went eagerly into Fiona's arms, then slid to the path. "Let's find Dustmop!"

"I thought you were going to show me your swimming hole." Chase cocked his head at Rose.

Rose demurred, caught between the idea of sharing her domain or of chasing the elusive, possible pet.

Although Fiona wanted to call off the entire tour, she opted to sway Rose in favor of the swimming hole. Whereas a romp after Dustmop might take up the entire evening, a viewing of their watery glen could be—if handled right—perfunctory.

She held out her hand to her daughter. "Let's show Mr. Chase the swimming hole. Perhaps Dustmop will come to drink while we're there."

"Okay!"

As Rose took her hand, Fiona felt enormous relief that her daughter was back where she belonged. Next to her. Unfortunately, the path widened to allow Chase to walk beside her as well.

She felt heat and energy—and *something* unnameable and untapped—radiate from him.

"Can you swim this early in the year?" he asked.

"If you're a polar bear," she replied curtly.

"If you're a polar bear," Rose repeated, softening the words with a giggle. Spotting the narrow waterfall that spilled into their private pool, she scampered ahead on the path.

Chase stopped and turned, preventing Fiona from following. "A word with you," he said, his manner one of order rather than request.

"Yes?" Fiona glanced around him to make certain Rose was safe.

"Earlier you suggested to Jodi and Raymond that you and I were partners."

"Of course. *Professional* partners."

"Then you served me lemonade on your front porch as if—"

"As if we were professionals discussing a work-related problem."

"Thank you, Dr. Applegate. You've just proved my point." His words caught her as certainly as if he'd reached out and grasped her arm.

"And what might that point be?"

"Any time we approach the notion of a relationship outside of work, you withdraw. Like now." He tilted her chin so that she had to look directly at him. "I thought we were approaching friendship on your porch."

Her pulse skipped a beat. "I thought we were approaching a solution to Jodi and Raymond's dilemma."

"And once we'd come up with that solution, you wanted me gone. Why is that?"

"Rose has had a tiring day—"

"This has nothing to do with Rose. She has more energy than a dozen Ribouds. *She* asked me to stay." Still cupping Fiona's chin with his hand, Chase brushed the corner of her mouth lightly with the pad of his thumb. "Why do you want me to leave?"

How could she tell him *because your presence fills me with a want that has nothing to do with either career or friendship?*

Turning her head to escape his touch, she replied, "I'm a very private person," then quickly added, "It's nothing personal."

Chase saw the untruth written in Fiona's body language as she set off on the trail after Rose. He didn't press the issue because he didn't trust his own motives in drawing Fiona out.

He wanted to gentle her as she wanted to gentle that half-wild dog, Dustmop. He wanted her to trust him, so that he could make her understand he would make a trustworthy father. But that understanding, when added to the truth of his situation, would surely leave her feeling betrayed.

Why did he pursue this convoluted route? Why didn't he come clean, right now and endure the consequences?

Why not? Because his mission to find his daughter had been clouded and complicated by her adoptive mother. He was attracted to Fiona in a way that went beyond professional respect, far beyond friendship. For brief moments throughout the day he'd allowed himself to think of the three of them as a family. He'd convinced himself he dreamed of a woman *like* Fiona. Sadly, he too lied, even to himself.

Because he wanted *Fiona*. Not someone like Fiona.

But how could he court her with so much left unrevealed between them? And if he told the truth now, wouldn't she shut him out, figuring his attentions arose only from the desire to take away her daughter?

For a man used to untangling other people's messes, he'd put himself in an untenable situation. He must prove himself trustworthy, at the same time he needed to look for the most auspicious moment to level with Fiona and break that trust.

"Mr. Chase! Come see!" Rose's cheerful command cut through his thoughts.

Following the childish voice, he stepped into a shadow-dappled glade that enveloped him with as much surprise magic as the meadow behind Alva Biggs's house. Surrounded by low-hanging trees, a tiny waterfall trickled over rock and moss to splash into a large, crystal-clear pool, the banks of which were dotted with small, cream-colored wildflowers. At the edge of the pool, Fiona sat on a boulder, one knee drawn up in a pose that made her look like some woodland sprite.

"Come see!" Although Rose had wanted to show Chase her swimming hole, she crouched now with her back to the water, staring intently at the ground. "Ants!"

Amid all this natural splendor, she found the tiniest of creatures fascinating. Chase smiled at his daughter's pleasure in the little things in life.

Would the Riboud nephews and nieces find her as sweet as he did, or would they ostracize her for her different perspective?

The question sobering him, he hunkered down beside her. "What are the ants doing?"

"Running."

"I can see that. Look at that little one move." He began to point, but Rose grasped his finger.

"Don't touch."

"I won't hurt them."

"Good." Assured he wouldn't disrupt the colony, she tightly pinched her index fingers and thumbs together. "Be careful. They can bite *you*."

It moved him that she would care about his well-being. "Do they swim in your pool?" he asked, wanting to stretch the companionship out with conversation, however inane.

Rose turned to look over her shoulder. "Do they, Mama?"

Fiona, watching them with a remarkable intensity, frowned as if to clear troubled thoughts. "Not unless a storm blows them into the water."

Patting him on the hand, Rose smiled. "Then they won't bite you when you come swim with us."

Chase glanced at Fiona to see if she seconded the invitation, but could read nothing in her cool, lichen-green gaze.

"Perhaps you'd like to swim today," she said, the corners of her mouth lifting slightly.

He flicked a hand in the icy spring water. "Are you trying to turn me into a polar bear?" He'd decline the frigid dip now, but he could picture swimming with Fiona here on a hot summer night, beneath a languid moon, oh, yes.

The clanging of a bell broke the woodland stillness.

Rose stood bolt upright. "Supper!" With an arms-extended, rolling gait, she trotted around the pool then down the path to the cabin.

"And so ends the tour." Fiona rose also. Was that relief infusing her pretty features?

He wasn't going to let her get away so easily. "Thank you for today," he said, willing her to remain a few minutes longer. "I enjoyed the change of pace."

"Thank you. Rose had a terrific time." She started down the trail.

He caught up with her. "And you?"

She stopped, then faced him, her expression guileless. "What are your intentions, Chase Riboud?"

"My intentions?" The open question took him off guard.

"Yes." She crossed her arms and solidified her stance. "You want to be seen in public with me. As a member of my team. The public part of our day ended on my front porch, but you stayed even after that." She cocked her head. "Why?"

"I like being with you." Without hesitation, he told her what was becoming increasingly, surprisingly clear to him. "I feel good in your company."

He reached out to touch her, but knew as soon as he did, it was the wrong thing to do. She backed away.

"I'm not ready for a relationship." The yearning in her eyes begged to differ.

"What happened to that little girl who took a chance and danced the polka on her uncle's shoes?"

"That was different." She looked down at the rocky path.

"I don't think so, Fiona."

His use of her name seemed to stir her. She looked up at him and seemed about to say something when the dinner bell sounded again.

"Martha and Rose will be waiting," he said, not wanting to push, satisfied with the gains he'd made today.

Without speaking, Fiona preceded him down the path to the cabin where Martha stood frowning on the back stoop, hands on hips, bell in hand.

"Sorry I'm late," Fiona said. "Has Rose washed up?"

Her chin set, Martha eyed Chase warily. "I didn't make enough supper for company."

"Martha!" Fiona flushed scarlet at the housekeeper's rudeness.

"That's okay," Chase replied. At least he knew where he stood with Martha. She didn't like him. "I have a date with a pizza."

"I'll see you to your truck." Fiona cast a warning glance at Martha who huffed, then disappeared into the cabin.

No sooner had they rounded the corner to the front yard than Rose came streaking off the front porch, her face and hair damp, her hands dripping. Obviously she had remembered to wash up for supper.

"Goodbye, Mr. Chase!" She lifted her arms to him.

Instinctively, Chase knelt to receive the farewell hug as he'd knelt on many occasions to receive those of his nephews and nieces. But this hug was special. It came from his daughter.

Rose encircled her short arms around his neck and squeezed. "Goodbye!" With a loud smack, she kissed his cheek, then backed away, grinning, the exuberant gesture bestowed like a benediction.

Rose took Chase's hand and placed it in Fiona's. "Now Mama." Clearly, she expected the adults to kiss good-bye.

Fiona's eyes widened.

He told himself this chaste kiss was for Rose's benefit, but when he pressed his lips to the softness of Fiona's cheek, inhaled her warm and womanly scent, he seized and stored this secret treasure for himself.

Fiona felt like home.

Chapter Seven

What a difference a weekend made.

As late as Saturday morning Fiona had steeled her will to forget Chase's penetrating gaze and his still-passionate-in-her-mind meadow kiss. Today, Monday, sitting in a booth at The Chat and Chew, having a cup of coffee with Sadie before opening the clinic, Fiona could think of little else besides the surprisingly sweet kiss Chase had given her before leaving her cabin two evenings ago. Taking a draw on the hot coffee, she sighed at the irony. Just as she'd cleared the table and washed the dishes from one sensuous repast, the man had provided her with new food for thought.

But what was the big deal about a peck on the cheek? Why did it have her humming to herself and smiling for no apparent reason? Was she daft with spring fever?

No. She was sane, but terrified, terrified from standing on the brink of a major leap of faith: she was prepared to allow herself to like Chase Riboud. Moreover, she was prepared to extend the hand of friendship and see where an initially platonic relationship might lead.

Why? Because the man had shown her a side of himself she hadn't dreamed possible. He had been kind to her daughter. More than kind, he had enjoyed her daughter's company with a fatherly ease that disarmed her, the protective mother.

And the kiss? The sweet kiss had finished her off. Whereas his loam-brown gaze had probed her inner spaces and disconcerted her emotional balance, his gentle kiss— a mere brush of the lips, as soft and fleeting as a spring breeze—had reassured her. He appeared to be a man of great strength with an enormous capacity for restraint. She would be a fool to pass up an opportunity to know him better—as a friend.

Sadie snapped her fingers directly in front of Fiona's nose. "You wouldn't happen to be daydreaming about the gentleman on the sidewalk?"

Fiona was surprised to find herself back in The Chat and Chew. "What gentleman?"

Grinning, Sadie cast a glance through the plate glass window. "The one trying to get that mangy dog to sit."

"Dustmop!" Fiona gasped, not believing her eyes.

Outside, Chase, a thoroughly perplexed look on his face, tried to keep the unkempt, half-wild dog from following him through the café door. The creature had never allowed anyone—not even Fiona—to get within arm's reach. It had always used the utmost stealth in making off with food the residents had put out for it, then disappearing into the surrounding forest, loath to associate with humans.

But now, it acted as if Chase Riboud were its long-lost friend.

"Will wonders never cease!" Dot, the waitress, exclaimed, opening the front door to get a better look.

Spotting Dot, the dog set off up the road, its tail between its legs.

Since Saturday and the now well-known confrontation with Raymond Hickock, Fiona had noted a subtle but distinct polarization in Bertie's Hollow where Chase was concerned. Hickock seemed to head up the Riboud detractors while Alva Biggs marshaled his supporters. When the man himself stepped into the small café, Fiona couldn't help but find herself on the side most inclined to admiration.

He stood inside the door, dressed simply in khakis and a white shirt, the long sleeves of which were rolled up to reveal strong, tanned forearms, dusted with dark hair. His large hands rested lightly on slim hips. If a woman weren't inclined toward friendship only, she might be swayed by his commanding physical presence, his powerful body, his handsome well-planed face with a strong jawline, framing a disciplined but potentially sensuous mouth. But Fiona—ever sensible—had set her sights on friendship. Period.

He scanned the room, appearing, once again, to search for her in particular.

"Got yourself a pet?" Sadie asked him, a twinkle in her eye.

Shaking his head, Chase strode to their booth, then, without hesitation, slid onto the bench beside Fiona. "What's with that dog?" he asked, bemusement clouding his eyes. "I thought you said he steered clear of people, Fiona."

He looked directly at her.

"He does. He did. He always has. He...hmmm..." With Chase's intense regard bathing her and with the length of his thigh pressed against her own under the table, she found herself babbling.

"How did you hook up with him?" Sadie seemed unfazed by Chase's presence but amused by Fiona's sudden lack of verbal skills.

"I nearly tripped over him this morning when I opened the front door. He was curled up asleep on my stoop."

In reaching for the menu, Chase brushed Fiona's arm, sending a jolt of physical awareness throughout her body. Coffee cup to her lips, she started and spilled her serving of Dot's strong brew across the table.

"Are you all right?" Surprise and question in her eyes, Sadie grabbed paper napkins to mop up the mess.

"Coffee...hot...wrong tube..." Fiona managed to mumble in a fine display of diction strangled by embarrassment. She'd return to all right if Chase would only move to another booth. Would only stop touching her.

"Careful." He slid a wad of napkins along the table in front of her. "It's going to drip on your lap."

The back of his hand brushed her breasts. Her nipples rising to attention, she jumped in her seat, knocking over the sugar, which spread in a crystallizing mess throughout the last of the spilled coffee.

Dot waddled to their table, sponge in hand. "You gonna join Merle and the boys at the convenience store, Doc? I've never seen you so clumsy."

"I'm sorry," Fiona mumbled under Sadie's amused stare. "I wonder what's gotten into me."

Sadie looked from Fiona to Chase. "Me, too."

"No harm done." Dot gave Fiona a motherly smile. "I'll get you a refill."

"No!" Fiona tried to get up, but Chase blocked her way. She felt like a teenager fleeing a disastrous blind date. "We have to open the clinic."

Sadie glanced at her watch. "We have fifteen minutes."

"Besides," Chase said, laying his arm along the back of the booth behind Fiona, "you have to tell me what I'm to do about this dog should he come back."

"What dog?" Fiona could only think of Chase's arm

behind her, so close she could feel the warmth he generated.

"The mutt." Chase grinned. "I thought you two were on first-name basis. Up at your cabin, you called him Dustmop."

Sadie sat bolt upright in her seat. "You've been to Fiona's cabin?"

Chase nodded nonchalantly. "On Saturday. After the movies."

"You two went to the movies?" Disbelief and pleasure lit Sadie's face.

"Three!" Fiona squeaked as Chase shifted his weight and rested his arm more on her shoulders than on the back of the booth. "Rose. Me. Him."

"What about the dog?" Chase repeated.

Fiona found it difficult to breathe in his presence, with his bulk crowding her and promising to touch her at every turn. "If he comes back, it's a sign. He's yours." Her voice sounded piping high as if she'd been partying and sucking on balloon helium. "Excuse me. I just remembered I promised the meds rep I'd meet her before we opened this morning."

It was a lie, but it was an out. Approaching sensory overload, she needed to get away from the sheer physicality of Chase Riboud. "I have to go! Sadie, stay! Pay! We'll even up later!"

A perplexed look on his face, Chase began to slide out of the booth, but Fiona couldn't wait. She actually tried to climb over him and instantly regretted the contact with his warm, firm body—a chest the size of Kansas and thighs that reminded her of the limbs on the mighty oak in which she'd built Rose's tree house.

Catching her foot under the edge of the bench seat, she plopped down again—hard—on Chase's lap.

He grinned.

Her pulse skittered as her cheeks flamed icy hot.

"No neckin' in the booths," Merle ordered with mock indignation as Doogie and Ernest smirked from their perches at the counter.

All eyes in the café turned toward Fiona and Chase.

So much for the mature approach, for offering her hand in friendship and waiting to see the direction that friendship took. She couldn't even have a cup of coffee in the man's presence without hyperventilating.

Bolting from the table, she left the café, all the while thinking it might be an excellent idea to keep a store of paper bags handy for those close encounters of the breathtaking kind.

With a smile Chase set the chopper down in the clearing beside the clinic parking lot. He'd been smiling all morning once he'd realized he had the power to fluster Dr. Fiona Applegate. In The Chat and Chew, when he'd settled into the booth beside her, her cool, aloof control had evaporated like morning dew on the sunny side of the mountain. She'd actually seemed tongue-tied.

And he'd been charmed.

That was why he jumped at the chance to deliver some surplus supplies Asheville General had targeted for the clinic. He wanted to see Fiona again so much that he didn't even complain about being used as a delivery boy.

Having shut down the helicopter, he stepped to the ground and inhaled deeply. The crisp spring mountain air took some getting used to. Unlike the air of Louisiana's steamy bayous or the arid deserts of his postings, this air filled his lungs with a remarkable vitality. The surrounding rugged mountains provided a formidable backbone, both physical and symbolic. The new green tree leaves drenched with noonday sunlight spoke of hope for the future. Here he could accomplish anything he set his mind to.

And he had a mind to see Fiona.

He grabbed the box of supplies and headed for the clinic's front door.

The waiting room was empty. Sadie sat behind her desk, checking information on a computer. Seeing Chase, she grinned a broad welcome. Whereas he'd begun to sense that not everyone in town was turning cartwheels over his arrival, he felt certain he could count the cheerful nurse among his growing list of allies.

"Doc in?" he asked, trying to sound indifferent over the eagerness of his heartbeat.

"She should be free in a couple minutes. She's with our last patient before lunch."

"Y'all take a lunch break?" Setting the box down on the counter, Chase brightened considerably. The idea of squeezing into a booth with Fiona a second time today gave him immeasurable pleasure.

"I think Fiona has a picnic date with Rose and Martha," Sadie replied as if reading his mind. "But I'm sure she has time to speak with you if it's important." She indicated the box. "Is it about this?"

"This?" Lost in thoughts of Fiona, he almost forgot his excuse for dropping in. "Ah...no...these are some miscellaneous surplus items Asheville General thought you could use. I...ah...wanted to update Doc on a project we had going." He had spoken with the head of the mercy program about Jodi and Raymond's situation, but the recollection just now came to him as he scrambled for a more pressing reason to be here than a run-of-the-mill delivery.

Standing and reaching for the box, Sadie raised her eyebrows until they touched her fringe of bangs. "You and Doc have a *project* going? Is that what it's called these days?"

"No! It's not like that." A retired army lieutenant colonel, a man of fortitude and self-discipline, Chase felt an unaccustomed heat rise to his face and silently cursed the weak chink in his armor. "It's a real project. Relating to the mercy flight program."

"If you say so." Sadie winked. "I'll tell Doc you're here." She disappeared down a short corridor, leaving Chase to examine his real motives in coming.

He wanted to see Fiona. But did he want to see her because she attracted him as a woman or because she attracted him as his child's mother? Such thoughts had tormented him in recent days as he contemplated establishing a father-daughter rapport with Rose. Was he looking to build a relationship with Fiona, the individual, or was he looking for a convenient package deal?

He knew the answer as soon as Fiona appeared at the end of the corridor.

Dressed simply in slacks and a long-sleeved blouse, she had the power to make him sit up and take notice. Take notice as a red-blooded, American male with no other ulterior motive than getting to know a fine woman.

She held her head with confidence. Her hair, pulled back in a long single braid, was a color to put the best of Alva Biggs's honey to shame. He wondered what it would be like to run his fingers through it, to wrap that heavy silken braid possessively around his hand.

As she walked toward him with an easy grace like that of a willow in a soft wind, he could picture her body pressed against his in willing embrace. A fresh, clean scent of wildflowers preceded her, reminding him that to experience Fiona was to experience all that was natural and good.

An openness in her demeanor threw him off guard, made him believe that she could sense his longing. And when she stopped before him, her hazel gaze direct, he wondered if she knew he wanted her.

"Yes?" She tilted her head. "Sadie said you wanted…to speak to me." Gone was the disconcerted Fiona of this morning. In her place stood a woman of cool control.

At the very moment he'd lost both cool and control.

"Hmmm." He balanced on the balls of his feet, as inarticulate as a teenage boy about to ask the prom queen for a date.

"Sadie said it was about our project." Fiona leaned slightly toward him in encouragement. "I assume she meant Jodi and Raymond."

"Yes." The word exploded from him in a sharp puff of air, unclogging both sanity and coherence. "We got the go-ahead to use the chopper."

"Excellent." Her smile was worth his adolescent awkwardness.

A middle-aged woman pushing an elderly man in a wheelchair emerged from the examination room at the end of the corridor just as Martha and Rose entered the front door, saving Chase any further attempt at small talk.

"Mama!" Rose flung herself at Fiona. When the child saw the man in the wheelchair waiting as his companion settled up their account with Sadie, she walked right over to him with great purpose, looked him in the eye, patted his arm and said with heartfelt solicitation, "Don't worry, Old Tom. It will be all right."

The elderly gentleman managed a wan smile. "If you say so, Rosie girl. If you say so, I'll believe it." He seemed to derive comfort from the child's presence.

The woman, finished with Sadie, turned to Fiona. "We'll see you next week."

Fiona knelt to the level of the seated man. "You let me know if that tea helps any."

"I will."

Rose bustled to the door, pulled it open, then waited patiently as the woman pushed the wheelchair through the entrance. The youngster aimed her farewell smile directly at Old Tom.

This simple kindness moved Chase. His special little girl, unlayered by social constraints, gave of herself freely. Her capacity to let her humanity shine through was her strength. The world could use more of the tender mercies Rose had to offer. How ironic and sad that society throughout history had tried to hide Down's syndrome individuals rather than pull them to its midst and learn from them.

He fought the constriction around his heart.

"Hi, Sadie! Hi, Chase!" Rose closed the door.

Fiona stood. "*Mr.* Chase," she corrected.

"I don't think so." As if she'd made a decision, Rose cast her mother a stubborn glance, then came to stand next to Chase. "Where's your hel'copper?"

"Didn't you see it? It's in the clearing behind the parking lot."

"We walked from the other direction." Martha's words were curt. Clutching a picnic hamper, she eyed him warily.

Chase moved to the window at the end of the waiting room. "Bet you can see it from here." He parted the mini-blinds. "Come look."

Rose scrambled up on a chair next to him. "Wow!" She turned to Fiona. "Mama! I want to ride!"

Chase watched the color drain from Fiona's face. "No, love," she said. "It's not a toy. We must stay here."

Remembering Fiona's own fear of flying, but pleased that his daughter appeared fearless and interested in this part of his life, he countermanded her mother's decision without thinking. "I could let you sit in it."

"Yes!" Rose clambered off the seat.

"That's not a good idea." Fiona's tone was icy, her body erect and stiff.

Her words made Rose pause, a shadow of rebellion crossing his little girl's normally cheerful face. "Want to, Mama," she muttered.

"I know you do, sweet cheeks." Fiona knelt beside her. "But it's for people who don't feel well, not for healthy little girls. It's for work, not play."

"Want ride!" The girl's thwarted desire had further stripped her spare language skills.

"Fiona." Chase felt frustration rise at her motherly overprotection. He wanted to share a moment with his daughter. He didn't see the harm in it. In fact, he pressed the issue. "It would be an important step to let the child feel comfortable in the machine." In case, God forbid, she should ever have need of it. "I'll be right with her."

Rose glanced from Chase to Fiona. "Want ride!" she repeated with a marked stubbornness.

Fiona cast a frigid glare in his direction before she turned her attention to their child. "Today is not helicopter day," she said, her tone firm. "Today is picnic day." She cupped the girl's trembling chin in her hand. "I want no sulky looks, Rose. You and Martha go choose a spot outside for our lunch. Mr. Chase is leaving *now*. You can watch the helicopter take off."

Rose considered this as Chase considered Fiona's veiled order for him to leave.

"Come, Rosie." Martha extended her hand. "I'll let you peel the hardboiled eggs while we watch the helicopter take off."

It wasn't much of an inducement, but it seemed to do the trick. Rose, still frowning, placed her hand in Martha's and the housekeeper led the child out of the building.

Fiona stood. "A word with you." Her tone of voice left

no confusion as to whom she spoke, for Sadie had made herself scarce.

"Why are you upset with me? I wasn't going to take her up. I was simply going to let her sit in the cockpit." His compromise had seemed logical to him. "As a mercy flight teammate, you know that it's a good idea for children to feel no fear where the helicopter's concerned."

"My tight schedule alone won't allow both a tour and a picnic. I value my time with my daughter. *As a mother,* I made a decision that today wasn't the day for the helicopter. It wasn't an easy decision for Rose to accept. By making suggestions against my wishes, you made her acceptance next to impossible and disrupted the little lunchtime I have to share with her."

It suddenly hit him. This wasn't about the helicopter. This was about parental authority. He had stepped on Fiona's toes, and he now realized he was going to catch a glimpse of her territoriality.

Fiona fumed inside. How dare he—this outsider—decide what was best for her child at any particular moment? Perhaps she'd made a mountain out of a molehill with the helicopter, but the doing was done. Chase Riboud needed to know that he could not come into Bertie's Hollow and *push.*

She tried to brush past him, but he caught her arm.

"Rose can have a picnic any day," he said, his words soft but underlined with a decided challenge. "How many days does she get a chance to sit in a helicopter? To broaden her horizons."

The suggestion cutting deep, she whirled to face him. "Are you intimating I don't wish to broaden my daughter's horizons? That I limit her?"

"Fiona." He released her arm. "You're a terrific mother." He hesitated. "Perhaps a little overprotective at times, but that's to be expected. I've seen it with my sisters—''

"Why, you arrogant busybody!" Drawing herself to her tallest, she skewered him with outrage. "Just how many children have you raised?"

He stepped back as if she'd slapped him.

Perhaps she'd overreacted. If Sadie had acted as he'd acted, had made a suggestion counter to Fiona's wishes, Fiona would have breezily told her to buzz off without putting a dent in their friendship. Why then did she feel so threatened by Chase's interest in Rose?

"I'm sorry." They spoke the words simultaneously, each looking anywhere but in the other's eyes.

"The program has me overeager," he offered, jamming his hands in his pockets and frowning in a way that reminded her of Rose at her most truculent. Clearly, he still felt offended.

"I only wanted to spend a few extra minutes with my daughter," she replied, not quite apologizing fully, but trying to make him understand that this was a parent thing and she, not he, was Rose's parent.

"Understandable." An emotional gulf had opened between them. He moved to the door. "See you round. We'll talk later about Jodi and Raymond."

Unwilling to bridge the gulf, she let him go without answering, then moved to the window to watch Rose's reaction to his departure. With great effort, Fiona inhaled deeply and tried to collect her thoughts and still her jangled nerves.

What would have been the harm in letting Rose sit in the chopper? None. Instead of diminishing the picnic, the experience would have enriched it. So why had she balked at Chase's suggestion?

Disgusted with herself, she turned from the window. She'd let him push her buttons, and her own undisciplined reaction had reduced her lunchtime with Rose from half an hour to fifteen minutes.

To her surprise, she found Sadie staring at her.

"Relax," her friend insisted. "Take your full half hour. I'll cover for you."

"Why do I let him get to me?" The question came out before Fiona considered the wisdom of it.

Sadie rolled her eyes. "Not long ago you said you couldn't get involved with a man who didn't show an interest in Rose. Today Chase did. And you snapped his head off, then threw the remains on the refuse heap. The man's damned if he doesn't and damned if he does." She smiled broadly. "Must be love."

Fiona ignored the last. "You didn't think he was trying to interfere with my parenting?"

"You're too suspicious, Doc. Must be those *feelings* again." She gave Fiona a quick hug, then steered her to the door. "I think he was just being nice."

"You do?" Fiona wanted to believe it.

"Yes. He deserves a heartfelt apology and a second chance." Sadie patted her shoulder. "Now, go have that picnic with your daughter."

Conflicting emotions dancing through her thoughts, Fiona opened the door, then stepped into an invigorating bath of fresh air and springtime scents.

She didn't dare believe she'd found a man who attracted her, who was attracted to her, and who showed a sincere interest in her daughter. For six years, she and Rose, with the help of friends, had built a fulfilling and independent life for themselves in Bertie's Hollow. She wished she had a crystal ball to determine if letting Chase Riboud into that life would enhance it or disrupt it.

The late afternoon sun illuminated the Asheville public library's facade as Chase pushed through the large oak double doors into the cool and quiet interior. His first few weeks on the job had been light, allowing him time to continue his research on Down's syndrome and to begin reading back issues of local newspapers, as Fiona had suggested, to get a feel for the area.

Fiona. No matter where he went or what he did, he was always reminded of Fiona.

Staff at the hospital sang her praises as did the residents of the hollows. Strong and self-reliant, she embodied the region's spirit. Her almost legendary compassion made her its angel. Yet no one seemed to really know the woman herself. Perhaps Martha did, but Martha wasn't talking.

Chase had thought he was making progress in gaining Fiona's trust until this morning, when he'd tried to add to his daughter's cache of experiences and Fiona had shut him out, setting him worrying about two recurring issues: Rose's education and Fiona's tenacious hold on motherhood.

His readings had made him understand the great need to guide and stimulate and educate Down's syndrome individuals. He had no doubts about the time Rose spent with Fiona—although she'd been unaccountably reluctant this morning to let their daughter encounter the helicopter—but he still wondered what kind of developmental experiences his little girl received from Martha and her daughter, with whom they shared a home schooling schedule.

The more he learned about Down's syndrome, the more questions he wanted to ask Fiona about Rose, about her education, about her health, about her future. But as this morning had proved, Fiona was willing to let people only so close before she closed ranks.

That thought led to his second concern: Fiona's fierce protective instincts where Rose was concerned. After much introspection, he'd given up the idea of gaining sole custody of his daughter. It wouldn't be fair to Rose or to Fiona, he now realized. But he worried that Fiona would never countenance even joint custody, leaving, to his mind, only one option. Marriage.

Such a huge step for two people who barely knew each other.

He'd never doubted that marriage lay in his future. And in Fiona he'd met his match. His mind and his heart and his body told him that. But somewhere along the line—it should be sooner than later—he must tell her the truth before they could build any kind of relationship short of marriage. And with the truth what would happen to their chances of happily-ever-after?

Was marriage an unrealistic option? He had to give this idea more—much more—consideration.

"Hey, Chase," Guy, the reference librarian greeted him. "What's it going to be today?"

He wiped fantasy thoughts of marriage to Fiona out of his mind. "I think I'll continue with the old newspapers on microfilm."

Guy rose to assist him. "How far did you get last time?"

"Up to fifteen years ago." He'd started way in the past, getting a feel for the history of the area, and had been working toward the present.

"Not too many newcomers would go to this trouble to get to know the area." The librarian turned on a machine, then took a spool of microfilm from the flat-drawered filing cabinet. "Most arrivals want to make us over in one way or another. Not you."

Chase flinched. If anything could be construed as making over a situation, his attempt to reconfigure Rose's family most certainly would head the category.

"It was Fiona Applegate's idea. Dr. Applegate. Over in Bertie's Hollow." He'd give credit where credit was due.

"Fiona." Guy smiled as he threaded the microfilm. "We were classmates in high school. She was something. Still is."

"What was she like back then?"

"Sweet and honest and devoted to her mother. And a born healer. We all knew she was destined to be a doctor or a vet or a social worker."

"How so?"

"There wasn't a stray, human or animal, that didn't find refuge at the Applegate cabin. Her mother took them in and Fiona nursed them back to health. She was a wonder." His expression grew serious. "I think she chose med school when she couldn't save her own mother."

A long thread of sorrow for Fiona's loss pulled at Chase.

What an amazing woman. In the brief time he'd known her, she had certainly touched and transformed him. Made him feel beyond himself.

"All set." Guy patted the microfilm machine. "Let me know if you need anything else."

He needed Fiona and Rose in his life. He needed a miracle toward accomplishing that.

Determined to banish his outsider status in this land Fiona so loved, he turned to the task of educating himself.

The old newspaper articles told of births and deaths and family reunions. They highlighted fishing contests and government-sponsored visits from Santa Claus. They detailed the area's economic trials and tribulations and successes. The columns of print chronicled the hopes and dreams and sorrows of a region as the grainy photos showed the faces—some Chase recognized—of determination and survival.

Turning the microfilm knob, he finished one issue and came to the front page of the next. He couldn't believe his eyes.

The banner headlines fairly shouted at him from the

screen: Local Woman Arraigned in Husband's Murder. The picture was of a younger Martha Ricker being led in handcuffs from the county jail.

Had Fiona entrusted his daughter's daily well-being to a murderer?

Chapter Eight

Evening's gray-gloved fingers crept across Fiona's front yard as Chase brought his truck to a skidding halt on the hard-packed dirt surface. Cool, pine-scented air and a chorus of spring peepers did nothing to soothe his anger. Leaping from the cab, he watched his daughter's mother emerge from the shadows of the porch. She had one helluvalot of explaining to do.

"Fiona!"

A scowl on her face, her index finger across her mouth, she hurried down the steps and crossed the yard to meet him halfway. "Hush!" she cautioned, glancing over her shoulder at an open upstairs window. "You'll wake Rose. It took me forever to get her down for the night."

"Where's Martha?" He lowered his voice but not his boiling point.

Fiona shot him a questioning look, but answered anyway, making each word distinct and faintly distancing. "Down the lane, visiting with her daughter, Anne."

"Why didn't you tell me Martha had been accused of murdering her husband?"

Fiona set her jaw. "It's none of your business."

None of his business? Rose was his business. "I'm making it my business."

"Why should you?"

"Why? For the same reason you make Raymond Hickock's drinking your business. Because you care about Jodi's safety and the well-being of her child."

Fiona seemed to consider this.

"Did Martha do it?' He grasped both Fiona's arms and held her firmly until their mutual gaze locked. "Did she kill a man? Yes or no."

"Yes."

Chase released Fiona so suddenly she stumbled backward. "And you let her care for your daughter?" Fury singed him inside out.

"Who told you about Martha?" Fiona's icy green regard remained unyielding, undisclosing.

"Answer my question. How could you let a murderer care for your daughter?" *His* daughter.

"I assure you I know full well what I'm doing."

"Then explain it to me."

Glancing up at Rose's bedroom window, Fiona reached out, encircling his wrist with fingers steely in their command of purpose, and pulled him to the far side of his truck. "I'll answer your questions, when you get a grip. When you answer mine." She compelled him with her resolve. "Who told you about Martha?"

"I read about her arraignment in an old newspaper. Now why—"

"Did you read about the trial? About the verdict?"

"You said she did it—"

Tightening her grip on his wrist, she shook him. "Did you read the *whole* story?"

"No." Looking deep into her eyes, he saw an anger rising to meet his own. "I came to you for answers."

"Why me?" Suspicion clouded her features.

"Because you're the one who's taken her in." His heart thudded doubletime. "Because you're the one who put Rose—an innocent little girl—in harm's way." Perhaps his initial plan to take his daughter back to Louisiana was the wisest decision after all.

"Rose is no concern of yours," Fiona declared, her voice low, but her words fierce. "But be assured she's safe with Martha Ricker."

"How can you know that? Were there mitigating circumstances? Did the woman kill in self-defense?"

"No. But—"

"Was it premeditated?"

"Probably. But there were extenu—"

"What's to say she won't hurt Rose or you?" Blood pounded in his ears. As much as he feared for Rose's safety, he couldn't stand the thought of any harm coming to Fiona.

"You've convicted Martha before hearing the whole story." Narrowing her eyes, Fiona dropped his wrist as if it—he—disgusted her. "Not even the courts did that."

He, in turn, clutched her hand and pulled her so close he felt the rapid in and out of her breathing. "How can you defend a killer?"

Stiffening in his grasp, she exhaled slowly and froze him with a cold, appraising glare. "You're a former soldier. Have you ever killed another human being, Chase Riboud? Have you ever planned that killing?"

The questions stunned him.

"Have you?" She slipped away from him to stand near the front of the truck. "Yes or no."

"It's not the same." As a soldier he'd killed, yes, but

under orders. Out of a sense of purpose and duty. To serve the greater good.

"Have you ever killed another human being?" she repeated slowly.

"Yes." He would not varnish the truth.

"Was it premeditated?"

"We planned campaigns. We expected casualties. These are conditions of military conflict. You can't compare—"

"But you have anticipated killing. And you have killed."

"Yes." He tagged her reasoning sophistic at the same time he recognized the pointed truth at its heart. "Yes."

"Then perhaps I should order you off the property. Keep you away from Rose. So as not to put her—or me—in harm's way."

He stared at her. Damn, but she sounded more lawyer than doctor.

"Now that I have your attention," she said quietly, "perhaps you'd care to hear Martha's story. Not that you deserve it. But you are a member of our community now. You need to understand."

She had a powerful way of commanding a man's attention.

"Come up on the porch swing," she said, turning. "It seems you could use a glass of ice water."

In stony silence Chase followed Fiona. Her verbal acrobatics may have made him pause, but he would not retreat until she'd explained to his satisfaction Martha Ricker's past and her present involvement with the Applegate household.

As Fiona went into the cabin, he took a seat on the porch swing. Was her absence to get ice water a ploy to make him cool his heels? He felt manipulated, and he didn't like it.

She didn't keep him waiting long, however. Returning

with two tall, already moist glasses, she sat beside him on the swing. In the few brief minutes they'd been apart, she'd composed herself. She seemed calmer now. More accessible.

"Martha was abused by her husband," she said, her words simple, her gaze never wavering. "God knows why, but she stayed in that marriage until...until her husband turned on her daughter." She took a long drink of water and seemed at the same time to force down a rising rage. "At the first attack, Martha got his hunting rifle and shot him. Dead."

Thunderstruck, Chase stared at Fiona, who waited for his reaction with a calm that belied the violence of her story.

"You said it wasn't self-defense," he breathed, realizing the situation's complexity. "It was." He understood decisive action for the greater good. Moreover, he was beginning to feel that a child is an extension of one's own self. "In protecting her daughter, she acted in self-defense."

"His family didn't think so. They pressed for the maximum sentence. Thank heavens, most of Bertie's Hollow and the courts understood. Joe Ricker was a cruel bastard. A bad husband and an even worse father."

It was the first Chase had ever heard Fiona speak ill of another soul, living or dead.

"What happened?"

"The judge was willing to give Martha ten years' probation if someone in town stood forward to accept responsibility."

"And you—"

"*My mother* took her in." Fiona looked away, her eyes misting.

He slipped his hand under hers and, with the toe of his shoe, started the swing gently rocking again. "But your mother's been gone since your senior year in high school, and you've been away in college. What happened to Martha during the interim?''

''She stayed here in the cabin, raised her children and took care of the property until I returned.''

''The judge permitted it?''

Fiona smiled. ''The judge was a very wise woman who respected the spirit as well as the letter of the law.''

''I understand now the depths of Martha's loyalty to your family.''

Fiona looked at him, warmth radiating from her expression, strength radiating from her posture. ''Martha is a member of my family.''

''And you saw me tearing up the mountain, aimed at attacking you and yours.'' He shook his head. ''I'm sorry. I should have read the rest of the story.''

''Why were you so intent on protecting Rose and me?''

''I care about you and Rose.'' He pressed her fingertips to his lips. ''I care about you, Fiona.'' It felt good to get that fact out in the open.

Fiona's heart did a little flip at Chase's admission. Perhaps that was what all the emotional push-pull had been about at noontime. Perhaps she'd pushed him away before he could pull her out of her safe world. She wanted to care for him but was afraid he didn't see her in any special way. Perhaps she'd decided she could only be friends with him because she feared he saw her only as a friend.

The warm and dusky look in his eyes as he lowered her hand but kept it firmly clasped in his, promised much more than friendship.

''Could you care for me?'' His voice was rough as if it cost a great deal to ask. His eyes showed an uncharacteristic vulnerability that drew Fiona into their dark depths.

She succumbed to temptation and touched his cheek, dared to run her fingertips down his rough, late-day shadow of a beard. Allowed herself to wonder what it would be like to watch him shave, standing at the sink before bedtime, chest bare, cotton drawstring pajama bottoms slung low on his hips. At home and at ease. A husband preparing for bed, perhaps to make love to his wife—

"Fiona?"

"I could." She blushed, remembering his question. "I do…care for you."

"Why?" He flashed her a boyish grin. "I can be hot-headed. And meddling. And, to top it all off, I'm an outsider." With simple intimacy, he brushed an errant wisp of hair off her forehead. "You tell me what the attraction is."

She shrugged. "Dustmop."

"That mangy beast?"

She loved his look of surprise. "Animals are good judges of character. That stray sees something to trust in you that he's never seen in anyone else around here." She grinned. "That's recommendation enough for me."

"Remind me to buy my new best friend a T-bone." Chase slipped his arm around her shoulder, drawing her close.

He was going to kiss her. And she could think of nothing she wanted more.

"Who's that?" The muffled question came from behind the screen door where Rose stood, rubbing sleepy eyes.

Fiona rose from the swing and Chase's far too tempting embrace.

"What's my girl doing out of bed?" she asked opening the door.

"Heard voices." Only half awake, Rose spied Chase. "Hel'copter man. Want ride."

"I don't have my helicopter with me," Chase replied,

"but I did buy you something today in the hospital gift shop." He rose, then headed for his truck.

"Want ride," Rose repeated petulantly, leaning up against Fiona's leg.

Fiona stroked her daughter's head, wondering if Chase would realize this wasn't the optimum moment for gift giving. Rose was not at her best when roused from sleep. Usually, Fiona gave her a drink of water, a hug and ushered her right back to bed, no discussion. Divergence from routine could end up on shaky ground.

Chase returned with a model helicopter. Kneeling, he extended it to Rose.

"No!" Rose turned her face into Fiona's side. "Want ride."

"I came in my truck, Rose," Chase offered, his voice even, his obvious intent reason. "The helicopter is on its pad behind my house."

"Want ride!" Rose wailed, waving the model off with one hand and clinging to Fiona with the other. Abstract explanations were difficult for her to comprehend when fully awake. When she grew overtired, they spelled tantrum.

"Waaannnt riiide!" Her wail became a keen as she flopped down on the porch floor.

Still kneeling, Chase looked up at Fiona. "What can I do to help?" he asked softly. Bless his heart, he didn't push, and—miracle of miracles—he didn't bolt and run at this unattractive display.

Scrubbing her teary eyes with balled-up hands, Rose kicked her legs out in front of her. Fiona recognized that her daughter was only taking a breather before the grande finale. What could Chase do to help?

"You can wait for me?" Fiona didn't know if he'd seize this opportunity as an easy ticket to escape. She wouldn't blame him.

"Sure thing." A distressed look on his face, he stood and moved the model helicopter behind his back, out of sight.

"Come on, Rose." With determination, Fiona gathered her quivering child in her arms. "We'll talk about apologies and thank-yous tomorrow. Tonight you need to shut those eyes and get your beauty sleep. Mama will not take no for an answer."

Chase held the screen door open for them, but remained on the porch.

Even as she protested, Rose pressed her little body to her mother. Fiona responded by cradling her daughter's head and murmuring, "Shaaa, shaaa, my sweet, Mama loves you deep and true."

And, oh, how she did. Rose was the center of her universe.

As Fiona climbed the stairs, her little girl's shrieks subsided into snuffles. Her tantrums came and went like mountain thunderstorms. Fast and furious, full of noise and threat, yet quickly over. And then the sun returned.

Fiona often wondered if Rose's outbursts came more from frustration than anger, a frustration at an inability to express herself in words. Of all her emerging skills, language had been the most difficult to master even with speech therapy. Fiona understood her as did Martha. But sometimes the little girl seemed locked within her inability to put voice to her feelings.

Standing in the middle of Rose's bedroom, Fiona swayed back and forth, rocking the increasingly limp form of her special child. It would take years of love and nurturing to bring Rose to her full potential. Fiona had all the time in the world. But she wondered about the man waiting below. He said he cared for both her daughter and her. Did he understand that Rose was not like other children in that she would be part child forever? Yes, she might achieve semi-independence, but Fiona's nest would never be completely empty.

Could Chase handle that?

Fiona knew she was thinking into a future the pilot hadn't yet offered, but, because of her special family configuration, she couldn't risk ignoring the possibilities.

Sighing deeply in Fiona's arms, Rose became unconscious weight, finally asleep and at peace.

Fiona gently laid her daughter on the single bed strewn with stuffed animals. Before returning downstairs, she brushed her hand over Rose's straight, dark hair. Kissed the tips of each short finger. Placed her palm over a little heart that housed so much love and joy. Pulled the covers up under the pug chin and found herself weeping.

"Would it be so much to ask, dear God," she whispered, "that Chase grow to love my Rosie as I do?"

Fiona swiped at her wet cheeks, passed a hand over her wrinkled shirt, fingered her mussed hair, then tiptoed out of the bedroom. She didn't expect Chase had waited.

But he had. He sat on the swing, looking as if he might want to take up where they'd left off. "You didn't think I'd stay?"

"That wasn't Rosie at her best."

"I know." He patted the swing beside him. "You forget my experience with the Riboud nieces and nephews."

He was lumping this experience in with that of his non-disabled family? Could it be that he was beginning to see Rose, the little girl, and not the disability? How awesome.

"I don't know how to put this." She sat down beside him on the swing. "Sometimes people see Rose throw a tantrum and they chalk it up to a nasty symptom of Down's syndrome."

He chuckled, a warm, rich sound. "Then *some people* would have no understanding of kids."

"You surprise me, Chase Riboud."

"That's only because you don't know me." He leaned closer. "I'd like to rectify that."

She wanted to touch him, but she felt a greater need to test him. "Do you realize that getting to know me means getting to know Rose? Do you know how intertwined our lives are, hers and mine? More than those of normal mothers and daughters."

"Yes. I understand." He said the words as if he believed them, as if they didn't frighten him. Moreover, in the depths of his eyes shone a great yearning, as if he not only understood the bond between Fiona and Rose, but craved it for himself.

Perhaps this was a special man for her special family.

He cupped the side of her face with his large hand. His palm felt rough and cool. "I want to know all about you. All about Rose."

"Even tantrums?"

"You handled this one well." He stroked her chin. "I admire your patience. Your loving firmness."

"Rose's situation may be special, but her wants and needs are normal. Just because she's a Down's child doesn't mean I should spoil her." She spoke plainly and discovered an ease in opening up to this man, who dared to probe where strangers shouldn't.

But Fiona had long ceased to see Chase as a stranger. In fact, her instincts told her he could play an intimate role at the very center of her world. If she would admit him. Her heart had already admitted him. Reason dragged its heels.

Sighing, she nestled into the circle of his extended arm and determined to give reason time-out this evening while she indulged her heart.

"I admire your ability to juggle the complexities of relationships," Chase said at last, pulling Fiona close up against him. "I've been out of the service only a few weeks, and already I'm beginning to see relationships in shades of gray. Not an easy thing for a career military man.''

''How do you mean?''

''In the army relationships are black and white. Superiors and subordinates. Regulated by clear-cut rules. Further defined only by one's assignment. Easily severed by reassignment. Relationships are easy to understand because they're essentially prescribed.''

She drew back to look at him, her sensuous mouth drawn up in an understanding smile. ''Are you finding civilian relationships difficult?''

''Complex.'' Like his with her. He swallowed hard. He'd just made strides in gaining her trust, and what did he want to do? He wanted to kiss her senseless. ''I admire the ease with which you handle them.''

She laughed softly. ''Oh, I just make it look easy. At the end of some days—like today—my neck pays.'' She rubbed her shoulder with one slender hand. ''The muscles are all tied in knots.''

''Muscle pain I can understand and ease.'' He made a circling motion with his hand. ''Turn your back to me. I'll give you a rub.''

Responding with a startled look, she didn't move. ''Did they teach you back rubs in officers' training school?''

''That's classified information, ma'am.'' He grinned. ''Now do you have a special reason for hanging on to that pain?''

''I…suppose…not.…'' Warily, she turned her back to him. The porch swing tipped precariously, forcing her to stand.

''Here. Let me stabilize this unit.'' He repositioned his right leg so that it stretched along the back of the swing. His left foot then rested firmly on the floor. Pressing his back against the armrest, he motioned for Fiona to sit in the protective V created by his open thighs.

As her eyes widened considerably, he had to admit he could conjure endless possibilities for the position. "Back rub," he reassured her, against the longing that rose within him.

Turning, she sat so primly on the edge of the seat that at no point did her body touch his. He corrected that by placing his hands on her shoulders. "Relax," he murmured.

"I'll try," she said, looking straight ahead. "I…give… Rose a daily massage. It not only helps calm her, it helps her form body awareness, a vital aspect of her education."

"And who takes care of you?" he asked, rubbing his thumbs in lazy circles over her upper back. "Who makes you aware of your body?"

She turned her head to glance at him over her shoulder. "Back rub," she warned. But her tone was playful, and her eyes heavy lidded as if she enjoyed his touch.

He increased the massage. Gently kneading her neck muscles, he watched in satisfaction as she rolled her head from side to side to take full advantage of his ministrations. Sliding his fingers around her head, he stroked her forehead, noting for his own pleasure her lovely, cool, smooth skin.

"That braid has too created tension," he said, referring to the style in which he'd always seen her wear her hair.

"I usually take it down after work. I got sidetracked tonight."

"Let me." Without waiting for permission, he undid the ribbon that tied the end, then threaded his fingers through the honeyed coil, loosening the heavy, silken strands of hair. He felt himself grow hard.

"Oh, that feels much better!" She raised her arms to massage her scalp and presented him with her arched back.

Placing his thumbs on the uppermost part of her spine so that his fingers wouldn't stray—he couldn't trust his longing—he kneaded as far outward on her back as he could reach. He moved downward, rubbing muscle and bone, feeling her vitality clear through the soft cotton of her shirt.

He didn't quite know when massage turned to caress. Perhaps when he reached her waist and found a corner of her blouse untucked from her slacks. Found a few inches of creamy skin exposed.

As with the braid, he neglected to ask permission as he slid his fingers into the opening, working the shirt fabric free from the slacks' waistband. He felt her stiffen, heard her gasp.

Encircling her waist, he pulled her against him, her back against his chest, her firm rounded bottom tight against his arousal. He whispered in her ear, "Do you want me to stop?" He pressed his hands against the warm, bare skin of her stomach.

She leaned back against him, making a half turn so that her mouth could meet his. "No." She spoke the word against his lips.

With a long, low, slow groan, he captured her in a kiss. He moved his hands over her skin until he felt the swell of her breasts, cupped their warmth in his palms, teased their tips with his thumbs, felt her quiver and whimper in surrender.

Fiona. His senses filled with Fiona. She was the woman he had wanted all his life. And he now knew she wanted him. He vowed to himself that, despite all obstacles, they would have their happy ending.

For Fiona this kiss was different. It wasn't the swept-away kiss of the meadow or the surprise chaste kiss instigated by Rose. This kiss was a conscious offering. She offered Chase more than she'd ever offered a man. More than her undivided attention, more than her body, she offered him her trust.

And in trusting him, she freed all former inhibitions, let her senses fly. She let herself float in the feel of his mouth on her mouth, of his hands on intimate parts of her body. His boldness made her brave. Slowly turning on the swing to face him, she undid the buttons on his shirt with trembling fingers, slipped her hands over the planes of his chest, over the wiry hair dusting sharply defined pecs and flat, taut nipples. She dared to claim him.

"Fiona." Trailing kisses across her cheek, he breathed her name. The urgent sound of it made her feel heavy, hot and moist.

She moved her hands down his chest and over the top of his khakis, reveling in the corded muscles of his thighs beneath, in her provocative position between his legs. This physical exploration came as such emotional release. Trailing her fingers up the inseam of his slacks, she found and stroked his arousal through the supple fabric. His low moan sent a trill throughout her entire body. Such power she exerted over him. And he, her.

With masterful hands, he turned her once again so that the back of her head rested in the crook of his neck, so that her back fit into his embrace, so that he cradled her on the swing in semispoon fashion, leaving her entire front exposed to the cool evening air. Exposed to his exploration.

She reached backward, twining her fingers behind his neck as his fingers outlined her cheekbones, her lips, her chin. He caressed the column of her neck, downward to her breastbone where he splayed his hands across her chest and captured her breasts. Even before her nipples tightened, his hands moved on, leaving an electrifying sizzle in their wake. He caressed her stomach, trailing the tip of one finger around the rim of her navel.

He whispered in her ear, "You are so beautiful."

He slid the fingers of one hand under the waistband of her slacks. She inhaled to accommodate the pleasure. Nibbling the outer shell of her ear, he stroked her wet heat, stroked her to rapid crescendo as he gently rocked the swing. The dual movement made her giddy, put her off balance. Down was up; up, down. She arched and turned her face to his neck to anchor herself. Softly called his name.

"Oh, Chase…"

His intimate caress became more insistent until she moaned her release and sank against him sated, yet wanting more. Much more.

At first she didn't recognize the pulse at her hip. Small, inorganic. Pesky. Her pager. She struggled to react, to clear her head, to sit up.

"What's wrong?" Concern limned his words.

"Nothing. Oh, my." Fiona ran hands over her dishevelment. Reached into her pocket. Recognized the phone number on the display of her pager. "I do believe Jodi's going to have her baby."

"Will we need the chopper?" His words were all business, yet his eyes still carried the sensuality of lovemaking.

"Perhaps. You'd better stick with me." She stood. "I have to call Jodi. Have to call Martha to get her back up here with Rose."

"Of course." Beginning to button his shirt, he looked nonplused, vulnerable.

Before entering the house, she threw her arms around his neck and kissed him quickly, full on the mouth. "We're going to deliver a baby!"

Just minutes ago Chase had made her feel so alive, so safe, so wanted. She would carry that joy with her as she ushered a new life into the world.

Chapter Nine

Chase felt like a giant in the Hickocks' tiny but immaculate living room. Fiona was in the bedroom examining Jodi. Raymond was nowhere to be seen.

"Everything's progressing nicely." Fiona rejoined him, a reassuring smile on her face. "Jodi's only dilated four centimeters, so, if she runs true to a first delivery, we have a wait yet."

"Do you need me?"

"Yes. But not to fly." She stopped smiling. "Raymond's down at Proud Mary's Dart Bar. He doesn't know Jodi's gone into labor. I need you to get him. Bring him home."

"I wouldn't be Raymond's first choice for a messenger," he said.

Fiona curled her fingers around his upper arm, sending a sensual heat throughout his body, a physical reminder of their caresses earlier. "I trust you to convince him his wife needs him." She smiled again, bestowing upon him the softest green regard. "Anyone who can bring Dustmop to heel, can bring Raymond Hickock home. I trust you," she repeated.

How could a man say no?

Jodi stood in the bedroom doorway, rubbing her belly. On the verge of motherhood, she was big and flushed and radiant. With an empty pang Chase regretted that he hadn't seen the stages of Marcia's pregnancy, hadn't been there to support her through labor and delivery. Had missed the first six years of Rose's life.

But if he'd been there for Marcia, he would never have met Fiona. Fate was cruel and beautiful at the same time.

"Do I have to stay in bed, Doc?" Jodi asked.

Fiona turned her attention to her client. "Not at all. In fact it will be better for your labor's progress if you walk around. I'm going to fix you some herbal tea."

"I wish Raymond was here." A shadow flickered in the young woman's eyes.

"I'm going to get him," Chase promised. As if making up for his own absence at Rose's birth, he'd be damned if he'd let Raymond Hickock miss this experience.

"Be careful." Jodi looked worried. "He might be ornery…if he's been drinking."

"He'll sober up quick when he learns he's about to be a proud papa." Chase doubted the truth of his own words, but he'd do his best to make the reality come close to the fantasy.

An ominous quiet descended upon the dim interior of Proud Mary's Dart Bar as Chase stepped through the doorway. When his eyes finally adjusted to the reduced light, he noticed Raymond slouched on a stool at the end of the bar. Everyone, from the beefy barkeep to the boys in jeans and bib overalls at the pool table, eyed Chase with a collective look of warning. He took a deep breath. He didn't relish MP detail under the best of circumstances. This was enemy territory.

A groundswell of muttering and conjecture met his walk to the bar where he took a stand next to Raymond. The man didn't acknowledge his existence.

"Doc sent me," Chase said quietly, looking directly at Hickock, willing him to look up, to begin to take responsibility for his family's well-being. "Jodi's gone into labor."

A flicker of interest stirred the father-to-be. He glanced at Chase, then scowled and turned his attention again to his half-empty glass of beer. "Ain't anything I can do. That's woman's work. Tell Doc to send word again when the baby's born."

Chase quelled the impulse to slam this self-pitying so-and-so into next week.

Instead, he turned so that his bulk crowded Raymond, so that the man knew he meant business. "Jodi asked me to give you a lift home. She wants you with her."

Raymond winced. "Why would she?"

He leaned closer to Raymond and spoke softly, offering the man a gift he might not deserve. "Why? Because your wife loves you and wants to share the birth of your child with you. You're lucky, Raymond. Don't push that luck."

Hickock rubbed his hand over his eyes. "I don't deserve her," he mumbled.

No, in Chase's opinion, he didn't. But the baby needed a father. And Fiona believed this man was salvageable.

"This child's your second chance," he urged. "Come with me. Prove to Jodi that you deserve both her and your baby." When he got no response, Chase leaned even closer so as not to shame Raymond in front of his drinking buddies, then growled low, "Be a man, Hickock. Stand up and be a man. For your family."

When Raymond began a shaky path to the door, Chase followed, making no unnecessary eye contact with the other bar patrons. Two things were for sure: as a new father, Raymond needed to find himself some gainful employment, and he needed to get himself a different set of friends. Chase determined to help him do both.

Call it compensation for seven missed years of his own life.

"Come on, Raymond." As Chase opened the door, the cool, refreshing night air swept in to offer relief from the stale, smoky pall of the juke joint. "Let's stop at the convenience store and get you some coffee."

He'd told Fiona once that you couldn't give a man purpose, and she'd responded by saying that you could nudge him in the right direction. Well, he'd just hunkered down for a long night of nudging.

Where was Chase with Raymond? Fiona wondered as she walked Jodi around the patch of yard next to the double-wide trailer.

For a first labor, Jodi's was progressing swiftly. Already her water had broken and her contractions were coming every five minutes. The young woman had held up with admirable courage, except that she wanted her husband. Fiona couldn't blame her.

"Can we go in and sit down?" Jodi slumped against her. "I'm tired."

"We can do anything you want, dear heart." Fiona helped the mother-to-be up the steps and inside. She brushed damp hair away from Jodi's forehead. "Would you like a bath?"

"I want Raymond."

"Of course." Fiona grimaced as she helped Jodi settle into a slipcovered recliner. Where was Chase? She'd counted on him to rouse Raymond out of his self-absorbed misery. If Raymond couldn't pull himself together even for the birth of his child, Fiona feared for the little family's future.

"Owww!" Jodi clutched the arms of the recliner as another contraction came upon her. "Where in blazes is my husband?"

"Right here." From the open door Chase nudged an exhausted-looking Raymond forward. The errant husband smelled strongly of coffee and soap from the convenience store restroom. Bless Chase's heart. He'd cleaned the man up as best he could.

"Ray, baby!" Smiling through her contraction, Jodi extended her hand.

Hesitantly, Raymond moved to the recliner, then knelt beside his wife. "I'm here for you, Jodi. I'm here." With a lost expression, he looked up at Fiona. "What do I do, Doc?"

"Anything Jodi wants you to do. Hold her hand. Massage her muscles. Let her lean on you. Take your cue from Jodi."

Tentatively, Raymond picked up Jodi's hand. "Okay, baby?" he asked.

"Okay," she breathed on a whoosh of expelled air, signaling the passing of her contraction. Clearly, she would be all right now that her husband had returned.

Fiona glanced toward the doorway. *Thank you,* she mouthed to Chase, who stood transfixed. His look—skepticism mixed with fascination—made her wonder if he'd ever experienced the ups and downs of a relationship as tight yet as flawed as the Hickocks'.

"Oh, oh!" Jodi cried. "Another one. So soon. And I need to push."

"Breathe into it, Jodi," Fiona commanded, quickly kneeling at the foot of the recliner. "And don't push until I've checked you." She slipped Jodi's nightgown to her knees and saw the baby crowning, saw the mother fully dilated. "Oh, my!" she exclaimed, joy leaping in her heart. "We're going to have a baby!"

"Not here!" Jodi wailed. "In the bedroom."

"I'll leave," Chase said, clearly interpreting Jodi's directive as modesty around an outsider.

"No. No," Jodi panted. "I...was...born...in...that... bed. My...mother...too. My...baby...pleeease."

"Your baby will be born in that bed, too," Fiona reassured her. "Boys, take an arm apiece. Support her back. And be careful. I have her legs. We'll carry her. It's not that far, nor too much to ask for three generations in one bed."

Raymond and Chase leapt to her command. Within seconds, they had Jodi propped up in her old cast-iron bed.

"Raymond," Fiona ordered, "kneel on the bed behind her for support. Chase, get a basin of warm water and a washcloth." Warm compresses on the perineum would help Jodi to a more gentle delivery should the pushing process become a long one. The errand would also give Chase something to do. "Jodi, girl, it's showtime!"

And to Fiona's mind, Jodi and the baby were the stars of this show. Raymond, Chase and she were merely the supporting cast. With that thought in mind, she let nature take its course. Luckily, the delivery proved textbook perfect. When the baby—a boy—emerged and began to squawk, her own heart raced in reaction to the formidable beauty of this circle of life.

"May I present your son," Fiona declared, giving the tiny boy a cursory wipe, then placing him on Jodi's bare chest. "He has a fierce sucking instinct. See if you can get him to nurse."

"A son," Raymond repeated, disbelief in his voice. "Jodi, sweetheart, I'm so proud of you."

Cradling her baby with one hand, Jodi reached back to stroke her husband's face. "I'm proud of you, too, Ray. I'm proud of you."

Fiona's heart constricted. With each delivery she made as a doctor, she relived the wonder of Rose's birth. The wonder of herself becoming a mother through Marcia's sacrifice. Watching Raymond and Jodi and their son, she silently vowed to do everything in her power to help this new family survive and thrive.

She noticed Chase standing still as a shadow in the corner of the room. His eyes glittered with unshed tears, as if this miracle moved him, too.

She thought of his strength, of his patience, of his willingness to make himself an integral part of this community. But when she thought of his kisses, of his caresses, of the frequent looks of intense yearning deep in his dark eyes, an unexpected conjecture leapt to the midst of her thoughts. What would it be like to bear Chase's child?

From his corner, Chase looked into Fiona's eyes and saw a woman who wanted another child.

He tried to suppress his awareness by concentrating on her professional skills and attributes, qualities he'd observed and admired tonight. Calm, reassuring, empathetic and supremely competent, she had delivered a baby and had brought a young family together. The residents of Bertie's Hollow might not all acknowledge it, but Dr. Fiona Applegate was the living, breathing spirit of this town. Its angel.

But the look on this angel's face said that she was not done with the earthly rewards of motherhood. More than delivering other women's babies, she wanted another child of her own…and perhaps his, if he correctly interpreted the emotional connection he felt as their eyes met.

Fiona's simple yearning for an expanded family twisted Chase's dilemma. He could marry her. But in all probability, he could not give her another child. If she wanted a sister or brother for Rose, he should release her in no uncertain terms so that she could find another man, the right man. But, dammit, he didn't want another man forging family bonds with his Rosie and Fiona. His Fiona.

As Raymond held his new son and Fiona finished with Jodi, Chase slipped out of the close bedroom, out of the too small trailer and into the big North Carolina night.

He sat on the tiny stoop and looked up at the stars. The stars in this part of the country were like no other stars in any other part of the world. Those over the arctic regions were brittle and laceratingly sharp. Those over the desert were too far away, inaccessible. And those over the bayou were drenched with such a humid haze they oozed together like a rich gumbo. But the stars over Bertie's Hollow were like individual fruit hanging heavy on a celestial bough, ripe for the picking, meant to be plucked and enjoyed by mortals. If not plucked, then wished upon.

He wished he knew how to sort out his personal mission, an endeavor that had once appeared so simple and now seemed tangled beyond reason.

His normal clear thinking had been further distorted tonight as he'd witnessed the emotionally charged birth of Raymond and Jodi's baby. It pained him to admit how much the experience inside the Hickocks' trailer had moved him, drawn him in. They weren't even family.

The Riboud clan, although large, was tight. Chase had younger brothers and sisters and nephews and nieces galore. But never once had he attended the birth of a Riboud baby. Never once had he been so close to such a miracle. He felt honored to have been a part—however small and insignificant—of tonight. The experience felt like a rite of passage, as if he now belonged to Bertie's Hollow.

And that feeling unnerved him.

He heard the whine at his elbow only seconds before he

felt the cool, moist muzzle in the palm of his hand. A rank doggy smell assailed his nostrils. Dustmop.

Chase looked at the mutt. "Go away. I don't need one more complication in my life."

The shaggy beast placed a huge, rough paw on Chase's thigh, lifted his head to the stars, and happily let his tongue loll out the side of his mouth as if they two were boon companions settling in for a long, lazy evening of swapping yarns.

"I have no time for a four-legged problem." Chase stiffened, tried to turn away without much success. "I can't even handle my two-legged challenge."

The mongrel leaned closer.

"Why me? Why can't you cozy up to someone who's known you longer?" Chase asked as he reached out tentatively to lay a hand on the big dog's head.

Dustmop placed his head alongside his paw on his hoped-for master's thigh and gazed upward with a look of utter devotion.

"Not so fast." Chase tried the gruff approach although his traitorous heart responded to the creature's warmth and simplicity. "What are you good for? Hunting? Protection? Or are you one of those lazy pot-licking hounds my uncles seem to get saddled with? Good for nothing but eating me out of house and home, aye?"

The dog's ears pricked up as if a pot-licking hound was just the kind of hound he wanted to be.

"And what about that name of yours? Dustmop. No self-respecting mutt would think of responding to that name. Who named you that?" He remembered. Rose had named him. Rose would love him.

"I give up." Chase knew he'd regret his weakness when his new truck's seats became a mat of dog hair. "Can you exist on human food until I can pick up some canine chow tomorrow?"

The cur thumped his tail in acquiescence.

"And flea soap," he added, scratching his new companion behind the ear. "Remind me to pick up flea soap."

"It will have to wait," Fiona said quietly behind him. "I need you to get the helicopter."

As the dog skedaddled into the woods behind the trailer, Chase rose, alert, concerned. "What's wrong?"

"I don't like the baby's color. There's a tinge of blue around his mouth. I'm hoping it's the least problematic of the possibilities, but I don't want to take any chances."

"Of course not. What about Jodi?"

"I don't want to separate mother and child. She needs to come, too."

Chase looked around. He and Fiona had arrived in his truck. The helicopter was on its pad behind his house not five ground minutes from the Hickocks' trailer, a building squeezed onto a tightly wooded lot. Landing here would be next to impossible.

"It would be better to transport them to the chopper." He made the decision quickly as his mind moved on to the safest way to execute his plan.

"How? We don't have a gurney."

"What about the mattress?"

"It's cheap. And foam. I noted they needed a better one when I changed the sheets under Jodi just now."

"Perfect. It will bend to accommodate the doorways and will protect Jodi and the baby in the back of the truck on the short trip to the chopper."

Fiona smiled. "I'm sure it's not exactly the textbook mercy lift Asheville General had in mind, but it'll work. Time is of the essence."

"Have you told Jodi and Raymond?"

"I'm going to now. I wanted to put you on alert."

"I'll back the truck up to the doorstep."

"Thanks." Fiona laid her hand on his shoulder. "I knew I could count on you."

Perhaps she couldn't in some ways, but he was going to try his damnedest to prove otherwise. For selfish reasons, yes. But even more than that, a change had crept into his agenda the moment he'd witnessed the birth of baby boy Hickock tonight. Before tonight, he, Chase, had only lived and worked in Bertie's Hollow. Now he belonged to it and it to him.

Fiona could think of no sweeter sight than Chase waiting for her in the hospital corridor, two coffee cups in hand.

He held one out to her. "How's the baby?"

"You mean Matthew Dale Hickock? He'll be fine." Fiona warmed her hands on the foam cup, inhaled the brew's invigorating aroma. "It looks as if the culprit in his bluish pallor is the least problematic possibility. An immature epiglottis."

"Will it require surgery?" Concern showed in Chase's every movement.

"Oh, no. It will require time and patience and a lot of gentle burping after feedings."

His relief was palpable. "And Jodi?"

"I have her settled into a room where the baby and Raymond can stay with her. They'll be home in twenty-four hours. I ordered her to let the nursing staff baby *her* in the meantime."

Chase frowned. "I know it's none of my business, but how are they going to pay? They can't have insurance."

It touched Fiona that he cared. "The hospital doesn't want to turn away patients. The administration is amenable to the idea of creative payment. Of medical service in exchange for skills. Raymond's good with his hands. We'll find some way for him to work off his debt with dignity."

A smile creased Chase's handsome face. "This program has the stamp of Dr. Fiona Applegate on it."

She blushed. "I admit to having a hand in it."

"I admire you." His eyes told her he did. In more ways than one. "Such a win-win situation."

"I can't say that the insurance companies think so." She rolled her eyes. "But my concern is the welfare of each and every one of my patients. And tonight—" She glanced at her watch. Five in the morning. "*This morning,* I want to thank you for your help."

"I want to thank you, too." Raymond Hickock approached them. He stuck out his hand toward Chase. "When I'm wrong, I say I'm wrong. I was wrong about you, Riboud."

He accepted Raymond's outstretched hand. "Congratulations. A son should make any man stand tall." His simple reaction with only a hint at the course Hickock should take, went a long way to building a bridge toward future communication. Perhaps Chase could find a niche in Bertie's Hollow after all.

That prospect made Fiona's pulse trill.

"Yeah. A son." Withdrawing his hand from Chase's, Raymond smiled. "You want to see him? All cleaned up, he's a corker."

"I'd like that." Chase turned to Fiona. "Am I allowed?"

"Sure," she said, then headed with the two men toward Jodi's room. "You're the uncle if anyone asks."

"Doc tells me," Raymond said with some hesitation, "that you'll give Jodi and me a lift into Asheville so we can go to parenting classes and I can look for a job."

"You just let me know the day and time." Chase maintained an air of encouragement without being patronizing.

Remembering full well his earlier negative assessment of Raymond, Fiona extended a silent blessing toward the pilot for giving the new father a second chance. She believed that everyone had gifts and everyone had special challenges, but that our humanity resides in the individual capacity to persevere, to accept, to forgive and to love.

"It won't be for long," Raymond continued. "I only have a few more weeks before the suspension on my driver's license is lifted. If I can get a job, I can afford to get my car back on the road." Raymond seemed determined to prove something to Chase. "I'm gonna get a job."

"I know you will." For a brief moment, Chase laid a hand on Raymond's shoulder. The gesture acknowledged Hickock's worth and proved Riboud a big man. "You have a family to support. Now show me this son of yours."

"If Jodi's asleep, mum's the word."

Like thieves in the night, they crept into the darkened room.

"Oh, hello." Jodi smiled brightly from where she lay on the bed.

"Come see." Raymond motioned Chase toward the clear plastic layette at the foot of Jodi's bed. Within, little Matthew slept soundly. "Want to hold him?"

Chase's dark eyes grew round. At that moment Fiona sensed the emotional layers dropping away from him. His look was unguarded and full of tenderness. "Yes," he answered in a rasp full of longing.

Carefully, Raymond picked up his son, planted a quick kiss on his forehead, then transferred him to Chase's arms.

He held the sleeping baby with an ease that said he was born to be a father.

"Matthew Dale Hickock, you're a keeper." Chase choked up as he looked from the newborn to each of the proud parents. "Jodi and Raymond, you are blessed." He said the words as if in benediction.

A proud smile on her face, Jodi reached for her son.

When Chase handed the baby to his mother, he caught Fiona's eye with a look so full of searing intensity that Fiona took a step backward. What had come over him? One minute he'd been tenderness personified, the next he seemed willing and able to gobble her whole. There was nothing professional or platonic about the yearning in his unwavering regard.

"I...we..." Her fingers fluttered to her throat. "Chase and I should move on. The clinic opens in a few hours. I have to shower and catch a few winks." She touched the foot of Jodi's bed. "Rest. All three of you. I'll be in to see you later this afternoon."

Jodi needed no urging to settle back on the pillows, her son in her arms. Raymond pulled a chair close to the bed. The couple murmured thank-yous and good-byes, but clearly they had eyes only for each other.

As Fiona left the room ahead of Chase, she wondered if she might ever find a third for her own family of two. Had she, in fact, found him already?

Here was a man who enjoyed her daughter's company. Here was a man, moreover, who not only respected her calling but who had just spent the night as her valuable teammate. The two of them had worked as one. The side by side had seemed a perfect fit.

Fiona admired Chase's piloting skills as well as his professional qualities. His clear-headed thinking. His flexibility. His devotion to a task until it was done and done well. But it was the man who attracted her. A man who was not afraid of a little girl with special needs, not afraid of giving a neighbor down on his luck a second chance, not afraid of who she, Fiona, was.

She chalked it up to an emotional honesty. And one trait she valued above all others was honesty.

"Ready to go home?" Chase asked, standing at her shoulder.

"Yes," she answered as she linked her arm with his. Yes, perhaps she was ready to go home with Chase Riboud.

Chapter Ten

For several days after the birth of Matthew Hickock, Chase did not see Fiona. He told himself his job left no spare time.

There had been a six-car pileup on I-40. Then a man fly-fishing with his buddies had imbibed too much beer, tripped over a rock near their campfire and broken his leg. His buddies had been too drunk to drive him to the hospital, but they'd called in the emergency crew from their cell phone. And last but not least had been the ex-senator hospitalized for a prescription drug problem. Once the former dignitary had stepped foot on the road to rehab, he'd wanted to be taken home in style—in the new mercy flight helicopter.

He'd been busy, yes. But that hadn't stopped him from thinking of Fiona.

Fiona and his reaction to her had complicated his life far more than he could have imagined. He'd begun by wanting Rose. He now wanted Fiona. If his male instincts were correct, Fiona wanted him. But Fiona wanted more.

The look of tenderness and longing in her eyes when she'd delivered Jodi and Raymond's baby, told him she wanted more children. He, Chase, would not be the man to give them to her.

Dammit, he hadn't even given her the truth.

He paced the living room of his small rented house. Dustmop, having decided he preferred living indoors with regular meals to roaming outdoors at the mercy of handouts, snored peacefully under the kitchen table, and Chase thought ruefully that the proverbial dog's life wasn't all that bad. Eat. Sleep. Run. At least it was a simple existence. Unlike his own.

He needed a sounding board.

Rubbing his neck in frustration, he reached for the phone and punched in his younger sister Marie's number.

"Hello!" Marie's sunny voice came through after the second ring.

"Hey, Ree. It's Chase. Do you have a minute to straighten out my life?"

"So much for pleasantries. Yes, I'm fine. Drew and the kids too. Now what's so important, big brother, that you put aside your manners?"

"At what point does a woman forgive a man a lie?"

"My, my, my. This is some serious stuff. Who've you gone and lied to?"

"It's more a sin of omission. But a big one." He took a deep breath. "I haven't yet identified myself to my daughter's adoptive mother."

"You haven't met her?"

"Oh, I've met her." *And kissed her and thought of her almost every waking moment and longed for her until I ache all over.* "I just haven't told her why I moved to Bertie's Hollow."

"*Maman* and *Papa* told us you'd given up your custody attempt."

"That's what they'd like me to do. But Rose is my daughter. Flesh and blood. And she becomes more my daughter—the child of my heart—each time I see her."

"So you've met your daughter and her adoptive mother on more than one occasion and you still haven't told them who you are?"

"Ree, you'd love them to pieces. Both of them."

"Be that as it may, let's back up a bit. You've been in town—what?—several weeks now, and you haven't told—*who?* I need a name, Chase. I can't talk about this woman whose future you hold in your hands without a name."

"Fiona." He didn't like the way his sister made his actions sound so cold and calculating. He didn't feel that way. Not now.

"You haven't told Fiona who you are? Why not?"

"At first, because Rose is a Down's syndrome child, I wanted to do some research. To see if I could handle being a father to a little girl with special needs."

"And can you?"

"Yes." Categorically. "And with Fiona by my side—"

"Hold on! You've fast-forwarded through some pretty pertinent information. You haven't told Fiona who you are, but when you do, you expect her to be cooperative?"

"Not in a court custody sense. I want her to marry me."

"Back up one more step!"

"I fell in love with my daughter…and I fell in love with her mother." He'd said it, now he couldn't deny. Not even to himself.

"And you want your sister to tell you how to keep them both once you tell them you're the child's biological father. Aye? Why weren't you honest from the start?"

"I had to be sure. Then, after I grew certain, I wanted to prove myself to Fiona. I thought, with us working so closely together, that she'd come to see the kind of man I am, come to understand.''

"Oh, Chase, I don't know that any mother could ever understand why someone would want to take her baby away.''

"But I don't want to take Rose away. Not now. I want to marry Fiona. I want the three of us to be a family. Here. In Bertie's Hollow.'' This was the first time he'd ever voiced his revised intention. A wave of relief washed over him. He'd kept his emotions in check too long.

"Then you'd better tell her you love her. Quick. Then tell her the truth. And pray.''

"This is your advice?''

"Hey, I'm better at planning than I am at damage control.'' Despite the scolding, her voice brimmed with both affection and sympathy. "For all the good it will do, I'll visualize you and Fiona and Rose, all dancing at the next Riboud *fais-do-do.*''

He hesitated in asking the next question. "It doesn't bother you…that…Rose is a Down's child? *Maman* and *Papa*—''

"Are from another generation.'' Marie gently completed his sentence. "They only said what they did because they don't know what we know. Little Drew has a classmate with Down's syndrome. Jean pitches a mean softball. And can eat a prodigious amount of pizza after the games. That's what my son notices about him.''

"Thanks, Ree.''

"You're welcome. And Chase?''

"Yes?''

"Next time call me *before* you do something stupid.''

"I'll try.'' He hung up with a smile and new motivation.

His pager pulsed at his hip. Dialing the number on the display, he hoped it wasn't a time-consuming assignment. He had to see Fiona. Had to talk to her. Tell her the truth.

"Riboud here."

"Can you get over to the consolidated school?" The dispatcher's voice was brisk, unemotional. "Tammi's at The Chat and Chew. You can pick her up on the way. Some kid got his head stuck in a schoolyard bicycle rack. The fire department's there already, but they're not sure what shape the kid's going to be in once they free him."

Chase felt a twinge of parental anxiety. Ever since the birth of Matthew Hickock, every child in Bertie's Hollow had been like his own child.

"I'm on my way." And he was as soon as he hung up the phone, not with the matter-of-fact ease of a professional doing his job, but with the concern of a father whose child needed him.

The truck windows rolled down, Fiona and Rose sang "The Wheels on the Bus" with great gusto. Martha, on her way to her quilting group, had dropped Rose off at the clinic. When Fiona was able to close early, mother and daughter had done a little food shopping and were now headed home for Rose's favorite meal of "pasghetti."

Rose spotted the commotion on the school playground before Fiona. "What's that, Mama?"

That involved a sheriff's department cruiser, a fire truck, the mercy flight helicopter and a dozen adults and children crowded around the bike racks. Fiona pulled her pickup up next to the brown cruiser.

Opening her door, she held out her hand to Rose. "Let's see if we can help."

"Yes, let's." Because helping was second nature, Rose slid across the bench seat to join her mother.

Once they recognized their doc, the crowd opened a path to where Ozzie Dunn, the sheriff, Ernest Whitehouse, a volunteer firefighter, Edith Pennyman, principal of the consolidated school, and Chase gathered around Rush Harmon whose head was stuck between the bars of one of the bike racks. Ernest held a crowbar, Ozzie a quart of motor oil, while Edith carried herself with a puffed-up sense of importance and utter indignation. Chase knelt beside the boy.

"What hap—"

"A dare." Chase cut Fiona off. "We disagree as to how to release him."

Rose, placing her hands on her knees, bent at the waist until her face was even with Rush's. "How you doin', Rush?"

"Not so good, Rosie."

Rose stroked his hair. "Mama will help."

"I'm glad you're here, Fiona," Edith declared imperiously. "Maybe you can resolve this." She glanced at her watch. "I'm due at a vital board meeting in twenty minutes."

"I should think the welfare of one of your students would be more important," Fiona replied, letting frost settle on her words. Edith was one of the reasons Fiona home schooled Rose.

Ernest lifted the crowbar in the air. "I can get him out in two shakes—"

"Ernest Whitehouse," Edith snapped, "I told you once before I will not have school property mangled. Those bike racks are *new*."

Sheriff Dunn turned to Fiona. "And Chase won't let me use the motor oil to grease the sides of the boy's head."

"I don't want to risk getting it in his eyes. We want to solve the problem, not make it worse." Chase, with Rose now kneeling beside him, looked up. "But the grease idea is a good one."

Rose smiled up at Chase. "Mama bought butter at the store."

"That's nice, dear," Edith declared in her usual dismissive manner. "Now, Fiona, what are we going to do? Talk some sense into these men."

"You didn't listen to Rose, Edith." Fiona turned toward her truck. "I'm going to get the butter we bought at the store."

"See." Undaunted by Edith's slight, Rose smiled at Rush. "Mama will help."

Fiona quickly returned with the tubs of butter which she smeared, liberally and without ceremony, on either side of Rush's head. She glanced at Chase and Sheriff Dunn. "You two pull on the bars. I think they'll give just enough to let Rush slip through."

They did, and he did.

The crowd cheered. Rose hugged Rush around his middle. Rush, rubbing his head, declared sheepishly, "I feel like a greased pig." Edith bent to inspect the bars of the bike rack. Assured that no damage had been done to school property, she glared at her watch, then stormed off to catch her important meeting.

She called back over her shoulder, "Someone needs to wipe that mess off the bars before school tomorrow."

Chase sidled up to Fiona. "I think I might start hanging around the board meetings too," he said with a decided edge to his words. "Especially around the time the board seeks to hire and fire."

Rose joined them, a triumphant smile on her face. She slipped one hand into Fiona's and the other into Chase's. "You saved Rush. Good job."

"Your idea saved Rush, Rosie," Chase replied, a look of pride on his face. "We three make a great team."

Fiona's heart did a little flip. She'd been thinking the very thing.

Rose tugged on Chase's hand. "Come have supper." She licked her lips. "Pasghetti."

Chase turned to Fiona, question written in his expression.

Fiona blushed. Her daughter, the child, was braver where Chase was concerned than she, the adult. "You're certainly welcome," she said, anticipation rising with the invitation.

Chase tweaked Rose's button nose. "Pasghetti it is."

"Have to eat honey on our bread, tho'." Rose lifted both legs and swung between Chase and Fiona. "No more butter!"

The adults laughed.

"Meet you at the cabin?" The exhilarating thought of meeting up with him again made Fiona glance quickly from Chase to Rush, who stood surrounded by children as if he were the new community folk hero. "I'll give our grease monkey a ride home," she added, trying to keep her voice calm, assuring herself that this upcoming meal together could be construed—if anyone should ask—as job consultation. "That way I can make sure he's okay."

"Can I bring a bottle of wine?"

"Yes...that would be nice." She felt color rise to her cheeks again. Wine—in the privacy of her cabin—ruled out any pretense that this supper was going to end up professional in nature.

"See you later." Chase reached out and tweaked her nose!

Flustered at his familiarity, she just knew her face had gone crimson. In self-defense, she called out to Rush and beckoned toward her truck. "Let's get you home to a shower and shampoo."

Pulling out of the schoolyard, Fiona tried not to catch one last glimpse of Chase. She'd see him in a couple minutes, for pity's sake. But her traitorous gaze homed in on him standing beside his helicopter. Standing and watching as if he expected her to find him. Their eyes locked in a look that declared, *We belong.* Fiona felt it so clearly that she was certain the entire town recognized it.

Rush Harmon sure did. "You datin' the pilot?"

"Yes," she admitted for the first time publicly. "I guess I am."

"Cool."

No, her feelings for and thoughts toward Chase were anything but cool. Hot. Molten. Sizzling. Any one of those adjectives came closer to the truth.

And he was going to be all hers for the evening. Well...hers and Rosie's. With Martha gone until late, Fiona counted on her daughter to keep dinner, if not professional, then friendly.

Nervously fingering the bottle of wine, Chase stood on Fiona's front porch, waiting for her to respond to his knock. This supper was a major step in their relationship. He'd been invited beyond the cabin's front door. By Rose. His daughter, who seemed to like him very much, to trust him. In her guileless way, she'd asked him into her life. And Fiona's.

He needed to tell Fiona the truth.

"Hey!" With a breathy greeting the woman of his thoughts opened the screen door.

He stood speechless before her transformation.

She had changed out of her no-nonsense slacks and blouse into a loose tunic and pants outfit of a gauzy green material that, when she moved, showed each and every delicious curve of her body. She'd let her hair down, and it swirled, freshly brushed and gleaming about her shoulders. Too, she'd put on perfume—something very light yet woodsy and tempting.

Erotic hunger rose deep within him. Supper? He wanted to skip right to dessert.

"Chase?" She cocked her head to one side.

He fought his way out of a sensual haze. "We…need to talk." He needed to clear the air so that she and he could develop a relationship based on trust as well as mutual attraction.

"Chase!" Rose, a bundle of expectation, barreled his way. She seized his hands as Fiona caught the wine bottle. "Come! Help me set the table!"

Despite his pleasure at his daughter's warm welcome, he needed to come clean with Fiona. He cast a *save me* glance in her direction.

"Sorry." Shrugging prettily, she turned, wine bottle clutched in a firm hand, toward the kitchen area of the wide-open cabin. "Remember the story of the little red hen?"

He fumbled with his memory of childhood fables.

"If you don't help, you don't eat!" Rose crowed, dragging him toward a large trestle table already set with napkins and silverware. "I did this!"

Viewing her precise handiwork, he felt a growing warmth deep in his heart. He knew abled six-year-olds who would never think to lift a hand around their homes. But Rose contributed to the Applegate household with a cheerful willingness that made him proud.

"What can I do?" he asked, feeling honored to be a part of this tiny family. There would be time later to talk to Fiona.

Still holding his hand, Rose tugged him to a sideboard. "You can reach plates and glasses." She waggled a finger at him. "Don't break them!"

"I'll try not to." Although breakage with Fiona just a few distracting steps away was a decided possibility.

"I'll get pepper." His daughter released him to climb a stool next to her mother and rummage in a spice closet.

"What kind of pepper?"

"Hot!" Rose replied, her back to him, her attention focused on finding a certain container among the myriad in the closet.

Standing at the sink, draining spaghetti, Fiona laughed. "Red pepper flakes, Tabasco sauce, it doesn't matter as long as it's hot. Rosie likes her food—from eggs to pasghetti—spicy." Smiling, she looked over her shoulder at Chase. "It's certainly an imported preference. Heaven knows where she picked it up."

He nearly dropped the glass tumblers.

The Ribouds always joked that hot pepper rather than blood ran in their veins. In his daughter's, too.

"Got it!" Triumphantly, Rose held the container of flakes aloft.

Yes, she certainly had *it*. Both the Riboud penchant for zest and an ability to seize an unsuspecting heart—his— and hold it fast.

Surely Fiona would understand that Rose was truly *their* child. Surely that understanding would only strengthen the relationship between mother and father. He would hope— as he waited for an opportunity to tell his entire story.

"Come, come!" Having placed the pepper flakes next to her place setting, Rose urged Chase to the kitchen counter where a large salad waited to be scooped into individual bowls.

He followed but discovered the small galleylike kitchen didn't leave much room for a child with a step stool and two adults. While helping Rose dish up the salad, he found himself inadvertently touching Fiona more often than was safe for his overworked senses.

"Oops!" She backed up against him while maneuvering the steaming plates of pasta to the table.

"Sorry!" In reaching across the counter for an errant piece of lettuce, he rubbed against her arm as she reentered the kitchen area to retrieve the grated cheese.

"Beg your pardon!" Fiona held the cheese aloft and

pressed her front to Chase's as Rose, finished dishing up the salad, pushed her stool back into the corner of the kitchen and forced the two adults into an intimate sidestep.

"Hmmm...I..." Nose to nose with a woman who smelled delicious and who felt too soft and warm for reason, he sought words to save his equilibrium. "Do you have...a...corkscrew? I'll...ah...open the wine."

"Yes." Reaching under his arm with her free hand, she grazed his hip on her way to the counter drawer behind him and sent a sizzle through his pelvis. "Here you go." Retrieving the corkscrew, she stepped back, her eyes glistening, her cheeks flushed. "I'd love a glass."

Forget the wine. He was on the road to inebriation without it.

"Let's eat!" Rose executed her rolling skip to the table, climbed into her chair, then announced, "I'll say grace."

Having uncorked the wine, Chase followed Fiona to the table where Rose extended her hands to them. Seated, Fiona at the head of the antique trestle, Chase and Rose on either side of her, they held hands and waited for the supper prayer.

Rose cleared her throat. "Bless this house. Bless this food. Bless this family. Amen." She squeezed both his and Fiona's hands.

The forthright simplicity of the blessing—and his inclusion—stunned him. With very few words his daughter had drawn him into the circle of her family. Or had he imagined the implication?

Still holding hands, he glanced at Fiona and saw within the depths of her shadowed eyes a mixture of longing and vulnerability. She had recognized the implication. But had she accepted it?

Because he wanted her, he needed to talk to her. But not in front of Rose.

His daughter's little hand slipped from his. "Pass the cheese, pleeease!"

Fiona blinked, smiled, then turned her gaze from Chase to Rose. "I like that *please,* young lady," she said passing the shaker.

"I like that cheese!" Rose replied, dusting her mountain of spaghetti with a flurry of Parmesan.

Fascinated, Chase watched his daughter crown her meal with hot pepper flakes. He loved her meticulous attention to detail. He loved her absolutely certain preferences. He loved her gusto.

He loved her.

Rose slurped a strand of spaghetti. Fiona raised an eyebrow.

"Sorry!" Rose looked at Chase and giggled impishly.

"In Japan," he said, winking at his daughter, "it's considered polite to slurp your noodles." He cast an innocent glance at Fiona. "Home schooling. A little bit of international studies."

"Oh, thank you," Fiona replied, motherly warning creeping into her words. "I'm still grateful for that grass whistle demonstration in your music lesson."

He smiled and caught himself dreaming that he could have it all—a daughter and a wife who loved him in a town that needed him.

Fiona closely watched Chase, and Rose's reaction to him.

Her daughter was a naturally accepting child, but Fiona had never seen her take to anyone as quickly and as easily as she had to this man.

And Fiona had mixed feelings about that.

Considering her own longing to explore a relationship with the compelling pilot, she was pleased that he and Rose had established a rapport. Fiona had refereed far too many bitter blended families not to appreciate an atmosphere of mutual acceptance. But a tiny, hidden part of her—a part of which she was by no means proud—suffered a pang of maternal jealousy. It was immature, she knew, but it remained lodged under her heart all the same. It wasn't as if she was loath to share her daughter. She certainly didn't begrudge the granddaughterly affection Rose showered on Martha. Or the special aunt-like friendship Rose enjoyed with Martha's daughter, Anne. Why then should she bristle when her little girl showed signs of liking Chase? Of trusting him. Of looking forward to his visits.

Perhaps it was because both Martha and her daughter were very careful to defer to Fiona in every way that involved Rose's upbringing. Whereas with Chase there were elements of his relationship with Rose—fleeting incidences, to be sure—which seemed designed to be shared by man and girl alone. Like the grass whistle. Like the shoulder ride. Like his mischievous subversion just now of her reminder in spaghetti manners. He didn't always take his cues from Fiona. Sometimes he struck out on his own with an almost fatherly agenda.

And Fiona worried what would happen to Rosie's feelings if he saw the need to move on.

"Fiona?" Question written in his eyes, Chase leveled his gaze directly at her.

"Pardon?" She glanced at her half-full plate and couldn't remember having eaten a strand of spaghetti.

"I asked how the Hickocks are doing."

Ah, she could answer this question. "Fine." Smiling, she pushed lettuce leaves around her salad bowl with a fork. "Mother and child are doing fine."

"I want to see the baby." Rose grinned, her mouth rimmed with tomato sauce.

Fiona touched her own napkin to her mouth and watched her daughter carefully follow suit.

"And Raymond?" Chase poured an inch more wine in each of their glasses.

"He's working at the convenience store in Jodi's place until they start parenting classes next week in Asheville and he can look for a better-paying job."

"Is it dessert time?" Rose asked.

"If you clear your place, you may bring the brownies to the table."

As her daughter carefully removed her setting of crockery and silverware, Fiona sat back. A new feeling blossomed deep within her. A contentment in the here and now. She liked sharing her concern for her patients with Chase. She liked the domesticity of a shared meal. Although it unsettled her, she liked this threesome around the table.

Rose returned with the brownies. "Would you like one?" she asked Chase.

"In a little bit, thank you." He seemed relaxed. "I'm going to finish my wine first."

Fiona could almost see the wheels turn in her daughter's head as she nibbled on her brownie and considered why anyone would prefer wine to dessert. She didn't dwell on that imponderable long. "Will you help with dishes?" she asked Chase.

Crossing his elbows on the table, he leaned toward Rosie. "Do you help with dishes?" He seemed genuinely interested.

"Yes!" Rose sat up straight. Proud. "Mama washes. I wipe. Martha puts away."

"Tonight," Chase said, "to thank you for this delicious meal, I would be willing to wipe and let you have some extra playtime. Would you like that?"

Rose looked at Fiona. "Can I take my dolly on the porch? Wait for Martha?"

Fiona hesitated at the thought of being left alone in the

kitchen with Chase. Even to do up the supper dishes. How silly. "Yes, you may be excused," she conceded. Why did she continue to shy away from him?

Rose clattered across the cabin floor, picked her favorite doll off the sofa, then pushed her way through the screened doorway.

"You'll spoil her," Fiona said lightly, less in reprimand, more to ease the silence between the two adults.

"I wanted a chance to talk to you." Reaching across the table's surface, he placed his hand on top of hers. "About us."

She was afraid of that.

Rising, she slid her hand out from under his and gathered her near-empty dishes. "Us," she repeated softly.

He stood, also. "I thought it was time we each learned more about the other."

She felt color rush to her cheeks, then tried to diminish the blush with an attempt at lightheartedness. "Goodness, we delivered a baby together. That's a pretty elemental experience. How much more do we need to share?"

"That was professional. I'm talking personal." A shadow flickered in the depths of his eyes. "I'd like to tell you a few things about myself."

He'd have to wait. At that moment Martha entered the cabin, her expression as stormy as a thunderhead. She glowered at Chase, harrumphed loudly—and most rudely—then marched toward the corridor leading to the wing of bedrooms.

Martha didn't take well to strangers. Fiona had always forgiven her, however, because she assumed her dear friend feared a stranger might judge her harshly if her past came to light. Chase, having read the old newspaper articles, had rushed to such judgment. Without Fiona's reasoning, what direction might his outrage have taken?

Moreover, Martha felt a fierce maternal instinct toward Fiona and Rose.

Not the most tactful woman in Bertie's Hollow, she seemed always to take the offensive before she had to take the defensive. With Chase, her prickliness had developed into a strong dislike, and Fiona needed to get to the root of it, especially if the pilot was to become a greater part of their lives.

"Please, excuse me," she said to Chase. "We'll have to postpone our talk. It looks as if I need to have one with Martha."

Chapter Eleven

While waiting for Fiona to wind up her talk with Martha, Chase remembered Rose out on the cabin's front porch. She'd been very quiet. Snagging a brownie, he headed outside to see what kind of activities she enjoyed when left to her own devices.

As he pushed the screen door open, he noticed her sitting cross-legged at one end of the porch. She didn't acknowledge his presence. Instead, she sat rocking back and forth, softly singing a song in a private language, focused on the doll, which she waved in the air about her head. His daughter seemed lost in a world of her own making. Strangely content. At peace. In fact, her repetitious movements and the chantlike quality of her voice reminded Chase of meditation.

So as not to disturb her, he took a seat on the swing at the other end of the porch.

In his research on Down's syndrome, he'd read so much

about the differences that set these individuals apart. But the more time he spent with Rose, the more he saw similarities to everyday, abled kids. Moreover, Chase felt that the population at large could learn a thing or two from those moments that weren't quite mainstream.

Take Rose's behavior now. Supposedly, she'd had a full day of home schooling. Then, late this afternoon she'd participated with concern and creativity in Rush Harmon's rescue. Early this evening, she'd been charming and helpful over supper. It must be very close to her bedtime. But instead of getting wired in front of the television, she sat in a peaceful, self-contained state, as if she were winding down from today, recharging her batteries for tomorrow. Who was to say that Rose's different behavior wasn't, in fact, what *normal* should be?

Fiona opened the screen door. She glanced at their daughter and then at him. "I'd like you and Martha to have a heart-to-heart."

No, he wanted to have a heart-to-heart with Fiona.

He sighed. Apparently there were hurdles he needed to clear even before that last formidable obstacle. "I didn't realize I had a problem with Martha."

"You don't. She has one with you." Coming toward him on the swing, Fiona smiled. "She didn't really go into it, but I think she's a little jealous."

"Of me? Why?"

"She sees you as a rival for Rose's and my attention." She stopped directly in front of him, her expression serious now. "Martha's part of my household. If I'm to see more of you socially, I'd like the two of you to get along."

"You want to see more of me?"

Her cheeks flushed with pink, she lowered her gaze to the floorboards. "I thought that was pretty obvious."

He stood, then tucked her into a light embrace. "I just wanted to hear you say it."

She leaned against him, nestled her head on his shoulder, slipped her arms around his waist. "Martha, having been hurt in her marriage, sees friendship, affection, love as finite. I think she's worried that if you come into our lives—into mine and Rose's—we'll have no room for her. That she's in some way expendable."

"I wouldn't want her to think that." He kissed the crown of Fiona's head and inhaled the scent of strawberry shampoo. "I'll talk with her."

"I knew you would." Fiona stood back and looked up at him, her eyes brimming with happiness and trust. "I'll put Rose to bed and send Martha out here."

She moved out of his arms and across the porch, then quietly knelt beside Rose, touched her and whispered something in her ear. Slowly, as if coming out of a trance, Rose stood.

Seeing him at the other end of the porch, she waved her doll. "Night, Chase," she said, her voice already slurred with dreams.

"Night, Rosie. Sleep tight."

"Don't let the beggar bugs bite." His daughter yawned, then followed Fiona into the cabin.

Alone, Chase leaned against a support post, listened to the spring peepers and wished it was Fiona, not Martha, he was about to have this talk with. He smiled to himself, however. Fiona had admitted she wanted to see more of him. There would be time aplenty, then, for soul baring.

Martha stepped out on the porch, her features stony. It appeared she wasn't particularly delighted about this chat, either. The whole idea had the stamp of Fiona—wonderful, caring, conciliatory Fiona—upon it. And for Fiona, he'd make peace with the devil herself.

He might as well make the first overture. "What concerns you, Martha?"

The housekeeper scowled. "Heard you've been digging into old newspaper reports."

So much for the privacy of library patrons. "Fiona suggested I learn a little about the recent history of the area."

"And you now think you have the dirt on me."

"Fiona explained—"

"You think I'm not good enough to care for Rose."

"At first, yes." He might as well begin to practice absolute honesty.

"Let those without sin cast the first stone."

Many of the folk Chase had met in the past few weeks were wont to revert to scripture, so Martha couldn't know how close she came to his secret, his own dilemma. Despite her ignorance, her words pierced deep. How could he, of all people, judge this woman?

"When I learned your whole story," he replied, trying to keep his words even, "I understood." He hoped Fiona would understand when she learned the whole of his story.

"You're an outsider." Martha said this as if it were tantamount to the plague. "You can't understand."

"I've been around the world. People aren't any different just because the geography changes. Believe me, I understand your situation. I'm not here to pass judgment." He did understand. Understood how the fates had conspired to render her powerless and how, subsequently, she had made a bitter choice to take back control. As he had.

Would Fiona champion him as she had Martha?

"I may have been an outsider," he added, trying to reassure her, "but now I want to make Bertie's Hollow my home."

Martha didn't look reassured. Instead, she seemed to grow distraught at his words. "You want our Fiona."

He bristled. "You make it sound as if I wanted to abduct her. I want to grow a relationship with her. I respect her.

I'm attracted to her. Surely, courtship takes place in Bertie's Hollow.''

Martha narrowed her eyes. ''You planning on courting her proper?''

''Yes.'' He winced inwardly as he thought how he needed to tell Fiona the truth before he'd consider the courtship *proper*. ''But you needn't worry I'll take her and Rose away from you. This is your home, too. Fiona has told me you're a member of her family. I'll honor that.''

''I'm not concerned for me. I'm a survivor.'' Martha crossed her arms over her chest and assumed an immovable stance before him. ''If you hurt my gals, there'll be hell to pay.''

''Is that a threat, Martha?'' He didn't like ultimatums.

''It's a promise.''

With those chilling words, the older woman turned and disappeared into the house, leaving Chase to ponder the weight of her pronouncement. If the truth of his arrival in Bertie's Hollow didn't lie so heavy on his mind, he might be able to make a joke of Martha playing the dragon before the castle of the princess. But, because he held back potentially hurtful information...

Fiona reappeared on the porch. ''How'd it go?''

''It's going to take a while.''

Fiona leaned on the other side of the support post from him. ''Martha's pretty protective.''

''Do you think she might have a problem with men in general?''

''I've thought about that.'' She peered around the post at him. ''But I'm counting on you to be the man in a million who wins her over.''

He was just about to ask her if they could talk—not about Martha, but about the two of them—when she yawned loudly.

''Excuse me,'' she said. ''I haven't caught up on my

sleep since we pulled that all-nighter delivering Matthew Dale. It seems I've grown soft since my days as a med student.''

Concern for her well-being jumped to the forefront of his thoughts. She didn't need another knotty problem dumped in her lap tonight. Not when fatigue already sapped her. He'd talk to her when she was fresh.

''I'll head home,'' he said. ''Would you have lunch with me tomorrow?''

''If I can get away. Fridays can be pretty hectic.'' Her eyes flashed with flirtation. ''Got any special inducement?''

''Only this.'' He swept her into his arms and claimed her with a kiss.

He wanted her to think of him between now and noon tomorrow. He wanted her to know that he wanted her. He wanted to leave his mark.

And so he pulled her up tight against him and his mouth captured hers, his tongue swept the sweetness of her lips, his nostrils caught the heady scent of her yearning. He wanted her to savor this moment long after they parted, as he would.

Offering up a little mewing sound, she pressed against him, deepening the kiss. Her hands slid around the back of his jeans, cupped him, drew him to her. She had to feel how very hard he'd become, how much he desired her. She moved her hips against his. She knew.

He groaned with longing. Holding Fiona in his arms, he thought only of her. Of her softness. Of her strength. Of her utter desirability. Of the overwhelming effect she had on his body, mind and soul. She was all he'd ever wanted in a woman.

His hands played the contours of her body. She fit his touch. Exactly.

Her tongue teased. Her fingers provoked. Her quick hot breath drove him to the edge.

She backed away, breathless. "That's some inducement."

"I aim to persuade." His blood still snapped and sizzled in his veins as he tried to hold on to her.

"Lunch it is." Slipping out of his grasp with one last feathery touch from her fingertips to his swollen lips, she entered the house with a smile that held exquisite promise.

Fiona scrubbed the remaining cheese from the scorched kitchen countertop. The use of the stove forbidden to her, Rose had attempted to make a grilled cheese sandwich, using Martha's new iron. They needed to add proper cooking lessons to the home-school agenda.

What a fitting climax to today's heat and frazzle.

Fiona thought with longing of the lunch she'd promised to have with Chase, the lunch she'd had to cancel because she'd been called to the consolidated school to treat the second-grade class for head lice and then to conduct a schoolwide check. She shivered at the thought. It was never her favorite public health duty. And in such heat.

It was far too early in the year for temperatures in the upper nineties, but tell that to the strange weather system out of the Pacific. Bertie's Hollow had awakened to an unaccustomed heat that had intensified dramatically throughout the day. Forecasters predicted the pall would hang over the mountains for the next several days.

Fiona wanted nothing more than to sink into the cool spring waters of their shaded swimming hole.

"I'm sorry, Mama." Rose appeared at her elbow, thoroughly contrite.

Fiona had already administered a stern lecture and time-out. "I know you are, sweet pea." She stowed the cleaning supplies under the sink. "We're going to have to show you the tidy way to make a grilled cheese sandwich."

"Now?"

"Not now." Fiona knelt before her daughter. "Now you're going with Martha to Suzie's birthday sleepover where you'll have pizza and cake and ice cream." Suzie was Martha's six-year-old granddaughter, and the annual sleepover had become a tradition.

Rose grinned. "Martha and I packed our bags."

As if on cue, the older woman appeared in the doorway with two small overnight cases. "All set."

Rose hugged her mother. "Will you miss us?"

"Yes." And no, she thought with a guilty twinge as she hugged Rose back. After today's chaos, she would relish tonight's solitude. Did that make her a bad mother or merely mortal?

"What will you do?" Martha asked.

"Probably go to bed early."

"Well, we're not going to do that, are we, Rosie, my girl?" Martha winked and extended her hand.

"No, ma'am!" Rosie hopped from foot to foot. "We're going to stay up late and have a party!"

Smiling, Fiona kissed the top of her daughter's head, then stood. "Give Suzie a big happy birthday hug from me."

"Okay!" Rose slipped her hand into Martha's. "Let's go!"

When the screen door swung shut behind the two, it took several minutes for Fiona to adapt to the silence. She rarely found herself without company and felt a little giddy in this newfound freedom, like a teenager whose parents had *finally* trusted her alone overnight. What should she do first? Call her boyfriend and tie up the phone all evening?

An even better idea would be to call up Chase and invite

him over for a picnic supper and a dip in the swimming hole.

Before she could chicken out, she picked up the phone and dialed his number.

"Riboud here."

"Can a woman make up for a broken lunch date with an offer of a home-cooked supper?"

"Fiona! I was just looking at peanut butter and jelly. I'll be right over."

"Bring your bathing suit. The swimming hole will be chilly, but it'll sure beat this heat. You do have a bathing suit?"

"No...but I'll manage something that won't offend Martha."

Fiona paused. "Martha and Rose are spending the night at Martha's granddaughter's. They won't be back until noon tomorrow."

"Oh." It was amazing how much punch he packed into that one tiny syllable. "I'll be *right* over."

His grin caressed her clear through the phone lines.

After hanging up, Fiona changed into her own swim suit which she covered with an oversize T-shirt, then concentrated on packing a no-fuss picnic.

As she gathered up towels and an old blanket, she couldn't suppress an anticipatory bounce in her step. Couldn't hold back the old sentimental love song that sprang unbidden to her lips. Couldn't dismiss thoughts that for a few hours this evening—and perhaps for longer if fate proved kind and fully realized her unchaperoned state—she had the pleasure of Chase Riboud's undivided attention.

Did she dare admit, even to herself, that she wanted this man?

A knock on the door roused her from her fantasies. He was here!

Gathering up the hamper, towels and blanket, she met him at the door. "Hi!" Did she possibly sound as eager as she felt?

"Hi, yourself." His voice husky, his dark gaze penetrating, he opened the screen door for her. Whereas he always seemed so spit-and-polish, this evening he dressed casually in T-shirt, cutoffs and moccasins. The relaxed look made him appear even sexier than usual.

"Let me carry something," he offered.

In reaching for the hamper, his hand grazed hers and sent a flash of physical expectation throughout her body.

"Ready?" she asked innocently as she thought how truly ready she was. She had been cloistered far too long.

"Lead on," he encouraged.

He walked at her side as they made their way up the path behind the cabin. With a proprietary air, he touched her back or her elbow or offered his hand as they maneuvered around granite outcroppings or bushes overgrown with new, far-reaching shoots. He smiled easily whenever she looked at him…which was often.

She looked at him and saw an extension of herself, a part that had remained, up until now, missing. Walking by his side felt natural. Right. As if they were destined to be a pair.

"What are all the pink-and-white blossoms?" he asked.

His speech startled her because it seemed as if they'd been communicating all along without words. "Why, those are mountain laurel. They've blossomed in the past few days."

"Pretty."

"Yes. They're one of the reasons I could never live anywhere else."

"Do you ever get an urge to travel?"

She grinned, feeling flirtatious. "Are you offering to show me Cajun country?"

"Anytime. We could run down for a long weekend and bring a year's supply of hot sauce back for Rosie."

"A year's supply? Do you have friends in the army, willing to loan you military transport?"

He shook his head. "I don't care. I like a girl whose tastes aren't wishy-washy."

"That's Rosie!" Fiona skipped up the path ahead of Chase, then stopped at the edge of the swimming hole. "She's going to be miffed that her new best buddy paid a call and she was elsewhere."

"I promise to make it up to her." Chase came up beside Fiona, slipped his arm around her shoulder, nuzzled her neck. "But tonight, I'm all yours."

Despite the ninety degrees, she felt a shiver of pleasure at his touch.

Happiness washing over her, she spread the blanket amid the purple shadows on the slope spongy with moss. The pungent scent of pine needles filled the air. The birds, settled in the treetops but not yet ready to call it a night, sang as if they were love's official ambassadors.

"I can't remember the last time I attended an adults-only event, picnic or otherwise," she said, trying for a light tone, as she settled on the blanket and reached for the hamper.

Chase lowered himself next to her, folding his long legs until he sat cross-legged. "You haven't dated much?"

"No." Pouring two plastic cups of dandelion wine, Fiona lowered her head as if in concentration, so that he wouldn't notice her blush. "I've been raising a child and doctoring in my spare time." She handed him a cup of wine. "How about you?"

"Not much. I didn't have the family, but I had the career." He seemed suddenly uncomfortable.

"Let's not talk about the past." The last thing she

wanted this evening was for either of them to feel uncomfortable. She raised her glass in a toast. "To the present."

Touching his glass to hers, he relaxed. "And the future."

She liked the sound of that.

He took a sip of wine. "But I would like to talk about the past—"

"Not tonight!" She placed fingers over his mouth, felt the moist residue of dandelion wine. Some of the hill folk believed that particular drink possessed miraculous powers. Perhaps it would give her courage to take what she wanted tonight. "Tonight you must promise to think only of the here and now."

He looked at her as if he'd like nothing better.

"We have food fit for royalty." She began to draw supper out of the hamper. "And if you hadn't noticed," she added, nodding toward the spring-fed swimming hole, "we have our own private Jacuzzi with cold and colder running water. I don't know about you, but I've had a tough day. I plan to indulge."

A lopsided, boyish grin creased his face. "Are you trying to seduce me, Dr. Applegate?"

"I most certainly am!" She giggled, not quite believing that she'd admitted as much. "But I'm new at this. I'll need help."

"Oh, I'm going to like this assignment." With a waggle of his eyebrows, he reached for a bunch of chilled grapes. "May I peel you a grape, madam?"

Her laughter floated on the evening breeze.

Chase could not believe the change in Fiona. She seemed freer, more lighthearted than he'd ever seen her, as if she'd come to some transforming decision—and that decision included him.

He ate of the picnic she'd prepared without the least attention to the process or to the tastiness of the food. He focused all his energies on watching Fiona, on drinking in her quiet vitality, feasting on her present glowing happiness. It thrilled him that he could make her happy.

Finished quickly with food, he stretched out on his side on the blanket, his head cupped in his hands, and looked up at Fiona. "I can see why you wouldn't feel a need to ever leave this place."

"The old folks say the fairies keep us here."

"Fairies?" He could almost envision Fiona as a woodland sprite. In the muted light of the setting sun, her hair frothed about a face enhanced with elfin green eyes and alabaster skin.

"There's such a Celtic heritage in these parts. It's almost blasphemy not to believe in the little people." Her eyes flashed mischief. "Have you never seen a fairy ring of toadstools?"

"The closest I've come is a mildew ring in my shower stall."

"Mercy! Did the military leech all romance out of your bones?" Shaking her head, she looked around. "Let's see if I can find you a fairy ring."

He sat up. "Those?" He pointed to a feathery white clump of what looked more like flowers than mushrooms.

"No. That's bloodroot."

"Such a gory name for such a pretty blossom. How did it get named?"

Lightly, she rose from the blanket, and, using her hands, dug up one of the plants, roots and all. "It's really wonderful. Steeped in folklore, history and medicine." She brought the specimen back to the blanket.

Her interest and animation fascinated him. He could see where Rose would learn more schooled at home with Fiona than in any traditional classroom.

She fingered the long delicate stem. "Native peoples used the sap as an insect repellent. They dried the root and used the powder to cure rattlesnake bite. Modern scientists have discovered that certain ingredients in the plant can be used in toothpaste to fight plaque and decay.''

He touched the white-petaled flower and the cabbagelike leaf. ''That still doesn't tell me why it's called *bloodroot*.''

Taking a knife from the picnic hamper, Fiona sliced the plant's root over an empty Dixie cup. The sap from the cut ran bright blood red. ''See? Appalachian craft stores are full of baskets dyed with this sap.''

He dipped his finger into the cup. ''Quite the versatile plant.''

''Oh, yes. There's more.'' She grinned, and a hint of deviltry seeped into her words. ''Take off your shirt.''

''Beg your pardon?'' He was beginning to like this botanical lesson.

She twinkled. ''Purely for historical demonstration.''

''I don't need any rationale,'' he replied, slipping his T-shirt over his head. He was fast becoming a champion of home schooling.

''Sit still.'' Cup in hand she inched closer to him. Dipping a slender finger into the sap, she painted a stripe across his left pectoral, across his heart.

Her touch startled him. ''And this demonstration would be about…?''

''War paint.'' She looked directly, deeply into his eyes. ''Native warriors used bloodroot to decorate their bodies before going into battle.''

''But I'm not going into battle.''

Her gaze never straying from his, she painted a second stripe above the first. ''You haven't heard of the battle of the sexes?'' Her voice held a come-hither huskiness that made him ache to take her right here. On the blanket.

She painted a third stripe above the second and made him dizzy.

''Did the warriors' women ever use this?'' He asked the

question only to see if he could still put two coherent words together. He could. But barely.

Her eyes flashed. "Native women had their bodies painted when they made a gift of themselves to their men."

"Take off your shirt." He whispered the order.

"Yes, sir." Handing him the cup of red sap with a thoroughly naughty grin, she shucked her T-shirt, then sat before him—expectantly—dressed only in a sleek, black, one-piece swimsuit with a gold zipper running up the front. The thought of the mysteries protected by that slender, interlocking swatch of gold made him hard.

"Well?" She cocked her head. If she wasn't fairy, and enchantress, she was only one generation removed.

He dipped his finger into the cup, hesitated for only a moment, then painted a long, slow stripe from her collarbone, over the swell of her breast, to the upper tip of the zipper. She inhaled at his touch. At his claiming.

The birds had gone quiet. The gentle spring breeze had disappeared, leaving the trees tremulous and waiting. The surrounding forest, cloaked now in deep shadow, seemed to hold its breath.

Chase didn't want to think. He wanted to take what Fiona offered. Yet he paused with his surroundings because her offering was of such enormous import, priceless. The gift of herself.

"Do you want this?" he asked.

"Yes," she breathed. "Do you?"

"Oh, yes." She couldn't possibly know how much.

He set the dye-filled cup on the moss, out of the way. With a steady hand he grasped her swimsuit zipper and tugged gently until the suit opened all the way down to her navel. The stretch fabric, released from the zipper's constraint, slowly pulled back to reveal a V of creamy skin luminescent in the light of the rising moon.

She sat before him a half smile wreathing her lips, a goddess of the night, enticing. She watched his every move, serene and assured, as if she were in no hurry, as if an eternity of uninterrupted exploration stretched out before them.

With his right hand, he touched her skin. Felt its silkiness, her warmth. He brushed the fabric of the swimsuit over her heart further back. Felt the weight of her breast exposed in his palm. At that moment, she reached out and placed her hand over his heart.

"I want you," he murmured.

"And I, you," she replied.

He pulled her into his arms, pulled her down beside him on the blanket, felt her nipples rise taut and brush against his chest, felt his corresponding arousal rise hot and needy.

Skin to skin, yet it seemed he couldn't pull her close enough.

He kissed the angle of her jaw, the line of her neck, the curve of her shoulder as he pulled her tight, rounded bottom hard up against him. His body thrummed with desire. He pulled back, to slow his headlong race to climax, caught her face in his hands, tried to find his center in her eyes open and drenched in moonlight.

He felt dizzy as he saw not two, but four eyes—two green, two gold.

The gold hovered directly over Fiona's shoulder and seemed to dance with amusement when they caught his attention.

"What the—" He sat up and thrust Fiona behind him.

A joyous bark filled the hillside as Dustmop's forepaws landed on Chase's shoulders. Damn. Hadn't he left this furred pariah sleeping in his fenced-in backyard?

Fiona shrieked.

"It's okay!" He rose and pulled her with him, tried to reassure her as he fended off the unabashed greetings of his new pet, the practical joker. "It's just my mangy cur with his impeccable timing. He must have smelled the food."

As if on cue, Dustmop turned his attention to the neglected picnic hamper. Within seconds he'd devoured the remains of the potato salad.

Fiona dissolved in laughter.

"I don't find it funny." He didn't. Neither did his body, once revved, now idling at the curb.

"Well, I do!"

"Am I doomed to a life of looking over my shoulder, watching for my canine chaperone?"

She grasped his jaw with her long fingers, drew his face close, planted a quick, firm kiss on his mouth. "Not if we take this picnic indoors."

"I like this line of thinking." He did. And he loved her unflappable sense of fun.

She grasped the bottle of dandelion wine. "Leave the food as a diversion. Let's see if we can outrun your shadow." With a whoop, she danced down the moonlit path toward the cabin.

The feel of her body still imprinted on his, he followed, hot on her trail.

At the back steps, he caught up with her, caught her hand, stayed her flight. "Fiona..." He placed her hand over his quickly beating heart. "I'm not coming in tonight unless I'm here tomorrow morning."

With a gaze drenched in longing, she drew him up the steps. "Do you eat a big country breakfast or just coffee and juice?"

"A big country breakfast. Definitely. I plan to be hungry." As he followed her into the cabin, he crossed a bigger, more symbolic threshold into a realm of commitment. This was no one-night stand. By staying the night, he declared himself a part of Fiona's life from this moment on.

Chapter Twelve

Stepping into the cabin with Chase's hand in hers, Fiona flipped a switch and wondered if, having shed a little light on the matter, she would change her mind about this adult sleepover.

Chase tugged on her hand, turned her toward him, then cupped her face in his hands. "This isn't just fun and games for me."

"Nor for me." Feeling an overwhelming connection between them, she knew she would not turn back.

He stood before her, tall and straight. The three crimson stripes across his well-muscled bare chest made him appear every inch a warrior from another century. Even though she stood before him, exposed and vulnerable in her swimsuit, she felt no fear.

She placed the dandelion wine bottle gently on the floor, then slipped her arms around his waist. Reveling in the feel of his taut, smooth skin against hers, she kissed his mouth. The freedom to express her want, to claim him, exhilarated her. She trusted him, and, because of that trust, allowed herself to enjoy the physicality of the moment without nagging doubt.

Chase Riboud was a man she could depend upon. He was more than raw masculinity and physical attraction. He was sensitive, understanding and upstanding. And he had begun to make her tiny town of Bertie's Hollow his home. He would not pull her from who she was and where she always wanted to live. Even as he excited her, he made her feel safe.

He kissed with a devouring passion, and she found herself responding with a sensual appetite that had lain dormant within her for many, many years.

"Fiona…" He breathed her name against her mouth.

She bit his lower lip. Not hard. But hard enough to let him know that he now belonged to her.

She had always guarded the combustible side of her nature very carefully. Had never given her sexuality free reign to smolder and spark, never before let her passion erupt in conflagration. She had always been mother, doctor, woman, in that order. Tonight she would be woman first and she would let the fires rage. With Chase. Although the prospect frightened her more than a little.

Threading her fingers through his hair, she leaned into him and steadied herself, for she found her knees growing weak, found her eyes beginning to cross. "Oh, Chase, come with me. I have the loveliest big bed."

"Damn." He hesitated, a frown crossing his firm brow. "I didn't bring protection. I wasn't expecting—"

"Do you think I'm a doctor for nothing?" She took his hand and, on wobbly legs, led him toward the bedroom.

On a chair in the short corridor sat her black bag. Reaching inside and pulling out a half dozen foil packets, she smiled. "As a public service, I give these out like candy. But what kind of product am I promoting? I think we need to run a quality control check.''

He threw his head back and laughed, and the sound gladdened her heart. The sight of his strong white teeth against sensuous lips made her pulse pound.

His eyes flashed desire glazed with amusement. His gaze, exquisitely fierce, promised a journey of challenge and self-revelation. She would accept the challenge, take the journey, for this man possessed an undeniable vitality that excited her, that transferred itself to her very marrow.

With Chase she felt so alive.

She led him to her room with the enormous antique sleigh bed, turned on the little shell night-light next to the door, drew him close in a possessive embrace.

With his big, strong hands, he skimmed the straps of her swimsuit off her shoulders, peeled the fabric over her torso, down her legs as she clutched the foil packets tightly with one hand and with the other caressed the planes of his chest, showing a thin line of wiry dark hair that led from just below his navel to the button of his jean cutoffs. She unhooked the button, unzipped the jeans and discovered the dark line led to pleasure, hard and ready.

He groaned as she worked her fingers under the denim, pushed the jean shorts over his compact hips, freed him as she was free.

Naked, he scooped her off her feet, into his arms, then carried her to the bed. Gently he lowered her to the soft cotton comforter. From now on, in her mind, this would be her bed and his.

Her body filling with a warm, tingling expectation, she raised her arms to him, beckoning. His cheeks flushed, his eyes filled with dark fervor, he knelt on the bed, and the old springs creaked a welcome.

Stretching out beside her, he raised himself up on one

elbow. "Let me look at you," he murmured and splayed his hand across the breadth of her lower abdomen. His palm felt hot and heavy, his fingers light and far-reaching.

She ran her index finger slowly from his neck to his navel. "I hope you'll do more than look."

His reply came with a soft chuckle. "If I don't slow down, the main course will be over before we've unfolded our napkins."

"Ah, but we have all night." She let the tightly held foil packets fall from her hand onto the bed's surface. "And I have plenty of napkins."

"In that case..." He kissed her long and hard as he explored her body with his clever hands. Her face. Her throat. Her breasts. All received his inventive attentions.

Deepening their kiss, she arched against him in a wordless invitation, a plea, and ran her hands down his sides, around his back, over the steely hard mounds of his buttocks. Gloried in possessing him.

He responded by sweeping his hand down her abdomen, creating an electric sensation that moved from the surface of her skin to her very core which was fast becoming more liquid, more eroticized by the moment. As he slid his fingers between her legs, she moaned against his mouth.

His silky massage wreaked havoc on what little equilibrium she'd managed to retain. She squirmed against him, her body magnetized and drawn to his touch. With each movement, he caught her in a spiral of newly heightened physical desire, until her center gave way and the stars fell behind her tightly closed eyelids.

She reached for him, slid her hand in a caress around his arousal, turned her mouth from his, and rasped, "Now. Oh, please."

She reached for a foil packet, ripped the packaging, sheathed him.

He rose above her, paused for what seemed an eternity,

penetrated her with a look from his smoldering, dark eyes—a look that said they belonged—then entered her with a low ragged moan.

He filled her. Exquisitely. And when he moved, she felt enveloped by him. Enveloped by his physicality. Enveloped by his powerful emotional aura. Inside, outside, he made her his. She wrapped her arms and legs around him to contain him as he contained her.

They rocked together with a slow rhythm at first, savoring their intimacy. Her first climax trailing her like charged stardust, she couldn't suppress a small noise—half hum, half purr—that rose in her throat. A primitive song of life. Of giving and of letting go.

Her need grew all too soon as her body not her mind began to conduct the rising crescendo of sensation that thrummed like a symphony through her. She moved with greater demand. He met her demands and raised them to a higher pitch, a greater intensity.

Their bodies slick, they gave and took until she felt her center give way. Again. This time surpassed the first.

"Chase!" she cried as the music in her body exploded into a shimmering jazz that played every muscle, every bone, every nerve with an unsettling syncopation.

"Fiona…" he moaned, clasping her to him, shuddering his release.

He sprawled across her, his greater weight to the side, his one arm and leg pinning her, possessing her, protecting her. From herself.

Time and time again she'd claimed she was not a letting-go kind of person. She had always been—until now—a hold-on-tight kind of person. She'd held on to caution, to responsibility, to a concern for the wants and needs of others over her own. Just now, she had let go and she had soared to the accompaniment of cosmic lights and celestial

music. Such universal high flying could grow addictive.
Yet how dangerous could it be with Chase at her side?

Her fingers trembling, she touched his face, felt the features that had grown ever so dear to her. Felt his heart beat
against her shoulder. With a rising tenderness she began
to hope that this night would be the first of many, stretching far, far into the future. She allowed herself to imagine
Chase a permanent part of her life. When all was said and
done, she was a simple woman. She would be content with
this man of her heart as her husband, the father of her
daughter.

"You are so beautiful," he whispered. "And so trusting."

How odd that he should mention trust.

She pulled away and looked deep into his eyes, eyes
still drenched in sensuality. When she placed her hand on
his chest, she felt something unspoken between them.
Something he'd held back even as they'd joined their bodies as one. There was a physical satisfaction in the relaxed
and heavy position of his body. But in his eyes lay a troubled shadow.

She had to ask. "Is something wrong?"

"Wrong? No." With the pad of his thumb, he gently
brushed her lips. "Incomplete."

"I don't understand." Suddenly, she felt cold, shivered.
"What's missing?"

"Let's get under the covers. And talk."

She hesitated. "I feel you moving away from me."

"Not away." He kissed her forehead. "Closer. Much,
much closer. That's why I have to tell you something
about myself."

"If it's about the past, I don't need to hear it. As far as
I'm concerned, we begin from tonight."

Chase looked at the woman in his arms. Fiona had
moved his body and touched his soul. She had given of

herself freely, no questions asked. She had trusted him. Now he needed to begin earning that trust with honesty.

"Come. Under the covers," he urged, holding up the comforter for her. "You're shivering."

Eyeing him cautiously, she slipped between the sheets. "Is this the moment when you tell me it's been nice, but you can't commit to a steady relationship?"

"Oh, Fiona, just the opposite," he replied, following her under the covers, taking her into his arms. "I want to build on what we've started."

She pushed away from him and propped herself up on the pillows. Beautiful but distant. "Something is troubling you. Tell me."

"It's not that easy. Only two other people know." The doctor and Marcia, and they'd known before he had. It wasn't information he'd freely volunteer, not even to his family. "But you need to know."

She waited patiently.

"When I watched you deliver Matthew Dale," he began, "I could tell that you'd like more children of your own."

Her expression softened. "I'd love to have more children."

Why was this so difficult? Perhaps because it struck at the root of his manhood—the ability to provide. Not only to provide *for* a family, but to provide the family itself.

"You don't want children?" she asked, clearly concerned.

"It's not that." He didn't want her to think he'd be a reluctant family man. "It's that I couldn't give you children."

She placed her hand on his chest. "Sterility?" There was no scorn, no pity in her voice, only a frank concern.

"More complicated than that." This telling pained him. Would she think him less a man? "Because of certain repeated exposures during my military career, there's a high probability that the children I'd father would have problems.''

''I've seen such cases,'' she said, her voice gentle. ''The only sure way to know is genetic testing.''

''I've been told that.''

''And this news angered you.'' She touched the warrior-striped place above his heart with her fingertips. ''I can feel your anger.''

''Wouldn't it anger you? Wouldn't you feel like damaged goods?''

''Ah.'' The look in her eyes grew sad. ''The desire for human perfection.''

Was that it? If so, it made him seem shallow. ''I wasn't looking to be perfect,'' he replied. ''Only normal. Is that too much to ask?''

''If I'd insisted on normal, I'd never have Rosie. And what a shame that would be.''

Dear God, he was digging himself into a hole.

''You're a special woman, Fiona.'' He tried to make his dilemma clear without sounding completely self-centered. ''You see the silver lining to every cloud. You're warm and loving. You have a rare gift of unconditional acceptance.'' He shook his head in frustration. ''When I received my medical report, however, I didn't even know that a woman like you existed.''

''Well, I do.'' Her smile was soft. ''But I sense that you're still conflicted.''

''I'm not a man given to introspection, but this whole issue has kept me thinking.''

''What bothers you most?''

No one had ever asked him. The question gave him pause. ''I'd have to say, expectations.''

She raised one eyebrow but said nothing.

''I'm a Riboud.'' He scowled. ''Riboud men produce

large robust families. I've always wanted my own branch on the family tree. Furthermore, I'm an ex-military man. By definition, I'm supposed to be...well..."

"Manly? Macho?" Her frown reflected his. "Do men define themselves solely by their ability to populate the earth?"

"No. Not solely. But the ability to be a father is part of what it means to be a man."

"Ah. And fatherhood is all about biology?"

"Not always." But he thought about Rose.

Would he have given her a chance if she'd not been his biological daughter? He didn't address his own mental question, afraid the answer might highlight some of his earlier, uglier preconceptions, misunderstandings.

"Answer this for me." She skewered him with a serious look. "Is fatherhood a right or a privilege?"

"Perhaps fatherhood is a privilege," he murmured mostly to himself, struck by this new notion.

Fiona smiled, as if pleased with his response. "The privilege of fatherhood can come in many guises. You have to be prepared. Open to possibilities."

"Such as?"

"Let's use a purely hypothetical situation." Her expression softened. "I want you to keep your answer to yourself." She took a deep breath. "Would you be satisfied if your opportunity for family consisted of...a woman with a job that was more calling than career and a Down's syndrome child? No more, no less."

Yes. Yes, he would. He started to tell her, but she placed her fingers on his lips.

"Don't tell me," she warned. "Remember, it's a hypothetical question you're to answer for yourself. To see if you're open to possibilities not related to biology."

He caught her wrist, removed her fingers from his lips. "Would *you* be satisfied?" he asked, thinking of the look of longing on her face when she'd delivered the Hickock baby. Part of his problem lay in thinking that he couldn't give a woman what she wanted. "You said you'd love to have more children."

"Funny you should bring that up." She leaned back on the pillows. "I consider myself one of the happiest, most fortunate women on earth. I love my hometown. I love my work. And I adore my daughter. I have all that I could ever want or need right here in Bertie's Hollow. Everything else is a bonus. Lovely, yes. But a bonus."

He scowled. "A husband would be an extra?"

"Don't get me wrong. A husband or a husband and more children would be a blessing, but because I lack them at the moment does not diminish the joy, the fulfillment in my life. I refuse to dwell on what I don't have."

"You think I'm dwelling on what I don't have?"

"Only you can answer that."

What did he *have?*

He had a daughter who delighted him, who made him proud to the verge of tears. He had a job he liked very much in a town that felt more and more like home. And he had the prospect of seeing Fiona every day.

She cupped his cheek. "I feel your anger subsiding."

With her probing, she had helped him sort out his feelings, helped defuse his anger. He remained in awe of her understanding, her empathy. "What hat are you wearing now, Dr. Applegate?"

"I'd have to say I'm not wearing a hat right now. I'm just a woman who cares very much for one wounded man." She touched the crimson stripes on his chest. "There are many different kinds of battles, Chase Riboud. But you don't have to fight all of them alone."

He captured her hand and kissed the tips of her fingers.

"Because you face a physical challenge and because you need to work through that challenge makes you no less a man." She trailed the fingers of her free hand down his chest, over his abdomen to where she stroked him intimately. "On the contrary..."

Amazement filled him to discover that she still wanted him. He'd feared that his disclosure would dampen the sensuality of their night together. Instead, he found himself growing hard under her touch. "But I thought—"

"That the feast was over?" She smiled, the devilish glint having returned to her eyes. "Heavens, no! We still have many napkins left to unfold." With a soft chortle, she held up a foil packet.

Taking the packet from her hand, he opened it and quickly sheathed himself. "I can't promise to hold back this time." Her understanding had fueled his passion to white heat.

"I'm not asking you to hold back. I'm asking you to join with me." She slipped her hand behind his neck and drew him to her for a deep, demanding kiss. "Now," she insisted against his mouth.

Too much had she asked earlier with her questions. Her probing had ended with unexpected revelations that made his mind spin. He no longer wanted to think. He wanted to feel.

He entered her and lost himself.

Her body, strong yet pliant, met his in a rhythm that soothed at the same time it excited him. He'd met his match in this woman who took him to new heights of physical intensity as she'd taken him to new depths of introspection.

Flushed with desire, she gazed up at him, held him with her passionate regard, even as her fingers bit into his shoulders, even as her hips thrust to meet his. This was no incidental coupling. This was a claiming. A mutual commitment. A future.

Unable to hold back, he thrust inside her and felt the

bittersweet liberation. For brief seconds he was caught in a free fall. Cleansed. Weightless. Without direction.

But as soon as he lowered himself to Fiona's side, as soon as he felt the warmth of her along his body, he regained his sense of self, his sense of purpose, his emotional compass.

They lay for a long time in each other's arms, silent and spent.

At long last Fiona spoke. Softly. "It took great courage to tell me about your fatherhood issues. Issues both physical and emotional." She sighed deeply. "Because of your openness, I want to share something about Rose and me that isn't common knowledge."

He held his breath. If she planned to disclose that Rose was adopted—something she'd never discussed with him—it would provide the perfect opportunity to complete his truth telling.

"Tell me," he urged.

"It ties in with my questions to you about the rights or privileges of parenthood. I know full well that I'm privileged to be a mother." She hesitated. "You see...Rose is adopted."

His pulse began to race. This was his chance. He must come clean. Now. There would be no more perfect opportunity.

"I know," he replied, his words catching in his throat.

She twisted in his arms so that she looked him directly in the eyes. "How?"

"There's no way I can prepare you for this...." He stroked her cheek and prayed she would hold in mind all that they had shared to this point. "I'm Rose's biological father."

Grasping the sheets to her nakedness, Fiona recoiled, staring at him in horror. He was not joking.

This then was the impending change she'd sensed when

first he'd come to Bertie's Hollow. This was the unnameable power he held over her. This was his shadowed mystery.

How could she have been so blind?

How could she have misinterpreted the intensity in his eyes, the yearning, the hint of darkness deep within him? How could she have let down her guard where her daughter's well-being was concerned? Why had her intuition, so strong in helping others, let her down in protecting her own?

Wrapping the sheet around her, she scrambled out of bed, backed into the far corner of her bedroom, her heart thudding with anger and fear. "Get out of my house."

He sat on the edge of her bed, anguish written in his eyes. "Let me explain."

"Go." She edged toward the bedroom door. He could never explain away this treachery.

"Fiona, please. I'm the same man I was a minute ago. Only now I'm your daughter's father."

A storm of emotions crashed over her. Revulsion at this sudden, unexpected exposure. Hurt at this betrayal. Shame that she had let herself love the betrayer. Fear for Rose's future...

And an inescapable desire to know more about the man who had impregnated Marcia and had abandoned their child. To know him would be to arm herself against him. She sensed they were about to do battle.

Her mind reeled with unasked questions. "What do you want?" She nearly choked on the words.

"I want to tell you how I came to find Rose."

He made it sound like an accident. Happenstance. With the same degree she'd trusted him only minutes before, she mistrusted him now. "You abandoned her. And her mother." The thought galled her.

"I didn't know Marcia was pregnant. She never told me. Never contacted me after I shipped out."

Fiona scowled. As much as she wanted to doubt his words, she remembered Marcia had a knack for shutting people out. Even her own daughter. That harsh realization forced her to listen to Chase. "When did you find out you had a daughter?"

"About a month ago. I applied for a job in the hospital where Marcia worked. She saw my lab results and the doctor's report before I did." With great difficulty, he seemed to suppress a rising anger. "She must have pitied me. Tossed me a bone. I shouldn't father children in the future, but she'd save my pride by letting me know I'd already scored in the past."

He sounded so bitter. Unlike the Chase that she had come to know.

She shivered. He wasn't the Chase she'd come to know. But she was determined to get to know this man so that she could protect herself and Rose against him if necessary. Why had he tracked them down? To replace the children he couldn't have?

He got up from the bed, moved to reach his clothing. His nakedness startled her, as if, in the soft glow of the night-light, she were seeing him for the first time. He was undeniably beautiful. He moved across the room as if he were completely at ease in his body...and at home in her house.

But, in reality, he was a total stranger. A stranger who had used her. And the physical beauty that she had found so compelling, she now found menacing. The man she had just made love to now threatened her world.

"Get dressed," she ordered, moving swiftly to the door in a wide arc that avoided him. "And meet me in the kitchen. We do need to talk."

She all but ran to the small laundry room at the back of

the kitchen where she tore off the sheet that still bore the musky residue of their lovemaking. In disgust, she threw it in the corner, then rummaged through the clean folded laundry for a sweatsuit and thick socks. Covered now from head to toe, she reentered the kitchen as prepared as she would ever be for an ugly confrontation.

Chase leaned against the kitchen counter, his arms folded across his chest. "I'm sorry that I wasn't honest with you from the start." He had the nerve to look her in the eyes.

"Why didn't you tell me immediately? The first minute you came to town." Her words came to a fast boil as they tumbled over her white-hot anger. "I was certainly accessible."

He reddened. His stance stiffened. "How can I explain this so you won't hate me?"

"Start at the beginning," she snapped, knowing she would still hate him. She had a sinking sensation that this story was not going to get any more palatable. That nothing he said would lessen the animosity she now felt toward him.

"When I first arrived in Bertie's Hollow," he began, his words deliberate, cautious, "I could only think of myself. I was blinded by a sense of betrayal and rage. Marcia had double-crossed me by giving up the only child I might ever have. She didn't even have the courage to tell me about the pregnancy, and then she gave Rose up for adoption without my knowledge or without my consent."

Fiona did not like the direction this discussion was taking. No, not one tiny bit. She sensed legal repercussions looming on the horizon.

"The adoption was private, but legal through and through," she replied between clenched teeth.

"A father has rights." A look of raw pain in his eyes, he took a step toward her.

Her heart clenched in fear and sudden realization. "You came for Rose. You want to take her away from me." She backed away from him.

"I did, but—"

"You used me to get to her!" Thinking of their love-making earlier, she found it hard to breathe. She had let herself go because she trusted him, an unimaginable thought now. "You used me."

"No! You changed me, Fiona. You and Rose. You've healed me. I don't feel the same as I did when I set out from that doctor's appointment. From that meeting with Marcia. Hell, I don't even feel the same as I did the first day I met you. The first day I met Rose." The longing in his eyes beckoned.

"Oh?" She eyed him suspiciously. "And how do you feel now?"

He extended his arms to her. "You know how I feel."

"How could I know how you feel," she protested, confusion threatening to overtake her thoughts, "when your presence here has been a lie from beginning to end?"

"It hasn't ended yet."

"It has as far as I'm concerned. I want you gone."

"Fiona…I'm staying. I have a job here. This is my home now. Rose is my daughter."

"I don't believe you." She shut him out. Tried to shut out the horror of him trying to take her daughter away. Her natural drive to protect Rose had malfunctioned, and, because of that failure, their safe haven on Smoke Mountain had been breached. "You will never take Rosie from me," she declared. "I will fight you on this."

He extended his arms to her. "I don't want to fight. I want to work things out."

"You planned to take my daughter from the only mother she's ever known." Thank God Rosie was safe with Martha away from this house. "That's not what I call working things out."

"I didn't think it through. At first all I could think of was my loss. The injustice. The need for Rose to know her father. I thought of it as a search-and-rescue mission. If I thought of you at all, it was as an obstacle. I'm ashamed now to admit that."

She glared at him. He would learn how difficult an obstacle she would become.

"But then I met you, and you were—are—so warm and kind and giving. Not an obstacle, but human. An individual. I had to find a way not to hurt you. I thought if you got to know me as an individual, you'd understand the motivation behind the truth."

"Which you failed to tell me."

"Things got complicated." A shadow of pain passed over his features. "When I learned that Rose was a Down's child, I doubted my ability to care for her. I needed to dispel my ignorance." He paused. "I spent a week doing research at the Asheville library, at the hospital."

Had he cared that much? That sounded like the old Chase. But she didn't want the old Chase playing on her sympathies.

"Did you see a lawyer, too?" she asked, a bitter taste rising in the back of her throat.

"No." He looked hurt. "We both love Rose. The two of us can figure out what's best for her."

"Oh, no." She marched to the front door, opened it. "You're going to need a lawyer and proof you are who you say you are. Until then I want you to go. And I want you to stay away from my daughter." A ruthless maternal instinct made her drive this man—this dangerous man she had almost loved—from her home.

He crossed the room to stand before her. The darkness

was gone from his aura. Only pain remained. And longing. His eyes had not lost their longing.

"What about us, Fiona?"

"There is no *us*." She fairly spat the last word. "I'll see you in court, if necessary."

His expression haunted, he turned and walked out of her life.

Slamming the door behind him, she embraced her anger to mask the agony of his going.

Chapter Thirteen

Aching with Fiona's rejection, Chase drove up Smoke Mountain, not down. She'd told him to leave her cabin, but, unable to bring himself to believe she truly meant to shut him out of her life permanently, he wouldn't go far. He felt like Dustmop, tail between his legs, shunted from pillar to post, unwanted yet hanging around the perimeter, desperate to belong.

He'd give Fiona a chance to cool off, and then he'd try approaching her again.

Clutching hope like a talisman, he drove all the way to the end of the gravel road, past Alva Biggs's cottage to where the road became a humped track, curved, then ended suddenly in her meadow on the mountain's peak. He parked his truck at the edge of the tall winter grass, spiky and pale in the headlights, made a call to the Asheville General Hospital to let them know he was available, then, by the silver sheen of a setting moon, walked out into the meadow where he had first kissed Fiona.

The memory now stung.

Stars hanging low overhead, taunted him. He could wish on each and every one of them, and he still wouldn't come close to repairing the damage he'd done. Not just tonight, but leading up to tonight.

Settling himself on the top of a giant granite boulder, he racked his brain to think of how he would change the past if given the power.

Should he have taken Marcia's news and gone on with his life as if nothing had happened? No. Rosie was his daughter, and finding her, getting to know her had enriched his life. He still firmly believed that her life could be richer for knowing him as her father.

Yet Fiona seemed set against allowing him a parental role.

Should he have told her who he was the minute he arrived in Bertie's Hollow? This was a more difficult question to answer even with the benefit of hindsight, but he'd have to say, no. When he'd arrived in town, he'd been angry, blinded by a sense of injury done him. He suffered from a cruel tunnel vision and could see nothing but his own self-interest. He was not in an emotional position to consider either Rose's or Fiona's needs or wants. To have revealed his identity then, when Fiona and he were strangers, would have ended in certain acrimonious turmoil.

When would have been the right time to come clean? And why had he missed the perfect opportunity?

He ran his fingers through his hair in exasperation. His perception of the situation had changed daily. The more time he spent with Rose and Fiona, the more he saw of their special bond, the more he felt he must honor that bond. To honor it meant backing off from his original mission.

He didn't want to sever Rose and Fiona's family ties; he wanted to be included.

The more time he spent in their healing presence, the issue revolved less around him and more around them. By the time he'd seen an opening in which he could present his case, he'd fallen in love with mother and daughter.

Fiona was a warm and empathetic woman. That was one of many reasons he loved her. She'd given Martha Ricker a second chance as she had Raymond Hickock. She'd understood their weaknesses and seen clear to their good qualities. This thought gave him hope.

With time, she must come to realize that he loved her, and that he would never hurt either her or Rose. Somehow he'd show her. He'd made a grave mistake, yes. He admitted to that. He'd been thoughtless, self-centered and clumsy. He was sorry to the depths of his soul for any pain he'd caused her.

But he was not going away. To go away would be to give up on a relationship, on a family that was meant to be.

Fiona paced her tiny kitchen, anger alternating with grief. She had kicked Chase out of her life before he'd answered all her questions. In a state of shock, she hadn't even known all the questions to ask.

He'd said he'd come to Bertie's Hollow to find his daughter. The implication was a custody battle although he said his plans had changed. What were his plans now? He said he wanted to work things out. What did that mean? And where did she fit in?

She shivered at the thought of their passionate love-making. She had thought it so beautiful, so real, such an act of sharing, but she now recognized it for gross manipulation on his part. Furthermore, every look, every word, every act of his from the beginning of their acquaintance now took on a more sinister hue. He had used her to get close to her daughter.

His daughter.

Feeling chilled to the bone, she moved to make herself a cup of tea. Mechanically, she took down chamomile leaves, her squat brown teapot that always made her smile but held no comfort for her now, and her favorite cup and saucer. She brought water to a boil in the funny old whistling teakettle that sounded more like a chick with the hiccups. Seeking solace in familiar things, familiar procedures, she found none whatsoever. Her heart held despair, empty and cold.

Having made the tea, she stood at the counter, trying to draw warmth from the steaming brew. Automatically, she reached for the cookie jar and drew out an animal cracker, Rosie's favorite.

At the thought of her daughter, Fiona couldn't breathe. Her heart became a stone in her chest. Anguish and insignificance filled her veins. In front of her eyes, a black, swirling vortex devoured all she held dear as sorrow and impotence leached hope from her bones, turned her dry and brittle, threatened to dissolve her into dust, threatened to suck her into the maelstrom, into oblivion.

She grabbed the edge of the counter to keep from falling.

Fiona felt a sudden sharp pang, an intensification of the black terror. She knew, although the vision was formless, it was about losing her Rose. Nothing else could wreak such utter emotional devastation, the sense of which persisted even under the bright kitchen lights.

Rosie.

Dropping the cup and saucer, she felt her socks soak up the spilled tea. The liquid was warm, yet she felt drenched in a cold sweat. Her chest and arms tingled with encroaching numbness. She had to tell her lungs to work. If a patient were to describe such symptoms to her, she would diagnose a severe anxiety attack.

Rosie.

She had to get to Rosie. This overwhelming sensation could only mean that her daughter was in trouble.

Dear God, had Chase tried to take her from the sleep-over?

Willing her legs to work, Fiona struggled to the phone. Punched in the number for Martha's daughter, Anne Windsor.

"Yes?" A groggy Anne answered after several rings. An eternity.

"Anne, this is Fiona. Please, check on Rose."

"Doc, the girls are fine on the family room floor. They just got to sleep after a very long party."

"Please, check." Fiona didn't want to alarm Anne, but she couldn't ignore the intensity of her vision. "This is important. I can't sleep."

"Neither, it appears, can I," Anne grumbled. But she added, "Hang on. I'll check."

Waiting was an agony. Fiona prayed Anne would come back to the phone and tell her this immobilizing fear was unfounded, yet the anxiety fueled by a mother's instinct grew with each passing second.

"Fiona!" Anne croaked as she picked up on the other end of the line. "She's lying in a pool of blood."

"Blood!" Fiona fought the urge to panic. "From where?"

"As if she started her period, but she's too young—"

"Wrap her up! Keep her warm! I'll be right there!" Slamming down the receiver, she grabbed her truck keys from the rack by the back door, then raced out of her cabin in her wet stocking feet.

Desperation pushed him down the mountain.

He'd received a call to pick up Rose Applegate at the

Windsor house. His Rosie. In some kind of distress. A medical emergency. Fiona was with her, thank God.

Trying to keep his truck on the narrow, winding, gravel road, Chase drove as fast as he dared. The predawn half-light made navigating tricky. He had to look for a mailbox, painted with the name Windsor. Once he picked up Rose and Fiona, his house and the helicopter were only another mile and a half.

He worried about Fiona. Would she hold up under this emotional blow, having just received one from him earlier? He'd admired her professional cool and calm on previous occasions, but this medical emergency involved her daughter. Their daughter.

He spotted the Windsor mailbox. No sooner had he pulled his truck off the road than the headlights picked out Fiona carrying Rose wrapped in a faded quilt. Martha draped her arm around Fiona's shoulders in support. Fiona's face was ashen. Rose's eyes were closed.

Throwing the truck into park, Chase leaned over to open the passenger door. "Get in."

Martha glared at him. "Where's the helicopter?"

"I'm on my way to the helicopter." He didn't like Rose's pallor. "Get in," he ordered Fiona. "Don't waste time."

Fiona glanced only once at her daughter, then climbed into the truck, clutching a limp Rose.

"Call," Martha said simply. "We'll pray." She closed the truck door.

Backing onto the main road, Chase made the tires spin. *Caution,* he admonished himself mentally. He needed to get a grip. For Rose. For Fiona. Levelheadedness would win the day.

"What's wrong?" Keeping his eyes on the road, he voiced his concern aloud.

"Any number of things. Only hospital tests will tell for sure." Her words were flat, cold.

"What do you think?" he asked, quelling the fear he felt in seeing his child's still form in Fiona's arms.

After twenty years in the military, he'd thought himself a man inured to fear. But, then, he'd only been a father for a very short while. And fatherhood could scare the pants off you.

Fiona hugged Rose to her chest. "She's bleeding from the rectum. It could be Meckel's diverticulum. A rupture. It's not unusual with Down's individuals. We've been warned, but I prayed…"

"She must have been fine only a few hours ago."

"That's the good news. We'll get her to the hospital. Get X rays. Get her into surgery if necessary."

Dear God. Surgery. His little girl. "What's the bad news?" He had to know. Had to prepare himself, steel his will, make himself a rock for Rose and Fiona.

"Don't even think of bad news." Her voice resolute, she bent to kiss their daughter's forehead. "Rosie? It's Mama. Wake up, sweetheart."

Rose stirred. "Sleepy," she murmured.

"Don't sleep. Let's sing 'She'll Be Comin' Round the Mountain'." Fiona began the song and Chase joined in, making up words when he forgot the original. He was neither singer nor doctor, but he knew Rose needed this tenuous connection.

He hit the state two-lane in a shower of gravel and pushed the accelerator to the floor. A minute, no more and they'd be at the chopper. A couple minutes to secure Rose on the gurney. Despite her fear of flying, Fiona would have to act alone in Reg and Tammi's place.

His house with the chopper behind it came into view. He'd never seen a more welcome sight. They'd accomplished step one in their journey.

"Hold on, Rosie," he said, a lump rising in his throat. "You're finally going to get that helicopter ride."

He pulled as close to the big bird as was safe for takeoff, jammed the truck in park, jumped out of the driver's seat and ran around to Fiona's side. She already had her feet on the ground, Rose in her arms.

"Go on," she urged. "Get everything ready. I can carry her."

He sprinted to the chopper. Unlocking the door to the ambulance section, he decided to keep the gurney inside. It would be quicker to lift Rose from Fiona's arms to his. He leapt into the entrance just as Fiona came abreast. "Hand her to me."

When Fiona complied, he took this precious little life into his arms, then placed her gently on the gurney. Before he could strap her down, he saw the blood seeping through the old quilt. So much blood.

Feeling a pain greater than if the injury had been his own, he froze.

Fiona climbed into the rear section. "I'll take over from here. You get us off the ground. Call ahead. Request Max Edelmann."

He started as if he'd been in a trance. *Procedure,* he reminded himself, moving toward the cockpit. *Follow procedure. Just play it by the book. This is second nature to you.* Procedure was a hell of a lot easier to follow when the patient wasn't your own flesh and blood.

Taking the pilot's seat, he went through the preparations for takeoff mechanically yet efficiently. He'd always said he could do this in his sleep. He hadn't prepared for a nightmare.

Call in. Prepare the hospital. Fly precise. Land safe. He made a mental mantra, but always the image of Rose underlined his thoughts. *Stay cool,* he added. He owed it to his little girl not to let emotion blind him. He was her

father, yes, but he was the pilot upon whose clearheaded
skills her life might depend.

"Are you secure?" he called to Fiona.

"Yes! Hurry!" Panic laced her words.

As he took the chopper up, the sun began to rise over
the distant mountains. A bright new day. He took it as a
sign. A good sign. But for added measure he prayed to
God that his daughter wasn't suffering because of his past
mistakes.

In the back of the helicopter, Fiona, suppressing her own
fear of flying, clung to her daughter's hand.

"We can do this, Rosie," she whispered and tried to
quell a growing nausea. "We're going to get you to the
hospital. If surgery's necessary, Dr. Edelmann will do it.
Do you remember him? He gave you a stuffed bulldog one
Christmas. You said Dr. E. looked just like that bulldog,
only not so pretty. He didn't see the humor, and right then
I decided I wouldn't date him."

Her daughter, her breathing shallow, didn't respond.

Fiona brushed the hair from Rose's forehead. "Now
Chase would think it funny. But Chase is special—"

As much as she tried to suppress them, tears slipped
from her eyes and down her cheeks. She shivered as overwhelming emotions buffeted her, blotting out her physical
distress. Such emotions. Worry for her daughter's well-
being. Regret for the tentative relationship with Chase
now lying in ruins. And guilt that she'd sneaked a little
time for herself and thus had not been at her daughter's
bedside when she'd most needed her.

Telling herself that she'd be no good to Rosie if she
gave in to sniveling, she pulled herself together, wiped her
tears on the back of her hand, concentrated on a future
when all would be well. For Rosie, at least.

"Rosebud," she said, laying her head next to her daughter's on the gurney, placing her hand over the tiny, beating

heart, "you'll love the pudding and whipped cream they serve for lunch. But they're going to have to dish up two because I'm staying with you every step of the way."

Although she would not entertain even a remote possibility of bad news—from the doctors or from Chase's inevitable lawyers—she wasn't about to leave a moment to chance.

She tried not to think about Chase. Tried not to think that she had kicked him out of her and her daughter's life only to need his skills immediately thereafter. His skills were not the problem. She trusted them. She had once trusted him. As a person. She no longer did.

On the descent from Smoke Mountain, he'd been cool and collected. But she'd seen the look in his eyes when he placed Rose on the gurney and noticed the blood. He'd reacted with raw emotion, as a father would.

After tonight, whether she liked it or not, he was forever linked to her and to her family. All that was left was to determine the extent.

"Hang in there, Rose of mine." She squeezed the little hand.

It seemed ages before her stomach reacted to the helicopter's descent. She prayed Max and crew were waiting on the tarmac outside Asheville General, prayed Chase had been clear in his radio call to the hospital. Every second counted.

She felt the gentle thud of touchdown. Before the rotors stopped spinning, the side door slid open. Max Edelmann's big, jowly face stared up at her. A full complement of nurses and technicians stooped behind him, blown about by the diminishing wind of the overhead blades. Two aides leapt into the helicopter, rolled the gurney to the opening, then to the ground where they engaged the wheels and began the push to the hospital entrance.

"Fiona, what do you know?" Edelmann jogged alongside the moving gurney.

Fiona kept pace. "Rectal hemorrhaging. I suspect a ruptured Meckel's diverticulum."

Edelmann brushed aside the quilt, palpated Rose's abdomen. "Let's get her to X ray."

"I'm coming with you." Nothing could keep her away.

The group moved as a well-coordinated unit. Edelmann fixed Fiona with a quick, hard glance. "As far as the hospital's concerned, you're in because you're a doctor. But I know better. Your real job is to be there for Rose. Emotionally. As her mom. I'm in charge professionally. Remember that. Let me make all the hard, intellectual decisions."

"Just as long as they're the right decisions," she replied as the automatic double doors of the emergency room swooshed open.

Turning to make sure the gurney had cleared, she caught sight of Chase running to catch up. "Chester!" She hailed the security guard, then pointed at Chase. "Don't let that man anywhere near my daughter."

Shock registering on his face, Chase stopped outside the closing double doors as the team raced through the emergency unit toward X ray.

"What was that all about?" Max growled.

"I'll tell you later," Fiona responded, out of breath more from emotion than physical exertion. "Until then Chase Riboud is not to so much as step foot on Rosie's floor."

"I'll write it up."

Adrenaline pumping in her veins, she followed the group as if she were a member of the team. She'd run this drill hundreds of times during her schooling. But she'd never run it with her daughter as a patient. Never run it as her mind reeled from thoughts of a possible custody suit.

Her heart beat double-time. Rosie lay so still and small on the moving gurney, her color sallow in the hospital's harsh lighting. Fiona tried to reassure herself. Rose was a good girl. Strong. And stubborn. It helped to be stubborn in the face of danger.

Fiona, too, needed to be stubborn in the face of danger. And right now, more than illness, Chase was the face of danger.

Tears sprang once again to Fiona's eyes. As much as she hated to admit it, Max was right. Unrestrained emotion should play no part on the medical team. It sapped one's strength and cluttered the decision-making process. In fact, she'd barely noticed their progress through the bowels of the hospital, down to X ray, even less the medical dialogue between Max and his staff. She had been in her own world of motherly distress. For Rose's sake, she needed to can the distress and channel her love and her empathy toward a happy and healthy ending.

Chase had watched Fiona and the medical staff rush his daughter into the hospital. Relief had washed over him that they'd delivered Rose in excellent time. Bitterness had gnawed at his gut because, as her father, he should have been right in the middle of that group. Instead, he'd been left behind. An outsider. Waiting and worrying.

To add to his pain, Fiona had ordered security to keep him away from their daughter. Surely she would relent. A parent herself, she couldn't leave him twisting in the wind.

Now sitting in the emergency room, he clutched the half-empty foam cup of coffee. The stale liquid felt like a corrosive acid in his stomach. The lack of news from either Fiona or the staff threatened to undo him.

He stood up and approached the emergency room desk clerk. A new hire possibly, for Chase didn't recognize her. "Is there any word on Rose Applegate?"

"Who?" The woman's dispassionate reply was cold even by emergency room standards.

"Rose Applegate. Dr. Fiona Applegate just brought her daughter in."

"Then I'm sure Dr. Applegate will do everything she can—"

"Has she sent any word on Rose's condition?"

"Why would she?"

Chase began a slow burn. "Because I'm waiting, and she knows it."

"And you would be?" The clerk eyed him insolently.

"Chase Riboud, the mercy flight pilot."

The clerk raised one eyebrow. "You follow up on all the cases you fly in?"

Chase bit the inside of his mouth. "Fiona Applegate's...a personal friend."

"That still doesn't change the fact she hasn't left word." The clerk turned to her computer screen. "Sorry." She wasn't and he knew it.

"Riboud." Chester, the security guard, approached him, his tone more perplexed than threatening. "You've got no call to be pestering the staff about that little girl. Dr. Applegate ordered me to keep you away. Now Dr. Edelmann's put it in writing."

"You don't understand."

"No, I don't." The guard looked away, uncomfortable. "But I've a job to do. I can't keep you out of the emergency room. You're staff. But you're to stay away from that little girl. And to my mind that means no questions, either."

"Just find out for me if she's going to be all right." Chase fought back the overwhelming sense of helplessness. "I can't stand the not knowing."

"No can do." Chester's frown showed more pain than

hostility. "Now, why don't you make my job easy and head home?"

"I'm staying."

"Then I'm watching." Chester moved away, near the water cooler, but kept a nervous eye on Chase.

Willie, one of the nurses Chase recognized, walked by. "I'll try to find out something," she said, her voice low in passing. "Don't worry."

Don't worry. As if he could shut off his emotions.

Worrying about Rose, worrying about his broken relationship with Fiona, he paced the crowded waiting area until even the sick and injured folks waiting to see a doctor looked at him in irritation.

Still no word from Fiona. Still no idea how his daughter, his only child, fared. Never before in preparing for or awaiting the start of any of his countless military missions had he felt this sense of dread. Never before had he felt so defenseless.

Reaching into his pocket for change, he headed for the pay phones. He'd do what he always did in moments of personal crisis: he'd touch base with family. Early risers, his parents should be sitting down to breakfast.

He punched in their number.

His mother answered. "Hello?"

"*Maman,* it's Chase."

"Are you all right, *cher?*"

"I'm fine. But Rosie's in the hospital. I don't know what's going to happen."

"*Bon Dieu!* Justin!" She called to her husband. "Pick up the extension. It's Chase. Our granddaughter is in the hospital."

Perhaps there was hope after all. His mother had automatically referred to Rose as their grandchild.

"What is being done?" His father burst onto the extension with his usual concern for family and demand for action.

"X rays right now. Possibly surgery, depending on what they find."

"What is wrong?"

"From what I can gather, there's bleeding. From the intestine, I think. I don't know exactly." Frustration at his lack of information dogged him. "Hell, I'm not a doctor."

"But the wee one's mother is. There is much hope." His mother's voice imparted solace over the distance. "You and she must be strong for each other and for our little Rosie. She must pull through this so that we might meet her."

A dark sense of despair crashed over him. "I don't know that you'll get to meet either one of them in the near future—"

"Why not?"

"I told Fiona who I was—just before Rose got sick." His blood grew cold with the memory. "Fiona's hurt almost as bad as Rose, *Maman*. And very angry. I can't say that I blame her. I blame myself for not realizing from the beginning the potential for pain in this whole situation. But I was caught in my own anger. In shock."

"Now she is in shock. What mother wouldn't be? Is she a good mother, this Fiona?"

"Oh, the best."

"Do you love her, son?"

"Yes." He slumped against the wall.

"Have you told her?" His father's gruff question jolted him.

"No, I never did." And therein lay an even greater problem than the issue of his identity.

"You must let her know," his mother urged. "You must prove yourself with the strength of your love."

"*Maman!*" Chase couldn't help but show surprise at

this change in attitude. "When I last called, you advised me against pursuing my relationship with Rose. You never even asked about Fiona."

His father cleared his throat. "Your sister, Ree, has been educating us. Perhaps we spoke in haste." An apology of sorts? It was difficult for his stubborn father to admit any fault in judgment. This gruff explanation was a big step in the right direction.

"We were harsh," his mother added. "But we can tell how much you love this child and her mother. I'm sure we'll love them as well."

"I'm afraid you may not get the opportunity," he admitted. "I'm guilty of a severe lack of judgment in handling the whole situation. If...*when* Rose recovers, I may have lost her. And Fiona."

"Take heart," his father said, his words choked with feeling. "Fiona may listen to reason, after all. We did. The first order of business, however, is to see our granddaughter recover."

"Go to her," his mother insisted. "Call us when you have news."

"I will." He couldn't bear to tell them Fiona had banned him from Rose's side.

"Our prayers go with you, son." His father's voice rang across the miles like a clear, sustaining bell.

"I love you." His own voice cracking, Chase hung up.

He wished he'd told Fiona he loved her. And Rose. The time had never seemed just right. But ever since he'd moved to Bertie's Hollow, his timing had been off.

Despite the fact that Fiona had exiled him, he had to create the right time.

But first he must make a phone call he dreaded. To Martha Ricker. She would be worrying. She deserved an update. Besides, if Fiona refused to consider him for emotional support, she still needed someone close, waiting at the hospital. Fiona thought of Martha as family. He'd even go get her, if necessary.

With profound chagrin, Chase thought how he would have to admit to Martha that he had hurt Fiona.

Delving into his pocket for more change, he felt a presence at his left shoulder. Turning, he found himself face to face with an unsmiling Martha.

"What do you know?" she asked. "That snotty little clerk will tell me nothing. Says I'm not family."

"We got her here in good time. I think they've taken her to surgery. A Dr. Edelmann—"

"You *think* they've taken her to surgery." Martha eyed him suspiciously. "Fiona hasn't sent word?"

"No." He took a deep breath. "Fiona's angry with me."

"Why?" Martha bristled defensively.

"Because I told her the truth." Chase looked Martha right in the eye. "I told her that I'm Rose's biological father."

She stared at him, stony and still. "Now it all becomes clear," she said, her words leaden. "Your pursuit of our Fiona. The way you and Rose bonded." She narrowed her eyes. "Why did you come to Bertie's Hollow? Why did you do this hateful thing?"

"Because Rose was conceived, born and given up for adoption without my knowledge or consent." He had no more secrets. He might as well tell her the whole truth. "And because I can't have any more children. I did it to preserve the only family I might ever have. Can you understand that desperation?"

"I can." A great sadness made Martha's whole face sag. "It looks as though you and I are more alike than not, Chase Riboud."

"But you made people believe in you again. How can I?"

"What are your true feelings?"

"I love Rose. I've fallen in love with Fiona. I want us to be a family. Marriage. The whole nine yards."

"Then tell Fiona."

How simple. His sister Ree had told him as much. As had his parents.

How much pain and grief could have been avoided if he'd been forthright at every stage along his journey? But he hadn't been capable at every stage. He wasn't now the same man he'd been when he'd started out on his mission, hell-bent to rescue his daughter; nor the same man he'd been halfway through when he'd begun to feel an attachment both to his daughter and to her mother but had been too emotionally layered to declare himself. Rose had taught him how to strip the layers away to the bare essential—love. Fiona had changed him from an angry man to a man capable of acting upon that love.

He must tell Fiona all this. He must find a way to make her listen.

Chapter Fourteen

Rose was going to be all right.

In the recovery room, Fiona held her daughter's hand and could not take her eyes off the small, still form in the big, white bed.

The surgery had been a success, and, in a moment of thankful bliss, Fiona had kissed Max Edelmann as the aides had wheeled Rose out of the operating room. The gruff surgeon had actually blushed. And then he'd told her that part of the success lay in the fact that the mercy flight helicopter had been able to transport Rose so quickly. A trip by ground ambulance would have taken at least thirty minutes and would have lost Rose precious time.

With a knowing look, Max had said, "Don't forget to thank your pilot."

Chase.

"Your father," Fiona whispered to Rose as she reached into her pocket for a crumpled piece of paper.

The note was from Chester in security, telling her that Chase still paced the emergency room. Waiting. Asking anyone who might know about Rose's condition.

Stubborn man. Just like his daughter.

Fiona stroked Rose's hair and allowed herself to think how alike the two were in many other ways. In addition to their stubbornness, their dark coloring. Their love of hot and spicy foods. A fondness for fiddle music...

She'd told Chase that she believed parenting was a privilege, not a right. Had he shown himself worthy of that privilege?

Although Fiona had ordered Chase out of her life and away from her daughter, she was a woman to whom fairness meant a great deal. She'd scolded him for condemning Martha before he'd learned the whole story. She'd cautioned him not to dismiss Raymond out of hand. Didn't Fiona, then, owe it to Rose, who had grown up so far without her father, to weigh the pros and cons of this thorny situation?

Right from the moment he'd first met Rose, he'd treated her as a little girl, not a little girl with a disability. If he'd compared her to anyone, he'd compared her favorably to the Riboud nieces and nephews. He'd chosen just the right movie to take her to. He'd shown a genuine interest in caterpillars and Henny Penny and ants, as well as a natural instinct for shoulder rides and gentle horsing around. And he hadn't run from Rose's temper tantrum.

Moreover, in six years Fiona had never known an acquaintance—not even Martha or Sadie—to do a week's worth of research on Down's syndrome.

She thought of Chase's actions in the community. His polite deference toward Alva Biggs. His silent strength during the birth of Matthew Dale and his subsequent look of absolute tenderness when he'd been allowed to hold the baby boy. Reg and Tammi and staffers at the hospital sang his praises. And then, of course, there was Dustmop. Animals recognized kindness in humans.

For all intents and purposes, Chase Riboud appeared to be an upstanding member of Bertie's Hollow.

But what about his treatment of her, Fiona? As a friend. As a lover. As a pawn.

It hurt her to think that he might have courted her to get close to Rose—she still hadn't emotional distance enough to gauge the legitimacy of his courtship—but that seemed a moot issue now. The real concern was his relationship with Rose.

Max Edelmann had told her to thank the mercy flight pilot. She needed no urging to give mental thanks. Chase had acted with his usual professional skill. She couldn't have asked for more...but he had given more.

In the race down to the helicopter, he'd joined her in singing "She'll Be Comin' Round the Mountain" as if he realized how Rose needed that connection to the waking world. His off-key rendition had touched Fiona even then, even when she still burned with anger at his withholding of the truth. And then when they'd arrived at the chopper, and he'd lifted their daughter onto the gurney, no actor could have faked the look of anguish on his face.

And why shouldn't he feel anguish? Rose might be the only child he'd ever have. How much had it cost him, as a man, to admit that?

Sighing heavily, she hugged her Rosie. Whether she liked it or not, Chase Riboud had the fathering instinct. He deserved to know that his child was out of danger.

She turned to press the nurses' button, only to find Willie Schumach standing in the doorway.

"Willie, will you take a message for me?"

"Sure."

"Please, tell Chase Riboud...I think you'll find him in

emergency…that his…that Rose Applegate came out of surgery with flying colors. She's going to be fine.''

''Wouldn't you rather I sat by Rose and you delivered the message in person?'' Willie's penetrating gaze held uncanny insight. Rumors traveled far too fast in a hospital. ''Chase seems mighty anxious.''

''I'd prefer to stay with my daughter.''

''I'll tell him then.'' With the squeak of her crepe-soled shoes, Willie disappeared.

Fiona turned back to Rosie. Instead of feeling relief, she felt guilt. As awful as his truths had been, Chase had delivered them face-to-face. And she couldn't even look him in the eye to tell him her good news.

With a change of heart, she quickly but thoroughly checked her daughter's vital signs, then snagged a passing aide and drew from him a promise that he'd sit by Rosie's side until she returned.

Then she headed for emergency, her heart pounding.

When the elevator doors opened on the ground floor, she could see Chase and Willie standing at the end of the long corridor. Willie must have just delivered the news, because Chase's face glowed with relief. As Willie walked away, Fiona began the longest journey of her life, down the hallway, keeping her eyes focused on the man who stood alone amid the bustle of the emergency room.

Careful to maneuver around a gurney parked in the middle of the corridor, she didn't see the instant his tears started, but by the time she looked up, his cheeks were wet with his silent weeping. He stood in public, openly vulnerable.

Whatever his feelings for her, she couldn't doubt that his love for Rose was genuine. And for that reason, she'd force herself to listen to any explanations he might offer.

Consumed with joy at the news Rose would make it, Chase stared into the face of an angel.

Fiona stood not a dozen feet away from him, her hair in disarray, dark circles under her eyes. Her face a conflicting study in compassion and cool distance, she watched him as if she might turn at any moment and disappear. Yet, having sent Willie, she'd now come in person. An obvious afterthought. A very good sign.

He moved toward her. "I'm so glad."

"Me, too." She stayed where she stood.

"Is she really going to be all right?"

Fiona smiled. "In a few days, you won't be able to keep up with her."

He wouldn't be able to keep up with her. Was that just an expression, or was there real hope Fiona would let him see his daughter again?

"What was wrong?" He asked, trying to keep the conversation on Rose. They both loved Rose.

"The X rays proved my diagnosis correct. It was a ruptured Meckel's diverticulum."

"You'll have to walk me through this. " He hated feeling in the dark. He hadn't even been able to give a cogent explanation to his parents.

"It's a projection the size of a finger that grows on the inside of the intestine. A long ballooning out. When food gets caught on it repeatedly, the end wears through and starts bleeding. Down's individuals are particularly susceptible to the condition."

"How serious was it?"

"Serious. But we caught it early, thanks to your safe driving and piloting skills. We've gained another mercy flight champion. Max Edelmann."

He caught the *we*, held on to it for dear life.

"Martha's here," he offered in the spirit of family. "In the cafeteria. Her son-in-law brought her."

"Then I need to tell her the good news before I get back

to Rose. They should be moving her out of recovery into her room soon.''

He reached out and touched her arm to stay. "Give me three minutes."

"I really need to get back to Rosie." The look in her eyes grew wary.

He drew her off to the side of the busy hallway, then took the plunge without preamble. "I love you, Fiona Applegate.''

Shock electrified her features. "But—"

"Hear me out." He touched his fingers to her lips. "Then think about it." He'd gotten in enough trouble for withholding the truth.

"You told me once," he began, "up in Alva Biggs's meadow, that we love or we perish. I thought I understood, but I didn't. Not really.'' He hesitated, searching for the right words. "You see, I thought that the loving itself was enough. I thought perhaps, because of my secret I could enter the back door of intimacy, could make you fall in love with me and then come forward—out the front door, so to speak—with the truth. Along the way, I forgot that honesty is part of the loving process.''

"Chase—"

"I'm not saying this right." He swallowed hard. "In my careers as a soldier and as a mercy flight pilot, my life and the lives of others have depended upon my good judgment. It pains me to have to admit to you that self-interest clouded that judgment...in this...the most important matter of the heart.''

She looked down at her hands. "I don't know what to say.''

"Don't say anything." He took her hands in his. "Several hours ago you asked me if I would be content with a doctor for a wife and a special-needs child for a daughter.

You told me not to answer right away.'' He squeezed her hands. "My answer's yes.''

"So much has changed.''

"Nothing has changed except everything is out in the open now. Look at me, Fiona.''

She did, and he saw doubt and yearning mixed in equal parts, shadowing her clear green gaze.

"I love you. I love Rose.'' He hurtled along in his speech, fearing he might not get another chance, unable to hold back any longer. "I want us to be a family. I want to marry you. But if you can't return my feelings...I'll leave you alone. I owe you that. You needn't worry that I'd try to gain custody of Rose.'' He felt tears sting the back of his eyes. "I'd only hope that some day you'd forgive me and find a way to explain to Rose about a father who loved her and had to leave despite that love.''

Fiona's eyes grew moist. "This is too much.'' She pulled her hands out of Chase's grasp.

"I know. That's why you need to think about it.'' He leaned toward her and gently kissed her cheek, tried to memorize in an instant the feel of her, the smell of her. "Rose needs you. Get back to her. I'll find Martha in the cafeteria.''

Without another word, Fiona fled down the long corridor and into the waiting elevator.

Fiona sat on one side of Rose's bed. Martha sat on the other. Rose had regained consciousness, but she was groggy. The two women sat an optimistic vigil.

"Are you going to let Chase come up?'' Martha asked. "At a time like this, a father should be near his child.''

Stunned, Fiona stared at her old friend.

"He told me,'' Martha replied. "Down in the emergency room while we were waiting for Rose to come out of surgery.''

"Did he tell you why he wasn't honest with me from the beginning?"

"He told me of his desperation. He saw Rose as his only chance at a family." Martha picked at the bedcovers. "I understand how someone can do something unthinkable when they fear they might lose a child." She looked up at Fiona. "We're all human. All flawed. But there's good in all of us, too."

Remarkably, Fiona was moved as much by Chase's admission of his flaws as by his admission of love. She was a person who experienced imperfection daily in her career and in her personal life. Yet, she had always believed that everyone had gifts and everyone had special challenges, and that our humanity resided in the individual capacity to persevere, to accept, to forgive and to love.

She had seen Chase's devotion to Rose, both in his day-to-day interactions with her and in his emergency room vigil. She had seen the joy Rose derived from her growing relationship with her father. Could Fiona afford, for Rose's sake, to toss all that aside?

As for herself, she had felt more alive in Chase's presence than she had in her entire life. Could she afford, for her own sake, to shut that feeling away?

If she were honest with herself, she must admit that she loved Chase Riboud. Could she now forgive and accept?

Rose's eyelids fluttered open. "Thirsty."

"Of course you are." Fiona held the straw to the glass of ice water to her daughter's lips. "All in one night you've gone to a birthday sleepover, ridden in a helicopter and had a visit to the hospital where Dr. E. made you all better."

In confusion, Rose looked from Fiona to Martha. "Where's hel'copper man?"

Martha cast Fiona a pointed glance.

"He's downstairs, sweetheart."

"Want to see him, too."

"Out of the mouths of babes..." Martha moved her chair closer to the bed. "I'll wait here."

Fiona stood but did not move. To walk downstairs and invite Chase to Rose's bedside would take an enormous leap of faith, because he'd asked not only to become a part of her—*their*—daughter's life, but also to become a part of hers. As a friend, lover and husband.

He'd just now said he loved her. He'd asked her to marry him.

If she opened the emotional gates now, it was for keeps.

"Want Chase, Mama," Rose repeated. Insistent.

So did Fiona.

"Go, child," Martha urged. "There's no denying he's a part of who you are."

Fiona raised one eyebrow. "When did you become so all-knowing?"

"Heavens! You don't need 'the sight' to tell. It's been written all over your face since the day he flew into town."

"That long?" And everyone, it seemed, had known but her. So much for her intuitiveness. She blew a kiss to Rosie. "I'll be right back with Chase."

She didn't even know if he remained in the hospital.

Her pulse started to race as she passed the nurses' station. *He'd made his offer, now wouldn't a wise man go home?* By the time she reached the elevator, her palms were damp. *What if she'd been so hideous to him he decided to rescind his marriage proposal?* She jabbed the down button, but barely waited two seconds before deciding the stairs would be faster. *What if he still wanted to marry her, but had been called away on an emergency flight, and she had to wait to tell him yes?* Clattering down the stairs, she had to remind herself to slow her pace. It would never do to walk down the aisle on crutches. *Was she really going to say yes?* By the time she reached the first floor, panting, she realized she looked a fright. *Some bride-to-be.* Her operating room scrubs were rumpled, her hair felt as if she'd stuck her finger in a socket, and she just knew her worry and lack of sleep had her looking like a raccoon.

She didn't give a fig about her looks. Far more weighty concerns propelled her.

If Chase remained in the building, she was about to invite him up into her daughter's room and into their life. Permanently.

Pushing the first-floor stairwell door open, she strained to catch a glimpse of him in the emergency waiting room. No Chase. Disappointment dogging her, she approached Chester.

"Have you seen the mercy flight pilot, the one I asked you to watch?" she asked, heat rising to her cheeks.

"Don't you worry," the security guard replied. "I'm keeping tabs on him. Last I saw, he was in the gift shop. I told the volunteer to page me when he leaves. I had to leave him for a moment. Had a woman locked out of her car...." He droned on, but Fiona had stopped listening.

The gift shop? The day shift was up and running? For a moment she'd forgotten time had not stood still throughout her daughter's operation. She looked at her watch. It was one in the afternoon.

And she needed to begin her new life.

"Chester," she said, beaming, "you don't have to restrict Chase Riboud any longer. He and I are about to clear up our misunderstanding."

"That must be why he's buying all those presents."

She hurried out of the emergency room area, around the labs, past the administration offices and into the main lobby. Through the gift shop's glass walls, she could see Chase standing in front of the cash register, wreathed by balloons, stuffed animals, candy and flowers. When he pushed the lot forward, then reached in his back pocket and produced a charge card, she realized he was about to purchase each and every one of those items.

Mercy, but they were going to start their married life as paupers.

She stepped into the gift shop doorway. "Chase Riboud, what do you think you're doing?"

"I wasn't going to take them up," he replied, a sheepish look on his face. "Willie said she'd deliver them for me."

"These are all for Rose?"

"Yes…well…the candy, flowers and balloons were an easy choice, but I can't decide on the stuffed animal."

"You'll spoil her."

He brightened. "You'll let me send them?"

"That depends…" She played the moment for all it was worth. She needed this lighter conversation before she could bring herself to begin the heavier, the more important. "Let's see the choice in stuffed animals."

His smile was tentative, but grew stronger as she approached. He held up a turtle, a bear and an owl. "I couldn't find an ant or a caterpillar," he explained, and then he held up what looked like shredded rags, like the fringe of her oldest chenille bedspread.

"What in—"

"Look closely," he advised. "Do you think Rosie would recognize—"

"Dustmop!" Right down to the bright button eyes, the floppy stuffed animal was a true clone. She laughed aloud. Grinning, Fiona put the turtle, the bear and the owl back on the shelf. "The choice is obvious."

"Ring it all up," he told the clerk with an air of satisfaction, and then turned to Fiona. "You'll tell me her reaction?"

She caught his gaze and held it. "Why don't you come up and see for yourself?"

"Do you mean it?" Jubilation lit his features.

"Absolutely." Suddenly shy, she looked down at her hands, willing herself brave enough to make this next leap of great faith. "In fact, Rose is awake. She asked to see you."

"How does that make you feel?"

"I have to admit it made me think."

"About...?"

"About you and Rose. About you and me." She looked up at him, and his expression of rapt attention made her catch her breath. "About you and Rose and me as a family."

"And...?"

"I'm still angry at you for not telling the truth."

"I understand that. But can you possibly understand why I reacted as I did?"

"As a mother, no." She paused, inhaling deeply. "But as a mother...yes. To find yourself a parent, whether biological or adoptive, is an overwhelming sensation. A responsibility. An elemental connection. If it's a bond of love, there is none greater." She touched her palm to his chest, over his heart. "I can't imagine how I would have felt or acted in your circumstances. I may have seen myself as trapped and done exactly as you. Or I may have tried a more direct approach...I can't judge."

"I'm sorry for the pain I've caused you." His sincerity appeared as no superficial mask. It emanated from the inside, out. "Can you forgive me?"

"From now on, it's total honesty between us?"

"Total honesty. From now on."

"Then I can forgive you."

He sighed, and his handsome features relaxed. "Is it too soon to ask you where we go from here?"

Her pulse picked up. To delay, to make a point, would punish her as well as him.

"When you were going through the options, earlier," she replied, "when I brought you news of Rose's recovery...what was Option A?" She felt herself fairly sparkle with joyous anticipation. "If I recall, it had something to do with marriage."

"Are you saying what I think you're saying?"

She blushed as the volunteer, a young candy striper, watched them, chin propped on her hand, stars in her eyes.

Surprisingly, Fiona didn't mind the audience. There had been too many secrets between Chase and her. She'd take openness—even with onlookers—any day.

"Let's start at the beginning." Taking both his hands in hers, she flashed him an impish grin. "I'm a traditionalist."

Helium balloons bobbing about his head, he said simply, "I love you, Fiona Applegate. Will you marry me?"

"Yes. Because I love you, Chase Riboud." She hadn't even hesitated in her response.

Applause erupted from the gift shop doorway where a crowd had gathered, among it some very familiar Bertie's Hollow faces.

"You're going to need this, then," the candy-striper offered, slipping a bride's magazine into the bag with the sweets and the stuffed animal. "My treat."

"Definitely." Fiona, soaring once again, laughed. "We're going to have to explain weddings to Rosie."

"What fun." The look Chase shot her was not, however, focused on any wedding. It was focused on the honeymoon.

Slipping his arms around her waist, he drew her to him. For all to see, he kissed her with a passion that reminded her of mountains and free-flying birds and the fresh spring breeze that blew through Bertie's Hollow. Home. He was as much a part of her as her town. As doctoring. As Rose.

Unafraid, she kissed him back and hoped that she could

impart with the touch of lips and tongue a sense of utter contentment, of welcome, of promise. In all her life, she'd never asked for perfect. She'd asked for real.

Chase Riboud was real.

But when his hands slipped down to cup her bottom, she remembered where she was and drew away, laughing.

The watching crowd burst into another round of applause.

"What the ding-dang is going on here?" Chester pushed his way through the onlookers. "Front desk says there's a riot in the gift shop—" Seeing Chase and Fiona, he stopped short. "Well, if this doesn't beat all."

Chase grinned. "I'd say that about sums it up."

"Don't worry," Fiona declared, grasping the bouquet of flowers. "We're taking this party upstairs, Chester. We have to give my daughter the best present of all. A new daddy."

Congratulations rippled through the crowd.

Picking up the bag of gifts and corralling the balloons, Chase caught Fiona's eye, and slowly, deliberately mouthed, *I love you.*

She reminded herself to kiss those lips often.

Chester ushered them through the crowd. "Good luck!"

Luck had nothing to do with it. Love ruled the day. And honesty.

"About that policy of total honesty…" As if reading her mind, Chase slipped his free hand around her waist.

"Yes…?" She braced herself.

"When I move in, you automatically get yourself a dog."

She laughed in relief. "Rose will love it!"

"And I snore—"

"I said *honesty.*" She jabbed him in the ribs. "Not confession."

Oh, she was going to love learning every little detail about this man of hers.

Epilogue

Cajun fiddle music squealed in the background as dancers of all ages spun on the make-shift dance floor beside the senior Ribouds' barn. Old men leaned against the barn door and swapped tall tales of duck hunting and pot-licking hounds. Children chased chickens and each other as the women set up the buffet, the centerpiece of which was a mountain of crawfish.

Maman and *Papa* had gone all out to make a *fais-do-do* worthy of their visiting son and their most recent daughter-in-law and grandchild.

His toe tapping to the insistent beat, Chase held Rose aloft on his shoulders so that she could experience her new family. Fiona was engaged in deep conversation not far away with Lulu Crochet, the ancient *sage-femme,* or local midwife.

As Chase executed a neat circle in time to the music, Rose crowed, "Look, Daddy!"

Great-Uncle Earl came dancing up to meet them. Earl never walked when he could dance, and tonight he was in fine form. A nonagenarian, wiry, and fit as a fiddle, the old gentleman was decked out in his usual partying outfit: his best white shirt, a black string tie at his neck and the brightest red suspenders one ever did see. No get-together, however, could convince him to wear his dentures. His tanned and leathery face looked like an implosion. No wonder Rosie was fascinated.

"Look, look!" Rosie pointed impatiently. "Down! Lemme see!"

Chase hesitated. Rosie loved details and always spoke her mind. And although his family had been warm and welcoming, he didn't know if Great-Uncle Earl would take kindly to having his toothless face inspected up close and personal. But Rosie wriggled until Chase feared she'd fall off her perch.

He put her down.

"How funny!" Covering her giggles with one hand, Rose pointed at Uncle Earl with the other.

Beside himself, Chase bent to whisper in his daughter's ear. "It's not polite to point." He prepared to explain to his uncle that Rose meant no disrespect.

"What's so funny, *'tite jolie?*" When Great-Uncle Earl grinned, the implosion in the middle of his face became a sinkhole. Even Chase had to remind himself not to stare.

"These!" Rose stepped forward boldly and seized the elderly man's crimson suspenders. "What are they?"

Bless her little heart, she hadn't even noticed his dentureless smile. Chase chuckled to think how his daughter surprised and delighted him on a daily basis, and continued to prove the adage, *It isn't how I look, but how you see me that counts.*

"Galluses, *chérie,*" Uncle Earl replied, snapping them against his chest for effect.

Rose giggled. "What are they for?"

"They hold up my pants when I dance." He winked. "Wanna dance?"

"Don't know how."

"You just stand on Uncle Earl's shoes, and I give you a dance you won't forget, I ga-ron-tee." He held out his gnarled and work-callused hands.

With the dignity of a belle at her coming-out, Rose placed her small soft hands in those of her great-great-uncle, then positioned her pink high-tops onto the toes of his scuffed work boots.

Chase smiled at the contrast. Smiled to think how his Louisiana family had expanded to include the young, the old, the eccentric, the different. How the bond of love had brought out their similarities. And because the Ribouds provided such a big extended family, Chase and Fiona were content to keep their nuclear family at three. Fiona and Rose had taught him that he didn't have to prove himself in some baby race.

Having spent time in Bertie's Hollow, he felt wiser coming home to visit Riboud country.

As Earl eased Rose into the eddy of dancers, she turned a beaming face to Chase. "Look at me, Daddy!"

Chase didn't know whether to laugh or cry, so tightly did emotion squeeze his heart.

"Did you lose your partner?" Fiona slipped her arm around his waist.

"Not for long." He swung her into his arms and into the dance.

She laughed and brought the cool ripple of a mountain brook into this steamy bayou country. "You've taught me a few new moves I didn't know were in me."

He slowed their dancing. "And you and Rose have taught me that fatherhood is less about biology and more about trust and love. That it's not a right but a privilege."

He hugged her tight. "I feel privileged to have found you two."

"I love you, Chase Riboud." Fiona kissed him on the chin.

"And I, you."

Who knew that this journey, begun with a sense of betrayal and a jagged mind-numbing anger, would end with this profound feeling of peaceful acceptance? He was truly blessed.

* * * * *

Silhouette Stars

Born this Month

Sean Connery, Elvis Costello, Patrick Swayze, Coco Chanel, Bill Clinton, Robert de Niro, Madonna, Danielle Steel, Magic Johnson, Princess Anne

Star of the Month

Leo

The year ahead is full of opportunity. You will need to make changes in your personal life in order to reap the benefits of all that is on offer. Career moves later in the year should bring financial benefits. Travel is also well aspected especially if taken in the autumn when it could well be linked to new relationships.

SILH/HR/0008a

Virgo

Events of last month should have made you wiser about exactly who you can trust. Having learnt this you should feel ready to move on in a positive and forgiving mood.

Libra

With renewed optimism you enter a new phase in which many of the problems that you have encountered lately vanish. A romantic relationship brings an added glow to your life.

 Scorpio

Your love life may have led you to neglect other areas of your life, although now you will be able to get the balance right. There could be exciting job opportunities coming your way.

Sagittarius

You have sailed into calmer waters after the upheaval of last month. You should feel pleased with the way you have handled yourself. You should start to move onwards and upwards, putting yourself in a stronger and more positive position.

 Capricorn

Changes in several areas of your life will cause a degree of tension. Take any offers of help and by the end of the month you should feel pleased with all you have managed to achieve.

Aquarius

Recently you have dealt with a great deal of upheaval. By mid month you should be reaping some of the benefits. A reunion with someone from your past may lead to a celebration.

Pisces

An excellent, positive month in which many of your plans will start to come to fruition. Friends and loved ones should be supportive and you may see a certain relationship in a very favourable light.

Aries

You should feel confident about the future and now that you have made the decision to move on you will be surprised how supportive those close to you are. Travel plans are well aspected, especially those connected with business.

 Taurus

There could be a few tricky moments as certain people seem determined to misinterpret what you are really saying. Take a break and allow the dust to settle and by the end of the month life will be back on track.

Gemini

Don't push yourself too hard as your batteries need recharging. This is an excellent time to take a break, catch up on family, or just relax at home pampering yourself. A lucky win late in the month gets you in the mood for celebrating.

  Cancer

After the upheaval of last month life quietens down and you can use the calm to assess what you do next. Your finances receive a boost and you may be able to buy something special.

Look out for more
Silhouette Stars next month

SILHOUETTE
SPECIAL EDITION®

AVAILABLE FROM 18TH AUGUST 2000

Surprise Delivery Susan Mallery

That's My Baby!

When Heather Fitzpatrick went into labour in a lift, she had reason to be grateful that Mr Tall, Dark and Handsome, her lucky companion, was made of stern stuff. And soon he was doting on her baby like a proud papa!

Hunter's Woman Lindsay McKenna

Morgan's Mercenaries: The Hunters

Rugged soldier Ty Hunter had let Dr Catt Alborak walk away from him once, but not even a passionate hellion like her could escape him a second time.

The Fatherhood Factor Diana Whitney

Brooding cop Ethan Devlin was fighting valiantly to reclaim his twin sons from his powerful parents, and suddenly he found he had an ally. Deirdre O'Connor was determined to reunite this family—for the sake of the children!

The Home Love Built Christine Flynn

Selling a house was routine work for Laura Barrett—when the parties involved weren't a harried sheriff and his vulnerable tomboy daughter. Suddenly she'd become a surrogate mum and the focus of a handsome man's attention.

Dr Cowboy Cathy Gillen Thacker

McCabe Men

Lacey Buchanon was only interested in Jackson McCabe professionally but she needed to get his attention before he'd listen to what she had to say. And she had an idea on that…

A Family Secret Jean Brashear

Boone Gallagher swore he'd never fall for a city girl again, but forced to share his house with curvaceous Maddie Collins for thirty days, his resolve was beginning to weaken…

0008/23a

AVAILABLE FROM 18TH AUGUST 2000

™SILHOUETTE®

Intrigue
Danger, deception and suspense

SECRET ADMIRER Amanda Stevens
COWBOY JUSTICE Patricia Rosemoor
TO SAVE HIS BABY Judi Lind
BEHIND CLOSED DOORS Carla Cassidy

Desire
Intense, sensual love stories

TALL, DARK AND TEXAN Annette Broadrick
CINDERELLA'S TYCOON Caroline Cross
HARD LOVING MAN Peggy Moreland
SAIL AWAY Kathleen Korbel
STAR-CROSSED LOVERS Zena Valentine
TOO SMART FOR MARRIAGE Cathie Linz

Sensation
Passionate, dramatic, thrilling romances

A PLACE TO CALL HOME Sharon Sala
IDENTITY: UNKNOWN Suzanne Brockmann
RIO GRANDE WEDDING Ruth Wind
FALLING HARD AND FAST Kylie Brant
THE MARRIAGE PROTECTION PROGRAMME
Margaret Watson
CULLEN'S BRIDE Fiona Brand

0008/23b

2 Books
and a surprise gift!

We would like to take this opportunity to thank you for reading this Silhouette® book by offering you the chance to take TWO more specially selected titles from the Special Edition™ series absolutely FREE! We're also making this offer to introduce you to the benefits of the Reader Service™—

★ FREE home delivery
★ FREE gifts and competitions
★ FREE monthly Newsletter
★ Books available before they're in the shops
★ Exclusive Reader Service discounts

Accepting these FREE books and gift places you under no obligation to buy; you may cancel at any time, even after receiving your free shipment. Simply complete your details below and return the entire page to the address below. **You don't even need a stamp!**

YES! Please send me 2 free Special Edition books and a surprise gift. I understand that unless you hear from me, I will receive 4 superb new titles every month for just £2.70 each, postage and packing free. I am under no obligation to purchase any books and may cancel my subscription at any time. The free books and gift will be mine to keep in any case.

E0ZEB

Ms/Mrs/Miss/Mr ....Initials............................
BLOCK CAPITALS PLEASE

Surname...

Address..

....

....Postcode ....

Send this whole page to:
UK: The Reader Service, FREEPOST CN81, Croydon, CR9 3WZ
EIRE: The Reader Service, PO Box 4546, Kilcock, County Kildare (stamp required)